"You gotta love a novel that open. ~~apter~~ Chapter One: A werewolf walks into a bar.' *Lars Breaxface: Werewolf in Space* is a galaxian romp. Beautiful vampire witches, a werewolf space pilot who is a heroic puncher of chins, washing down cat with quaffs of ale from his on-board keg-rack, sword-winged Fishman, a mirrored villain, and Frank the tree—they all take off on a tale of planetary revenge. I love the language and wordplay of this story, (something may not be 'superstitious' but it could be a 'littlestitious') never explained, you just get it and flip pages as it rockets you from a cantina bar fight to an epic library blood-wall battle and into far away subspace on a ride in a ship called *Sheila*. *Sheila* roars like a souped up '67 Chevy when a rabbit-foot chained key fires up her engines. And she keeps you cozy on light-speed auto pilot in her custom flame-painted body, with Death Metal tunes blasting from her speakers. I can't wait to see the movie. Hell, I want to be in it."

- Tom Atkins, actor, *Night of the Creeps*

"There's high concept, and then there's high concept with monsters, space opera, and a throwback to all those awesome nostalgic memories you have from the '80s and '90s. That's what Lars Breaxface has in spades. Featuring a vibrant band of ragtag heroes, this is one incredible ride through the recesses of time and space, as werewolves, witches, and other beasties chew up scenery and pursue every adventure they come across (and then some). Perfect for those who love their science fiction with a shot of pure adrenaline and fun, *Lars Breaxface: Werewolf in Space* is a rhapsodic good time."

- Gwendolyn Kiste, author, *The Rust Maidens*

"How to describe something like *Lars Breaxface*?! Lars is like a punk Han Solo adventuring through the sleazy space underground, trafficking in the occult and supercharged with gore. It's as colorful as The Fifth Element but mixed with the gritty irreverence of Heavy Metal; it's a teeth-gnashing action throwback; it's grind house science fiction."

- Tom Sweterlitsch, author, *The Gone World*

"This is the book you find in the far corner of the used bookstore where the lights flicker and the employees refuse to go. This is the book you find under your older sibling's mattress and when your parents catch you reading it they send you to military school on the other side of the country. This book is *Lars Breaxface: Werewolf in Space* and it's the new gold standard for cult classics."

- Seth Fried, author, *The Great Frustration*

"Lars the space-faring werewolf is a mercenary asshole whose obsession with getting drunk, paid, and laid makes him the galaxy's one and only misanthrope lycanthrope. He's the kind of person whose arrival at the party means it's time for you to leave (unless you want blood and vomit on your shoes). And frankly, I can't remember the last time I had so much fun following someone around the chaos of their own narrative. Lars and his posse of increasingly outlandish clients and hangers-on barrel through alien cities, backwater space stations, blood-splattered churches, and even the naked vacuum of space itself in pursuit of their goals. These places and their residents are rendered with prose so deft and loving that the only thing I want more than to live in these spaces is for Lars to take a shower and a nap."

- Angela Quinton, editor, *Werewolves Versus*

LARS BREAXFACE
WEREWOLF IN SPACE

BRANDON GETZ

SPACEBOY BOOKS

Denver, Colorado

Published in the United States by:
Spaceboy Books LLC
1627 Vine Street
Denver, CO 80206
www.readspaceboy.com

First printed October 2019

ISBN: 978-1-951393-75-5

For Benji
and Hillary

Awooo!

PART I

A WEREWOLF WALKS INTO A BAR

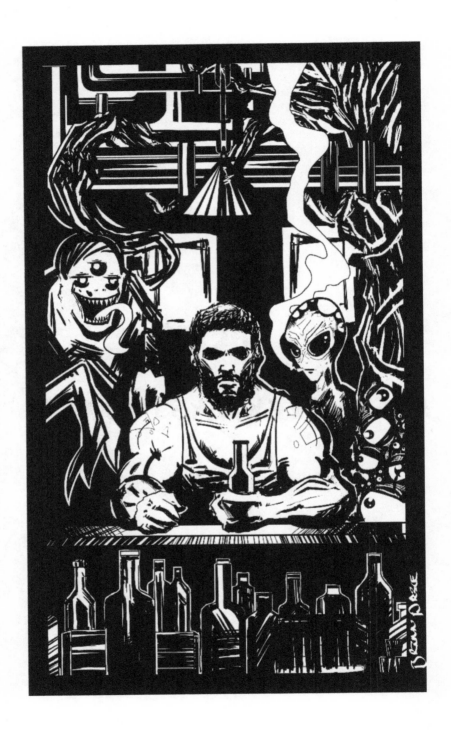

CHAPTER I

The bar he'd slunk into was a grungy space saloon called the Pickled Quasar. The kind of place where cantina jazz played loud so you couldn't hear the guy next to you and the lights were kept low to keep you from seeing the critters belly-up in your cocktail. A dice game went sour, some Siskelian asteroid smuggler muttered a crack about Mrs. Breaxface, his sainted mother, and Lars growled like a rabid moondog, faraway lunar juice pulsing in his veins. He tossed his pint of purple toward the dim light of the rafters, punching that smuggler and each of his crew in the chin before the glass crashed and shattered and purple mixed with bloodspatter on the chockablock steel floor of the bar. Because that's what Lars Breaxface does. That's who Lars Breaxface is: He is a puncher of chins.

The one-eyed bartender had a tentacle around the trigger of a blaster, and everybody, even the reptilian barbacks, gawked at the thick-necked, tattooed Earthman surrounded on all sides by unconscious Siskelians.

"Fuck off to some other gin joint," the bartender spat, spraying the bar with its mouthfoam. "We don't truck with brawlers. It's bad for our insurance premiums."

Lars shrugged heavy, hirsute shoulders and tossed a couple of coins on the table for the spilled pint.

"They started it," he grumbled. "I just finished it."

"Insults don't break my furniture." The bartender motioned toward the entry tube with the nose of its gun. "Now get the fuck out. I see your ugly puss in here again, I call StatSec, and those greasers drop you out an airlock."

A couple of the smugglers were moving now, groaning. It was easy to hear them—even the music had stopped in the Quasar. You could hear a tremuloid flex its root system in that kind of silence. And one did, in a corner, a prehensile branch wrapped around a bucket of chlorogin. Its leaves sagged with inebriation, and it watched Lars through the myriad, yellowed eyes in its trunk, giving the wolfman the willies, even more than the rifle aimed at his big, pulsing throat.

"Backspace shithole," Lars said, almost loud enough for the bartender to hear. He maneuvered his large frame toward the sphincter of the entry tube, the multi-hued crowd parting to give him a wide berth. The sphincter dilated as he neared it, and he stepped into the blue neon of the tube, shuffling toward the main hub of the waystation, hoping there was someplace to get a shave and a blowjob, not necessarily in that order.

○

Neon and trid flashed everywhere: an unbridled space disco selling everything from dick to dried vegetables. Victor's Halo was the biggest little shithole waystation in that sector, spinning right on the border between Federation space and the wide-open final frontier. Anyone passing through that far-flung corner of the galaxy had to stop there for snacks and fuel and sundries before a psychedelic jaunt through subspace. What Lars needed was to ice his hand and slap uglies with somebody decent-looking and humanoid. He passed a

4

greasy vendor selling t-shirts that said I WENT TO VICTOR'S HALO AND ALL I GOT WAS COCK ROT and eyed the hookers in the red-lit archways, looking for a biped or at least some species that wouldn't require too much creativity. He'd been in the black for weeks after his last gig, jetting FTL in his cruiser from one backspace fuel station to another, jerking off so much his sock drawer looked like a hive of tube worms. He was smiling at a feline pygmy with a big wet mouth when he felt a tongue on his ear. He turned to see the proboscis of one of the escorts extending three feet between the cavity in her chest and the silver rings in his earlobe. She batted the lashes on all of her eyes, and he was almost convinced. She smelled like wildflowers, some kind of cheap duty-free perfume. Then the scent in the air turned suddenly sickeningly sweet, like rotting fruit, and he felt a shadow on his back. Flies buzzed around his shoulders.

"You lost?" Lars didn't even turn around. He knew the smell. Proboscis girl slunk back into her archway, swinging her protrusion toward another customer. "There isn't a forest within ten lightyears of this spinner. Maybe you oughta fuck off back to the land of Oz."

Something hard and wooden crunched. Leaves rustled.

Lars turned. "Speak an actual language," he said, tapping the silver chip pinned to his collar. "This baby'll translate."

The tremuloid towered over him, sagging heavily, eyes bloodshot and reptilian. Deep cuts scarred its trunk, and some of the eye sockets were hollow, grayed. Bark flaked away as it moved its branches to shrug.

"What, you lose your speaking bits? No wooden tongue in that trunk?"

The eyes blinked. Lars had run into trems on a dozen different planets, usually minions and drudge workers—strong, not too bright, used to following orders. This one seemed dumber than the rest. Just a walking tree. He still felt the throb in his cock, and his knuckles ached from the chin-punching he'd done in the saloon. He needed a hooker and a bowl of ice—definitely in that order. He wondered what tricks that proboscis could do.

"Unless you're paying me by the hour, beat it. I'm on shore leave."

A thick branch around his arm stopped him from ducking through the red arch.

"Fuck you doing, sticks? Didn't you see the show back at the bar?"

The branch tightened. Bark dug into flesh. It reminded Lars of the Indian burns his brothers used to give him, only a thousand times worse. With his free hand, he slugged the tree-alien's trunk, thudding against living wood until his knuckles bled. The yellow eyes blinked at him heedlessly. The lights of the hub danced across its body, bright reds and blues and yellows: a haunted tree from a forest of nightmares. Lars put his hands up, and the tremuloid slackened its grip.

"Take me to your leader," he said. And the tremuloid shuffled its root system toward the opposite end of the hub.

CHAPTER II

The tremuloid sagged through neon and noise, parting the crowd with its branches. Lars scratched himself and inhaled the stink of the station: sweat and secretions, blood and slime, menstruation and ovulation, rotting flesh in the butchers' stalls and overspiced goop simmering in streetfood carts. In odd corners, religious pilgrims in bright robes burned incense on their shaved heads, and buskers maneuvered unlikely instruments of chitin and brass as travelers and smugglers and soldiers on leave scattered coin at their feet.

The tree-thing skulked into a swank, blue bar glowing with aquarium light, the trem's top branches shedding leaves as it scraped against the archway. The place was full, as noisy as the hub outside. Slinking across the tables and bottle shelves, translucent station cats eyed the freakish fish in the aquariums, green musculature shifting beneath their skins. Lars salivated. The cats smelled like lunch. No!

"If you want to take me to dinner, sticks, just be a gentleman and ask."

The tremuloid hobbled to the left, finding some chance vacancy in the crowd large enough to accommodate its foliage. At the table directly in front of him, Lars saw a gothic knockout of a woman who put to shame even his deepest spank-bank fantasies. She sat with legs crossed, a dark leatherette dress shrink-wrapped to her athletic alien body. Her skin, pale as death, was pocked and lined with ritual-

7

JAY

8

istic scars like scriptures for the blind, radiating from a complex brand that bubbled in the flesh above her breasts. Where hair would've been on most humanoids, tendrils hung like living rubber tubes. Ornamented here and there with silver rings, the tendrils were nearly the same purple as the grog he'd swilled and spilled in the Pickled Quasar. Her eyes: translucent ovals of amethyst with disco balls inside, flashing at him. She reached for one of the cats, brought it toward her, caressed its sticky skin with a sharp purple-painted nail.

She opened her mouth—a row of razor teeth behind black blowjob lips—and said, "You're the wolf."

The tremuloid's yellow eyes were watching. It had another cup of chlorogin glowing fluorescent green in its prehensile branch.

"That your pimp?" Lars said. "Doesn't say much. I like him."

The woman almost smiled. "You misunderstand," she said. "You're not buying me. I'm buying you."

"My lucky day. Been a while since I've been paid for it." He pulled a chair from another table and slumped into it, leaning back. "This one of those DNA gigs? Impregnation from a stud with good genetic batter?"

"I'm not buying your dick, wolf. If it even twitches in my direction—" This time she did smile, showing that mouthful of shark's teeth, blazing white and dangerous. Lars winced instinctively. Even the cat skittered away, a waste of a good meal.

"Listen, I've been in the black for a long time. Weeks, months. I'm just looking to get fucked, fed, and drunk. I've seen enough jobs to last me a decade in one of these shithole waystations. You hear about the Cacotopian civil war? Or that shit with the cyborgs on the metal planet out by Vega, the one whose name is in binary so you sound like an asshole rattling off all those zeroes? Been there and a hundred others—casino systems, outlaw moons, vagrant desert worlds, wherever somebody needs somebody like me to break somebody else." Lars grabbed someone's drink and chugged it, slapping it back on the adjacent table. "I don't need your job. The dick, however—give that away free."

9

The tremuloid shifted beside him, and the woman's tendrils twitched like snakes dreaming bad dreams. She uncrossed her legs and leaned forward. Tits bulged forward like halfmoons, making his blood uneasy.

"Let's start over," she said. "My associate beside you is Frank. He can't speak because of a blight he picked up from a flytrap whore, but he's loyal. I'd tell you my name, but you wouldn't be able to pronounce it with your primitive tongue. Call me Jay."

"Jay," he said, liking the taste. "Lars."

"I know. Lars Breaxface—the werewolf in space."

"It's got a ring to it."

"Show me."

Jay settled back into her chair, crossing her arms under her breasts. Sparks flashed inside her heliotropic eyes.

"It doesn't work that way," Lars said. "It's the moons. Place like this, it isn't even orbiting a planet, just some half-dead star. No moons out here." He scratched his neck and smelled the cats and creatures pulsing in the corners of the room. He could smell the meats for sale in the hub, too, beckoning. Fuck, he was hungry. And horny. Sometimes it felt like the same thing. "I've got plenty of lunar batteries in my cruiser. Rig them up, I can turn even if I'm lightyears from moonscape. But they're expensive—not wasted on demonstrations."

"Then how do I know what I'm getting?"

Lars stood, hulking. "You sent sticks—Frank—here to find me. You came all the way out to this borderland spinner. You already know what you're getting."

She cracked another smile. A cat rubbed viscously against her pale shoulder.

"They say you're quite the killer," Jay said. "A wild animal with a massacre or two behind him. Might be that's what I need."

Lars knew what she meant. Officially, Dys-7—a farming planet with delusions of independence—had succumbed to some exploding plague dug up from alien soil. But word gets around. Dys-7 had been a massacre, his only massacre. From before he'd learned to control the beast inside him. It still gave him nightmares when he went to sleep sober. He didn't list it on his résumé. "You heard wrong. I'm a merc, lady. Soldier of fortune. Sellsword. Private contractor. Bodyguard. Et cetera, et cetera. Just happens to be I'm a bodyguard with some unique lupine attributes."

"I have a bodyguard," said Jay, nodding toward the drunkard tree. "I need a monster." She reached into the purple hive of tendrils and pulled out a small cylinder. In the blue light, it took a moment for him to see what was inside: a solid black cube, enough negativium to power his cruiser till the next Big Bang. He could only sell half and still be disgustingly rich.

"Jeezus butt-fucking Joseph," he muttered.

Jay closed her hand, and the cylinder was swallowed back into its hiding place in her living hair. "Payment. For the job and for transit. The route Frank and I took to this system is no longer viable. And we have a few more stops to make before we get where we're going." She stood, and the cat behind her hissed.

"Where are we headed, then? You, me, and Treebeard over there."

"It's not on any starmap. Not even backspace."

"You make it sound like Hell."

"Close," she said. "Home."

CHAPTER III

Tethered along the docks of the station were a hundred ships from every corner of the galaxy: chrome rockets and effervescent orbs, heavy cargo clunkers and thin starcruisers, a few clockwork gearships with foil solarsails folded like wings. And there among them, bright yellow flames painted along its nose, golden spoiler above its tachyon engine, SHEILA in silver cursive beside the naked pinup girl on the fuselage, was his cruiser. Lars stared at it out through the bubbled porthole in the hub, some busker-wannabe beside him cranking an aluminum hand-horn.

Where's home? he'd asked.

We'll get there. Ran her black tongue across the points of her teeth. *When it's time.*

He couldn't say no. It meant retirement, if he wanted it. Sunside hut on some paradise planet, all the booze and pussy he could buy. No more cruising the black, finding brawls and battles to shove his mercenary snout into. No more oil-and-sweat waystations like this fucking spinner. He looked out the porthole at the row of rocketships, imagined never seeing another like it, maybe even hocking old *Sheila*, though he doubted he could. She was the only constant, the only friend, he had in the big black empty. He'd probably get her a new paint job.

"Where's our ride?" Jay said. She was behind him, a thin black bag on her shoulder; its leather-mimetic fabric matched her dress. Frank stood next to her, branches laden with luggage, a growler of chlorogin full and fluorescent in his primary limb.

Lars nodded toward the porthole. "Little number to the left, with the flame job."

"About what I expected. Except shittier."

Lars snarled. "That's *Sheila*. Two things I don't abide: shit-talking *Sheila*, and shit-talking my mother."

A voice hissed in the crowd, "Your mother's had more cock in her ass than a two-ton Plasticon whore."

Lars whirled, and there in the hub throng was a gaggle of Siskelian smugglers, mouths askew, bruises still blooming on their chins. The leader, the one he'd knocked out first back at the Quasar, had an old acid scar down one side of his face, blue keloid flesh where his left eye was supposed to be. The rest were a motley gang in pirates' armor bedazzled with meteorite, some bluer than others, all of them big and pissed off and swinging heavy asteroid-hauling chains.

He felt the wolf in his veins, trying its best to make him turn even lightyears from the nearest moon. He swallowed the urge—too far from a lunar recharge to go wolfing out for this blue waste of life—and instead rested his hand on his blaster.

"She look like you, motherfucker? Some half-evolved ape swiveling her hindquarters toward anything with a nickel and a hard-on?" The one-eyed Siskelian cracked his neck. His one jaundiced eye was a slit between cheekbone and brow.

Sinews, leverage, kinesthesis. Animal motion. The hub seemed to hush. Lars' blaster cleared leather before the smuggler knew to stop smirking. The Siskelian stood for a moment, mouth frozen in a gap-toothed sneer, dark blue blood seeping over his lips from the simmering jag of flesh where the rest of his face used to be. Blood, bone, and brains sprayed the smuggler's comrades, their faces progressing through a stop-motion animation from shock to rage as

13

their leader toppled and Lars blew imaginary smoke from the blaster's barrel. Around them, a wave of realization rippled through the crowd, radiating from the dead man. Sound came back, muffled screams growing loud in the claustrophobic hub.

"Lars, holy fuck," Jay was shouting behind him. "You never heard of keeping a low *fucking* profile?"

"Never let Greedo shoot first." Lars holstered the ray gun and kissed the knuckles of his chin-punching hand. "Besides, already punched the bastard once."

Those in the crowd who'd noticed the gore were panicking, pushing into the oblivious, the screams drowning out chitin music and chanted prayers. The smuggler gang was charging through the crowd, their heavy chains reared back to whip the wolfman. And then they weren't, snatched into the air by tentacles of wood and leaf, flung into sections of the crowd not yet disrupted by the panic. A tornado of white, black, and purple landed blows on the necks and kneecaps of the rest of the smuggler crew before they even had a chance to raise their chains. The smugglers collapsed, blue hulks bleeding all over their stone-studded suits.

Jay settled into some kind of ninja pose and surveyed the fleeing crowd. "StatSec will be here any second. They must be in the brothels tucking their dicks into their fatigues. We should run."

Lars looked around the hub for the proboscis girl, or even the little cat-person. Nothing but folks tripping over each other, giving him cold white stares like he was some kind of monster, which he was.

"Hello? Breaxface?" She punched him hard in the face, a sudden crunch in her fingers, and she swore loudly. "I said let's go."

He wasn't ready. Goddamn smugglers, trash-talking his mother. He hadn't gotten that blowjob. He hadn't loaded up on crates of jerky and salty snacks for the long haul. He was nowhere near drunk enough to drive.

"Just wait," he said. "Just a minute."

He felt himself lifted, the bite of rough wood grinding his arm. He was on his feet, and Frank was collecting the luggage, his growler smashed and glistening green on the station floor. All of the tremuloid's eyes looked heavy with melancholy, sticky sap-tears forming at their edges.

"We don't have a minute," Jay said, walking quickly past him. "You blew somebody's face off in a neutral station. In front of hundreds of witnesses. They'll throw you into the black alive, won't even waste a bullet. And I can't allow that—I need you."

He smirked, feeling the blood crack, already drying on his face. "*Sheila's* got a king-size bed. Thousand thread-count sheets. A little stained, but—"

"Shut up." Jay shook her punching hand, as if considering hitting him again. "Shut your mouth. And don't open it. Not even to breathe." There were shouts in the distance, official-sounding. Station Security. "Come on. The ship. We need to leave now."

Some of the smuggler crew were starting to rouse, all of them soaked in blue-black blood. Lars could take them, if he wanted to. Even without Jay and her pet plant's help. That blaster had charge enough to make a hundred shots at that power level before clicking empty. And there was always the wolf—however long he could last without a nearby moon. But what was the point? Jay was right. They had to go.

"So," he said, "no snacks?"

A branch thumped him heavily in the back. He nodded, surrendered. StatSec was louder, too loud, too near, nearly through the crowd. Jay started for the docks, her pace almost a run, and Lars kept lockstep. Behind them, the vegetal Frank, lumbering with surprising speed.

- reminds me of starwars / cowboy Bebop
- chapters work like scenes → very cinematic visual

CHAPTER IV

They ran, pushing past arriving crewmen and cybernetic stevedores. Crates tumbled as the dockmen's hand-clamps lost their grip, and more than once Lars almost went sprawling, only to feel Frank's wooden limbs reach to steady him; Jay vaulted each obstacle with ease. Behind them, concussion slugs dented the walls. A couple of bystanders, hit with the dull shells, dropped like sacks of moondust.

In a spinner this big, there were too many docks. *Sheila* was too far away.

"They're gonna route us," Lars shouted over crashes and gunshots. "Second squad rounding the other end to head us off, no doubt. They'll pop us like a dick blister."

Jay glanced back, amethyst eyes sparkling in the fluorescent light. She skidded to a stop. "Give me your hand."

"Are you fucking crazy?" A slug thudded against the ceiling above them, bounced hard to the corridor floor. "You said it yourself. We need to run."

Frank lurched past them then turned ponderously, his tree-bulk menacing behind Jay. From some enchanted pocket in her boot, the pale woman pulled a long knife, curved and ornamented with baroque blood grooves. She repeated: "Your hand."

He thrust his hairy mitt toward her, and she slid the blade across his palm. He barely felt it. Slugs pounded, and he thanked his luck that StatSec at a station like this were so poorly trained. Not like the jackbooted fascists he'd run into near Fed Prime. Red bubbled to the surface of the thin cut across his hand. And then it rose. Blood lifted from the wound. Not the chaos movement of zero-grav, but a deliberate rising: liquid sculpture, his blood given shape.

"The fuck is this?" he said. He didn't dare move his hand. He felt a sucking in his veins.

Jay's brow furrowed with concentration. "Shut up."

Blood twisted in the air above his outstretched palm. It became a storm, a miniature hurricane, crimson and gore. He felt it pulling from him, his heart pumping, feeding it. StatSec were on them. Riot guns raised. He could smell their sweat and fear. Slugs wouldn't kill you, not unless they hit your braincase, but fuck did they hurt. Lars tensed his back, expecting impact. Blood swirled. Blood roiled. Then Jay thrust her hand toward the security force, and blood flew. Lars turned in time to see the armored officers raise their arms against the bloodstorm; some fired at it impotently. With a wet slap, his blood flattened and spread, stretching across the width of the corridor, pitted with the slugs it stopped.

A blood wall.

Jay dropped her hand and wheeled. Bystanders and stevedores hugged the walls of the dock tunnel, terrified. Someone was vomiting.

"Fucking *run*," she said, and Lars shook the last drops of blood from his hand, boots thundering as he ran.

○

18

Sheila was unguarded. Near the airlock, a couple of sailors from a neighboring slip were playing a card game on a pair of crates. They didn't even bother to look up as the trio raced into the dock. Lars punched the lock interface the way he'd punch a chin—*hard*—and the sphincter constricted, interlocking, a kaleidoscope of flat steel blades closing between the wolfman and the two oblivious sailors. Lars fished his keys out of his jeans. As he turned the tumbler in his cruiser's bay door, a pink rabbit's foot dangled from its keychain.

Thuds against the airlock door, but the sphincter blades didn't dent. Even armor-piercing rounds wouldn't scratch an airlock. All a concussion slug would do is bounce.

"They're through the blood," Jay said.

Lars pulled the door open, reaching in to unfasten the trip wire inside. "You think?"

"They'll have that door open any second. Now that they know where we are."

"Thank the hot Cosmic Jeezus for bureaucracy. Union dockers won't haul ass, even for StatSec. We got two minutes, at least."

He stepped inside the cruiser just as the sphincter began to dilate.

"Well," Lars said, "fuck me. Overachievers on this crew."

A slug slapped against the starship, scuffing *Sheila*'s paint.

"Hey, assholes, that's a custom job!"

Jay drove her shoulder into his ribs, forcing him into the cruiser's cargo bay. They tumbled and flopped into a maelstrom of empty beer cans and crusty takeout containers. Taking the impact of the conc-slugs in his hard trunk, Frank ducked into the cruiser and pulled the door closed behind him. Jay was on her feet, cans rattling as she ran for the cockpit.

"Don't you touch my baby," Lars called after her. He pulled himself to his feet. His hand stung. Frank was looking at him with all his morose, sallow eyes. "What, Frank?" The eyes blinked. "Sorry about the growler, man. Some hooch in the fridge. Take what you want."

The tremuloid was hunched under the ceiling of the small bay. He rooted himself where he was, waiting, that spooky smattering of eyeballs now fixed on the door. Slugs rained against the hull.

Jay was already strapped into the pilot seat when Lars found her. He saw the pink rabbit's foot in her hand, the ignition turning. The cruiser shuddered as the engines fired. Her long, white fingers skipped easily over the holographic displays, punching in coordinates and travel codes faster than Lars could read them.

"That's my seat," he said.

"You should hold onto something."

"Nobody flies *Sheila* but me. Nobody."

Trid holograms flashed across her eyes. "I'm serious."

As she pushed the throttle, a pre-recorded soundbite blared from the stereo: the revving engine of an oil-burning muscle-rig. Nineteen sixty-seven Chevy Impala, if the sound library was to be believed. Metal whined as *Sheila* tore from the airlock, and the cruiser was free, suspended in space between two blocky cargo ships. Lars gripped the pilot seat to keep from toppling.

"Goddamn," Lars muttered, "you probably just killed fifty people with that depressure."

Her pale shoulders shrugged. "It was us or them."

The cruiser dropped below the cargo ships, and Jay steered it left, the big dying sun coming into view through the windshield.

"Is there anything uglier," she said, "than a dying star?"

"This hooker I met back in Sibyl Twin. Moon populated by ogres. She was ugly as sin, that one, teeth all busted out. Had its advantages, though." He shrugged. "Come to think of it, a lot of—"

Jay punched the throttle, and the small white dots of the cosmos began to stretch into lines, splinter into crystalline psychedelia, the universe breaking up as the cruiser burrowed into subspace, FTL-drive grinding in its chassis at the back of the ship, *Sheila* futtling as she'd done a thousand times but without the werewolf at her wheel, Lars watching space uncouple with itself—and then velocity finding him, carrying him, his whole weight up and slamming into the back wall of the cockpit, knocking him flat out on his ass with a dull metal thunk.

CHAPTER V

He is floating. The junk of the sky—abandoned space-race capsules, orbit station discards, the thousands of dead satellites decommissioned over the centuries—hangs around him in the thermospheric strata, barely in the pull of a dark and haggard Earth. He sees it, through the slow swirl of metal: Home. Brown continents, gray clouds, the sky a velvet nighttime blue. He's tagging old telecoms, he remembers, marking their dark solars for salvage. Rare-earths embedded in their panels. Singer and Muerta somewhere else among the wreckage, tagging the same, the rest of the crew sleeping off hangovers in the orbiter till shift change, and then he sees the piece of scrap like a razor, and he sees his tether, his link to the orbiter, severed, and he grabs for it, the far-off end of it frayed and snaking away in zero-grav, kicks the mini ion-thrusts on his ankles, tether still out of reach, and he's gasping now, oxygen leaking out, reserve tank kicking in but nominally, it isn't much, five minutes, maybe ten. His helmet slams into a heavy piece of junk, a windowless capsule turning on its own slow axis, the red flag of the Asian Union rolling in and out of view, he turns the airlock, no rust in space though it must be a hundred years old, the Union down below, on the surface, still radioactive and burning decades later. The airlock gives. Dust scatters as air rushes to fill the universe, or to try, and inside is a corpse in a red suit, mummified and skeletal, but it isn't right—too much hair on its face and limbs, fingernails long and black like talons. He closes the hatch and seals the lock, gasping, smelling his own acrid breath, the reserve tank empty, he hits the capsule's emergency trigger, O_2 flushing the small cylindrical room, Lars unlatching the suffocating helmet, and that corpse, the desiccated skin of its face retracting, a sick smile of jagged, animal teeth.

○

His bunk was so soaked with sweat when he woke he thought he'd pissed himself. Wouldn't have been the first time. His boots were still on, and his mouth felt like the hair on a buffalo's asshole. He needed a drink.

Blue bits of brain still clung to his shirt, so he peeled it off and crawled into a new one, a black T-shirt with military-grade thermal weave. Five minutes in open space, and only his arms and head would freeze off. He flicked a skull fragment from his pants and figured they were good enough. He didn't want to have to take his boots off to change.

Outside the bunk, Lars followed the sound of music—the raging rock 'n' roll that comprised his playlist—back to the cargo bay, where Frank was opening another beer and sucking it into his system through the siphoning end of his prehensile limb. Old trash had been pushed into a pile near a rack of salvage tools, and a new set of empties clattered in a ring around the drunken tree. Frank's eyes seemed to focus on Lars for a moment, vaguely, then he dropped the empty can and opened the nearby fridge for another.

"What is it," came Jay's voice from behind, "that werewolves dream about? Fat full moons? Pastures full of virgin sheep?"

He turned; she'd changed from the leatherette minidress into black fatigues, heavy boots, and a fitted sleeveless top that shimmered with spider-silk sheathing. Bulletproof. She wasn't

Oh, hello. I'm Jay. And I'm taking you to hell.

23

dressed to tease his dick anymore, to sap the blood from his animal brain. She was dressed to kick ass.

"All my ex-girlfriends, a never-ending erection, and a couple gallons of bacon-flavored lube."

"You were whimpering like a kicked dog."

"Must've been my ex-wives then." Then, with a growl, "You took my ship."

"You're the idiot who murdered somebody in the middle of a crowd. We had to get out of there, and you were bumblefucking around, whining about chipped paint." She pushed past him, grabbed a beer from the fridge, and sat on a steel crate that was secured to the floor with nylon. "Keys are in the ignition."

"The popped seal," he said. "StatSec blown into the vacuum, plus a few dozen crew. Sure, I killed one asshole. You killed half a hundred did nothing but park at the wrong dock."

She chugged the beer then showed her sharp white teeth. "Collateral damage." She rested her elbows on her knees, fumbling with the label on the can. "Anyway, we're clear. Even if the station beams our faces to central authorities, we're too far from Federation Prime, going nowhere they'd care to follow. It's the frontier, Breaxface. People die out here every day. Little people on little spinners, whole planets burned up in galactic genocide. Shit happens."

"Nowhere they'd care to follow, huh?" Lars nodded to Frank, big hand gesturing, and the tree-hulk tossed him a cold brew. "Where we headed, then? I mean now, in the immediate. Don't give me that need-to-know bullshit again."

"Canal City," Jay said. "Someone there knows something about toys. He might be useful later on."

"No thanks," Lars said. "*Persona non grata* on that pond planet. Ran a job there once for some up-jumped gangster-wannabe puppeteer. Job was too hot, I bolted. He wasn't too keen on that."

"Then let's hope we avoid a reunion."

"I said no, lady. Find another rock with a toy store."

"Canal City," Jay said. "There is nowhere else."

Lars growled but the look in Jay's eyes said no arguments—the mission, for now, was Canal City, and if he wanted to see payday, he'd have to suck it up. He slumped against the hull, nylon cargo nets dangling from the ceiling above him, grabbing one of the nets for the hell of it, resting his arm there. The music thumped. He sipped his beer. Despite a dull, constipated feeling in his gut that said he was headed for a barge-load of trouble, Lars felt better already. Hair of the fucking dog. Tasted like Valhallan glory.

"That blood thing," he said finally. "Back at the spinner. What was that? You a witch?"

Jay took a long gulp from her can then ran a fingertip over the braille of scars on her forearm. "It's something I learned a long time ago."

"Cruise control's got *Sheila* blazing the wormhole highway all the way to Canal City. Unless I was passed out all damn day, I'm guessing we've got an hour or two before we bump out of subspace and start docking."

"Three hours thirty-six minutes. Galactic standard."

"That's three hours to swap stories, get to know who we're working with." He drank. The beer was cold and bitter, the way he liked it. Frank's eyes, all of them, were fogging over, foliage sagging before them; Jay's flashed like violet galaxies. A guitar solo howled on the stereo, a good one, notes blitzing up and down the neck. He said, "So. Are you a witch?"

CHAPTER VI

She'd learned bloodhex as a kid, hardly big enough to fill out her black spider-print training bra. It was part of her schooling, she said. Blood magic and martial arts, right after ancient literature and music class. She could still play a mean fire-tremolo, her long fingers dancing across its pistons, though she only remembered a few songs. As for hex training, it'd been cut short, along with everything else, when her teacher had dragged her kicking and screaming away from the burning castle as her family, and her family's attendants—the guards, the scribes, the advisors, the priests—were murdered while she watched, the little bit of hex she knew helpless to save them.

"So, no," Jay said, finishing another beer. "I'm not a witch."

"Shit," Lars said, "that doesn't disprove witch. They burn witches. You could be a whole witch family."

Even before he finished the last syllable, Jay's long knife was at his throat, straining against an artery.

"Say it again, wolf. Call my family witch." Her eyes burned purple.

"All right, you're not a witch," he said, hands up in surrender, feeling the point of the knife nick his skin as he swallowed. "Nobody's a fucking witch."

Jay whipped the blade back in a blur of silver, and it disappeared into the length of her boot. She settled back with another beer, cracking open the can and watching it foam at the mouth. Lars sipped his. He still felt like six tons of oiled brick, and the dream made the hair on his arms feel like insects. At least it hadn't been Dys-7. The smiling skull he could handle. Dys-7 was deep-fried Hell. Near the fridge, Frank slouched against the hull surrounded by empties, his yellow eyes all blank and ringed with sap, smelling sick and saccharine and surrounded by flies.

"What about the scars?" Lars said finally.

"What about them?"

"They aren't battle scars. Precise. Tribal." He thrust his chin toward his own tattooed arms. His skin was covered wrist to neck in ink, much of it faded and hidden under thatches of dark hair. "These, they all have a story. Some military, some salvage-crew. Most of them, though, are hex. Witchy shit." Her eyes seemed to scan his arms. She was leaning forward on the crate. He thought he saw a smile grow at the corner of her lips, but if so, it was brief. "Found a witch on some godforsaken forest moon, guy I heard knew something about binding ink. Worth the cash. Hurt like the devil pissing razorblades, but it was worth that, too. Helps to control the turn. Before that—"

"Your massacre."

Lars scratched at one of the runic tattoos on his elbow, then scratched his beard because what else was there to do. "Yeah. That mess."

"Military," Jay said. "You don't walk like a soldier."

"I walk like a goddamn werewolf badass."

"You walk like a pirate."

"I swashbuckle a little." Lars shrugged. "Part of my public persona." Jay raised a scarred eyebrow and said nothing, so he went on: "I was born and raised on the Nevada coast. Back on Terra. My hometown, when you grew up, you joined the flood crews and crank-

ed out your own assembly line of starving brats with some local piece of ass, or you enlisted. No way I was getting stuck in that rotting stilt-town. I wanted offworld. Got stationed on an asteroid, our garrison officially on orders to guard a mine but everybody knew we were there to put down a rebellion if any of the miners had ideas about their pay or work hours, both of which were shit. One day the workers strike, so I get orders to shoot a few in the face and hang them above the shaft elevator. And me, I'm a good grunt. I know how to follow orders. So, I take each of these guys who just want a fair shake, and I put a bullet through each of their eyes and I tie them up by their feet, like cattle. I get a promotion.

"And then I resign. Dishonorable discharge, since my contract isn't up, so the only work I can get is salvage—all those fuckers are one step away from criminal anyway. I wasn't going back to the surface, not to the flood crews and the corn blight and the radioactive wind blowing in over the ocean. Worked salvage for a while. Then I got the wolf in my veins. Military groundcrew found our wreck, me wolfed-out and berserk, covered in gore, bits of my crewmates still in my teeth. Took twenty of them to take me in, six dead. Banished me from the planet after that. They were too scared to kill me—they didn't know what would happen if they tried."

The music had stopped, and the only sounds in the ship were the heavy thrum of the engine and the creaking of wood from a drunk and passed-out Frank.

"The scars are my name," Jay said. She looked down at her chest, the brand mostly visible between her cleavage and collarbone. As old as the scar was, it still looked wet, painful. Its design was intricate and hard to follow, an optical puzzle he couldn't parse. "Family crest. Branded when I was born. The rest of it they cut on my nameday: date of birth, zodiac, my rank within the family."

"That's a lot of fucking syllables for a name."

"Yeah."

"You're high society, then, huh? Some kind of space princess? I've always wanted to fuck a space princess."

Jay ran a finger across the hilt of her knife, still in her heavy boot—for now. "I'm just an orphan, Breaxface. I've been waiting a long time to avenge my family. Now you're going to help me do it. You, Frank, a few others. Even a witch."

Lars chugged his beer and tossed the can into Frank's pile of empties. They rattled and the cloud of flies scattered, briefly, but the tremuloid didn't budge.

"Well, shit," he said. "I didn't realize we were on a mission of righteous vengeance."

"We are."

The air was cloying with Frank's sap stink. Lars banged on a ventilation duct, and something dislodged, recycled air pumping in from the processor. They sat for a while, saying nothing, having said a hell of a lot already, whole biographies, so they listened to the small sounds of the ship. The vents, the flies, the machinery of propulsion, Frank. Lars' nuts were still aching from being cock-blocked back on the spinner, and he had to piss from all the beer. He stood up, steadying himself with the straps hanging from the ceiling.

"Put some tunes on," he told her. "When I get back, we'll play cards."

"Cards?"

"This is outer space, baby. Nothing to do but beat off, rock out, and sit pickling in your own farts." He dug a deck of cards from one of the pockets in his jeans and tossed it toward Jay. "At least this round I don't have to play solitaire."

As he drained the snake in the ship's chemical toilet, he heard thrashing heavy metal begin to blast from the cargo hold stereo. He imagined Jay banging her head to the beat, purple tendrils whipping like a squid with palsy, and felt his cock turn rigid in his hand.

A mission of righteous vengeance. For a magic ninja space princess.

There were worse ways to earn a paycheck.

CHAPTER VII

Sheila sloughed the wormhole like an old, stiff tube sock, and right in front of her, in a swirl of white clouds, was the ocean planet. From orbit, all Lars could see was the wild blue of the planet's turbulent surface sea, but he knew that down somewhere near the southern tropic was the world's only landmass, a small island continent crisscrossed with filthy, stagnant canals, the algae-slick intergalactic trade port of Canal City, a crime-ridden gangster town just out of Federation reach. It reminded him of Freewheel, without all the fun. Beyond the blue world, a couple of moons swung like a pair of celestial testicles. Lars could feel them trying to pull the wolf out of him. He grit his teeth and pushed *Sheila* toward the atmosphere, radioing the city's maglev aerodock for permission to land.

As for the card game, Jay had won every hand.

○

When they landed, it took a couple of slugs from an engine wrench to rouse Frank. The tremuloid shook his foliage, blinked the sap out of his eyes, and lumbered toward the hatch. He stood just outside the cruiser, drinking in the fading sunlight through his leaves. Jay climbed out behind him, then Lars, who took note of the shape of her ass in the fatigues and of the blaster hanging from an ammo belt that sat loose on her hips.

"Expecting trouble?" he said.

Without looking back, she answered, "Hoping not."

Lars glanced at the water-city rising below them. He could see the whole city stretching across the island from up there, on the port's floating mag-lev docks. "Keep the safety off. This whole town's trouble, battered and deep-fried."

○

A shuttle spat them out on the platform of a busy terminal, its vaulted ceilings alive with holograms and screeching birds, crawling greenery, and the echoes of loudspeakers calling out departures and arrivals. Frank and Lars followed Jay through the crowds of travelers and panhandlers, toward the wide-open archway that led into the city.

Canal City was teeming. The port metropolis stretched into the shallows of the continent, its waterways clogged with glass gondolas and amphibious taxis with heavy electric engines, bipeds of a hundred alien races weaving between traffic on levitating riverbikes. Sunset reflected on the upper stories of skyscrapers—towers of thick, barbed coral which rose from the green water like the bones of leviathans. A film of algae and slime clung to their brindled foundations. Birds that looked like twists of rubber tubing arced in the light, diving the polluted canals for twitching red fish, while cicadas screeched a constant white noise under the shouts and rhythms of the city. Canal City was old and alive, beautiful in its labyrinthine architecture, and stank of sewage and brine. The salt in the air made Lars' beard itch.

Jay walked the canalside planks with purpose, and Lars kept pace, scanning the crowds for any sign of the re-animated trash puppets of Quillian Nine. He knew the gangster puppeteer still held a grudge for the job he'd skipped out on, Lars absconding offworld in the dead of night with the up-front half of his fee with him for his trouble. Though the wolfman had figured them squared. The job hadn't been as advertised. Lars Breaxface beat people up for money, broke some faces, even killed a few assholes now and again if they needed it, but it was just a paycheck. He didn't get his rocks off to violence and pain, and didn't trust anybody who did.

As they turned a corner, a brace of the tube-birds flocked to Frank's foliage, twisting to roost in his beleaguered branches. The tremuloid swatted at them irritably. Before Lars could quip that the tree looked too damn sober, a small boulder spattered with moss and lichen scuttled into an alley, hissing and barking its head off. The sounds sent the birds fleeing from Frank's upper regions as the boulder—a crab thing, with thick legs and rough asymmetrical claws— kept up its racket. A brood of boulder-crabs bubbled from rain gutters and sewer runoffs, all the size of spaniels and all raucous. In one fluid motion, as if busting a dance move, Jay booted one over the walkway's edge, its shriek and splash a warning to the rest. As Lars caught up behind her, the barking creatures slunk back to their gutters, claws clapping angrily.

Lars smirked. "What'd it do, catcall you in crabspeak?"

"This city is a cesspool."

"Yeah," the wolfman shrugged, "but the sunsets are all right."

The princess glanced up at the sun beginning its slide behind the coral towers. "Come on. Before it's dark."

They resumed their trek across the boardwalks, Jay again taking the lead, a chorus of hungry claws clicking behind them.

○

The sun had fallen behind the skyline, calcified towers in long, bright beams. Ja business district, down a side terrace lower floors of a coral block, and fi nondescript storefront in the middle of

A bell dinged as Frank ducke ninja princess, and Lars followed the

34

making his blood race. If there was a sign above the shop's door, he couldn't read it.

○

The fish-man was standing beside a display case polishing his knob. The knob was glass, or some kind of crystal, and the green-scaled alien rubbed it thoughtfully with a soft cloth before setting it back into the case with knobs of varying sizes, shapes, and colors. Some were ribbed or rippled. Some looked like anemones. The fish-man blinked wide frog eyes, made all the more bulbous by the copper-rimmed steampunk goggles he was wearing, and his thick rubbery lips stretched into a salesman's smile.

"Look at you, big guy," he said to Lars. "You're a heck of a specimen. All that sculpted muscle, yes. You got one of them, whaddayacallit, one of those mushroom tentacle things in your trousers? How big is it? Could I take some measurements, some molds maybe?" He started fumbling in his shirt pockets before his gaze darted back up, taking in the whole bulk of Frank. "What is that, you guys horticulturalists? I don't think I have anything vegetal. Maybe some kind of root vibrator or something," adding in a yell that was aimed for Frank's uppermost branches, "Just how kinky *are* you, sir?"

Lars nudged Jay. "Fuck is he talking about, 'mushroom tentacle'?"

"Sorry, you guys just window shoppers? Welcome anyway, come in, come in." The fish-man bowed theatrically. "Arcturus Fishman, proprietor of Arcturus Fishman's Fucktoy Emporium. Coital pleasure enhancements for thirty-six different species and the number one supplier of erotic appurtenance for twelve planetary systems. We do custom jobs, too, for trickier bits. What are you guys packing? You two here together? Either of you got one of those egg sacs that squirts, or is that those half-naked apes from Xaxx-Planton? I get you primates confused. All that hair. So, what'll it be? A sex swing? Artisanal lube? Flavored with local fruits. I make it myself in the back. Makes a great sauce for ice cream, too."

It was then, as the piscine salesman grinned expectantly in the white light of the display case, that Lars began to understand what he was looking at: The whole shop was stocked with sex paraphernalia, from holographic gimp masks to cybernetic genitals. Half of the stuff he could only guess at its purpose. In his travels across the cosmos, he'd tried to stick to sexing with more or less humanoid plumbing. Pussy was pussy, even if the chick was electric blue.

"Mr. Fishman," Jay said.

Arcturus Fishman, proprietor of Arcturus Fishman's Fucktoy Emporium, waved a webbed hand. "Call me Fish. Everybody around here does. Of course, everybody around here has a clit-sized brain and no imagination. But you don't get to pick your own nickname, right? I wanted to be called Razor. Never stuck."

Jay leaned forward, resting her arm on a display case. Her other hand was on the grip of the blaster. "I want to see the Rubber Room."

"Rubber Room?" Fish picked at a fan of dried scales on his neck. His frog eyes avoided Jay's. "Where'd you hear about that? There's no rubber room. Heck, there's no room rubber or otherwise. Who told you about that? What you see is what you get, rubberwise. You see that dildo there? Rubber. That's about it, rubberly speaking."

Lars picked up the rubber dildo, and it flopped forward, the grotesque head of it smacking against his wrist. He set it back on the shelf and picked up a sleek metal number that he could see his face in, shrunken and skinny.

"Jay, what the fuck?" he said. "This guy just sells dildos. The fuck good is he for the mission?"

"That's not just a dildo," Fish called to him over Jay's shoulder. "That's a *space* dildo. Specially engineered for maximum zero-grav and subspace satisfaction, for the long haul through the black. On sale this week, twenty percent off." Fish glanced at Jay, then at the gun on her hip. "Two for one. Fifty percent off. Whatever you want."

Jay slipped the blaster from the ammo belt, and instantly it was trained on Fish. The bright red triangle of its laser sight glowed between his eyes.

"I want," Jay said, "to see the Rubber Room."

"Fuck, whoa, Frog Mother and all the fucking blue gods of the sea, oh fuck," Fish stammered, both webbed hands way up, "This is a private establishment. You can't just, with a gun, fuck. There's no Rubber Room. Oh fuck. There's no any kind of room. Even if there was, I couldn't—"

A bell jingled as the front door opened. Jay swung the blaster toward the door; Lars brandished the space dildo. Flanking the door stood two figures: the first, a knotted assembly of jagged coral and thick, gray driftwood, the other barely more than a pile of rock, algae-festooned and spattered white with bird shit. Debris-men, held together by some arcane force, in the vague shape of human giants and standing taller, even, than the towering Frank. The rock golem's head was rough-hewn and eyeless, the other's a jagged crown of conch shell, their faces blank and dull in a way that couldn't be mistaken for something alive. Between them stepped a man with skin like silver nacre, a mirror man, reflecting the sex shop like a funhouse attraction. Lars clenched the dildo so hard it crumpled. *So much for the long haul in the black*, he thought. *And so much for a fucking low profile*. Quillian had found him. And the mirror-faced gangster didn't look pleased.

CHAPTER VIII

The red triangle of Jay's gunsight glowed and refracted on the gangster's silver throat.

"Emporium's closed," she spat. "This is a private meeting."

Quillian's sharp cheekbones shifted, an expression that passed for a smile. "If it isn't Lars Breakfast, asshole from space," came the gangster's ethereal voice. The silver gangster spoke without a mouth, but his sense-language translated like any other. "I don't think your friend likes me."

Jay's head swinging to stare down Lars was the only movement in the room. Even the gimp masks on display seemed to be frozen on a particular devil-horned hologram. "You *know* this guy?"

"I told you we shouldn't come here." Lars was watching the debris-men for movement. "This is Quillian Nine, a genuine silver-plated piece of whale shit. It's Lars *Breaxface*, you tinfoil bastard. How'd you tail me? You got eyes in the algae now?"

"Things have changed." The shifting cheekbones again, the invisible smile. "You're a wanted man. Bounty Guild is beaming your mug all over Federation space and beyond. Something about a bunch of dead StatSec. I didn't sweat the details."

It was sticky in the shop, the city's humidity seeping in even with the A/C running. Lars scratched idly at the back of his neck. He grumbled a little, watching Quillian's enforcers for any sign of movement. *Shit.* Now they had a bounty on their asses. He didn't figure it could pay much—who gave a fuck about some far-flung rent-a-cops? But Quillian, he knew, wasn't in it for the paycheck.

"Please, Mr. Quillian," squeaked Fish from behind a display case, "I don't know these guys. I thought they were customers. They said they wanted rubber, I told them I don't know rubber, I don't even *have* rubber, right? No rubber in this place, that floppy piece over there, it's not even rubber, it's just rubber-*like*. Rubber-*ish*."

"Don't worry, Mr. Fishman," Quillian said. "They'll be leaving momentarily."

"We've got business here," said Lars.

Quillian raised his arms, and under the cuffs of his sleeves, Lars glimpsed heavy bands of metal circling each wrist, both flashing with circuitry.

"Like I said, things have changed. There is no business in this neighborhood unless I say there is." The gangster moved his hands, and behind him, the golems of sea-trash each lifted their own deadly fists. "And I say your business is done."

Fat stone and coral feet stepped forward in a lumbering march. Lars had seen the destruction the gangster's golems could do, had watched them splatter the enforcers of a rival family with one hammering punch. Quillian could only puppet two at a time, that's as far as the hex would work, but most of the time, two were enough. He saw Frank move to shield Jay, felt the pull of the planet's moons. Lunar power, stored and throbbing in the virus in his blood. His eyes narrowed on the approaching debris-men. And then Jay fired the blaster, and his shoulder burned hot white fire.

"*Fuck*, Jay, what was that? Shoot the goddamn *bad guys*!" Lars shouted, reaching to put pressure on the sizzling wound. Hot cosmic Christ did it hurt. Like fire ants eating the muscle from the inside.

"Move your hand," Jay yelled back, firing at the approaching golems.

39

Wood splintered as a stone fist slammed into Frank's trunk. The tremuloid had prehensile branches snaked and squeezing around the stone golem's neck and left arm, roots coiling around its knees, but the golem's free hand was pounding through hard bark to the fresh white flesh of Frank's outermost rings. The other golem was crashing through Fishman's displays, heading straight for Jay. Bursts of black energy exploded from her blaster, chipping shards of coral from the golem's shoulder. With her free hand, the space princess worked a mystical hand jive. Lars felt the tug inside his veins, his blood being pulled through the shoulder wound. As the golem neared striking distance, ropes of blood lassoed its ankles, and it crashed in an avalanche that sent Fish's sex toys tumbling from their shelves. She kept blasting. Bits of calcium carbonate broke from the hulk as it struggled to its feet. It burst through the bloodrope, splashing whatever coital enhancements hadn't yet been shattered. Blood kept pulling from Lars's shoulder. He felt heavy, woozy. Quillian hadn't moved, just stood mirror-faced and placid as his golems pursued their carnage. Frank, his side looking like a lumberjack had taken an axe to it, had captured his attacker's punching fist, but the coiled branches were creaking ominously, threatening to break. Blood wrapped the conch-shell head of the other golem. Blood bound its hands. Black energy chipped away its driftwood skeleton, and each time it kept coming. Fish had disappeared, and Jay was backing further and further into the store. There was almost nowhere left to go.

He felt it first, as always, in his hands.

Time slowed. He could almost pick the debris from the air, shards of glass and metal from exploding sex toys. His knuckles arched and cracked, claws climbing under the skin. He could smell the change in his own flesh. Raw and animal. His knees buckled; his jaws wrenched forward, dripping. Ribs broke and widened, bones fused in new shapes, and muscle and organs swelled to fit. Hair turned thick and coarse and gray, black around his throat and shoulders. His shirt stretched and burst. Tail, blooming, punched through his fatigues, and his boots were left ragged. As Jay landed a shot square in the golem's chest, Lars stood hunched and snarling, werewolf of mass destruction, swelling with a thirst for ultraviolence.

41

He went for Jay's golem first, tackling it into a rack of zentai suits. Beast and puppet tangled in shiny fabric, shredding it. Jay shouted something, but it was lost in the crash and growl of brawl. The werewolf ripped at the coral man. The golem thrashed. Its craggy fists thumped against his ribs, but the wolf kept tearing until, defying the force of its creation, one of the golem's arms was wrenched off, dropping in a pile of rubble. Lars howled. Fur and muscle met coral and shell, and the two were rolling, the puppet holding its own even minus an arm. Then the werewolf was airborne—a crash, another display case shattered, the wolf back on all fours in a moment, the coral automaton already marching forward with its only arm swinging like a great calcified club.

Lars hauled back his wolf-fist, felt moon power pulse through his veins, and did what he always did when some wily son of a bitch didn't know when to stay down: He punched it in the chin.

The golem's face rippled and cracked from chin to crown, bursting in a rain of shell shards. The rest of Quillian's enforcer fell into a heap of dead coral in the middle of Arcturus Fishman's Fucktoy Emporium.

"Lars," Jay was shouting, it was hard to know how long she'd been yelling for him. She was behind the cash register, her own black blood coiling across the room from a cut on her palm. The blaster was discarded, empty. "Lars, get Frank!"

Frank was surrounded by splinters and loose leaves. Two of his branches had been ripped away. They lay like dead worms on the store's polished floor. The tremuloid's wounds were still oozing. The golem he'd been fighting had lost one of its fists, the shit-spattered stones scattered among the wood. It was covered in Jay's blood. Bloodropes twisted around its neck, trying to cut through its impossible throat. The werewolf hefted one of the coral golem's driftwood arms, shouldering it like a baseball bat, and thundered toward Frank's attacker.

"*Frank*," Lars growled, "*duck.*"

The tremuloid untwined his branches, falling back, and the golem was momentarily free. As it spun to ready its heavy fists for Lars, the wolf leapt off a dildo display and soared, bringing the thick

42

chunk of driftwood around in a wild arc. Wood cracked as it made contact, and the golem's stone head rocketed from its shoulders, crashing through the shop's front window in a hail of glass. The debris-man's body fell into a heap of boulders. The wolf, still holding the cracked driftwood, sneezed at the cloud of stone dust. He dropped the wood and snarled through the haze. Hackles bristled on his neck.

Quillian still stood under the arch of the door. He was clapping his silver hands.

"Wonderful," said the gangster. "Just what I'd always wanted to see. The legendary space werewolf. One and only in the universe. It's what I paid for, Breaxface."

"*You wanted*," Lars said, "*a massacre.*"

"Stop pretending," said Quillian, "that you have some kind of moral high ground. Your reputation preceded you. It's why I hired you in the first place. You're a killer, Breaxface. Murderer of so many I bet you've lost count. What was one more family? Mama, papa, couple of kiddo snacks... Beast like you could've done it blindfolded."

The werewolf stepped forward, but something grabbed his leg. He looked down. Several space dildos clutched his ankle, each gripping like a finger in a chrome hand. Pieces of bondage gear—steel spreader bars, titanium cuffs, straps and whips and hogtie sets fashioned from alien substances—began to fit themselves together into an arm, a shoulder, a ramshackle set of sex toy ribs. Behind him, the toys rose, debris pulling together through its own gravity, a hulking monster of nipple clamps and polished cock-knobs and alien-proboscis ball gags. On its gag-and-collar neck it wore one of the holographic gimp masks. The mask was still frozen on the devil setting. Pixilated horns of red translucent light curled from its head. It lifted Lars by his ankle, and he fell hard on his wounded shoulder before dangling in the air, the gimp golem's hand squeezing like a vice on his leg. He worried his bones might break. The werewolf kicked and clawed at the air, reaching for the golem. It lifted him higher, looking on with blank black eyes, and its zipper-mouth curled into a ragged smile.

CHAPTER IX

The last time Lars had been choked by a sex toy, he'd been in a brothel called Orion's Belt. He'd seen stars and visions and came like an eight-legged Asgardian god-horse, but the vicious look on the reptilian domme had scared him and he'd sworn off the whole asphyxiation thing, at least temporarily, though you never could tell what you might be up for when some big-tittied hotness was tickling your short-and-curlies.

The gimp golem's look, hollow and hideous, scared him more than the domme's.

Its vibrator hand was a vice around his wolf throat, and it was still smiling its mask smile. The orange horn holograms lowed and menaced as it choked him. Frank's limbs were around the golem, prying it, like a great arboreal octopus. The tremuloid might've loosed the golem's toy-flesh, given time, but Lars didn't have time. He was fading. Bloodropes wound the golem's legs and neck. Jay had pulled her long knife, but she held it more like a talisman than a weapon. She didn't seem to know where to strike.

"Ki—" Lars gasped, "Ki—Quill—ian."

On some arcane wavelength, Quillian Nine beamed his golemological mojo into the ersatz skulls of his debris-men, made them move and grip and kill, and since the two he'd been pulling strings on had just been separated soundly from their head regions, the gangster's hex was reaching to anthropomorphize some new trash. Quillian's blank, pocked face wore its invisible smile as he watched Lars choke and squirm.

"*Quillian—*" he managed again, "*Quillian—is—controlling—it.*"

Jay heard him. Her dark blood splashed across the floor planks as she dropped the bloodropes and ran for the gangster with her terrifying knife. Quillian pulled his diamond-plated pistol-cannon from his vest, lifted its wide, gleaming muzzle, and let loose a volley. The cut on Jay's hand bloomed with blood, a shield instantly rippled with halted rounds. She dropped blood and bullets and leapt, body spring-loaded from a ninja crouch, blade arcing forward. The knife clashed with the pistol, Quillian wielding it now as a jeweled bludgeon, and the pistol, glitzing in the shop light, flew and clattered under the feet of the golem. Jay whirled and brought the blade into the gangster's side, biting an inch into his mineral flesh. Quillian laughed.

"Not a bleeder, sweetheart."

He wrenched at the knife with one hand. With the other, he punched her square in the face. She reeled, blinked and glared, fangs showing in her clenched mouth. Lars' vision was tunneling. Darkness licked at his periphery, shadow flames. He couldn't see Jay anymore. Only the gimp face. Zipper mouth. Brand-new shining chrome, the interlocking teeth of his nightmares. From now on, he'd only wear pants with buttons. And then: a singing column of laser-green light, and the gimp golem was headless, crumpling, no more zipper, no more holo-horns, just mangled sex toys falling around him and Frank in a heap. The collar, where the mask had rested, burned with green flame.

Lars barely registered his fall. His snout sucked breath as he watched Fish, still wearing his shopkeeper smock, step out from the hidden back room of the emporium with a big fucking gun on his scrawny shoulder. The gun was some kind of cannon, a sleek matte-

45

7/17 '91

46

black cylinder with fancy gizmos all over it.

"*Nice shot, Fishman!*" Lars roared. The werewolf pushed himself up to stand, and Frank reached a limb to steady him.

"I was *aiming* for *you!*" Fish shouted, cannon shaking in his webbed hands. "This boutique is the number one supplier of erotic appurtenance for *twelve planetary systems.* Do you understand the meticulous storage logic and polishing rhythms for each of these quality items? Are you aware of the precise lighting angles which optimize a space dildo for the perfect shimmer? Do you have any idea how long it takes to alphabetize Y'klarian cloacal stimulators, when the first half of every word in that language is the same six letters?"

Fish fired again, and Frank pushed Lars onto the floor. The column of laser light singed bark from the tremuloid's limb as it zapped across the shop. They heard, from no certain origin, Quillian's sense-scream, and Lars jerked his head to see a perfect half-circle carved out of the gangster's shoulder, tatters of his suit jacket burning neon green. Quillian dropped the long knife and fell to his knees with a hard clunk. Jay, wiping blood from her nose, stood over him, spat, and karate-kicked him in his chiseled chin. The silver gangster fell flat back against the door, unconscious. Above him, about shoulder-high, was a perfect round hole, smoldering.

Jay's blade scraped wood as she lifted it from the floor. She turned eyes and knife toward the laser-holding Arcturus Fishman. "You missed."

The fish-man dropped the canon and held up his hands. "The R-Rubber Room," he stuttered. "Oh, fuck, just go, just fucking fuck everything. No way my insurance'll cover this. Those philistines won't know the true value of my lube stores or comprehend the artisanal craftsmanship of a hand-cut mooncrystal sex knob. I'm ruined. You've ruined me. Twelve systems," Fish wept, "I was the galactic king of fucktoys."

Lars stretched and felt the claws on his fingers begin to sheath. Bones broke back into place, muscle and organs shrinking, snout receding into bearded human face. He lay shirtless and shoeless and in shredded pants in the middle of the remnants of the golem for a brief moment, until Jay nodded at Frank and said, "Help him up. We need him to carry a bag."

At the sales counter, she bent low to look Fish in the eye. "You ruined yourself, tadpole. You should've let me see the room as a paying customer. Now," she brought the knife tip to the dry patch of scales on his throat, "I'm just going to take what I want." As she disappeared into the back room, she called back, "Somebody pick up that cannon. I want that, too."

CHAPTER X

The Rubber Room was just that: a whole second display room lined wall-and-ceiling with hard white formtex. Hooks and arcs of formed rubber curled from the walls, holding an armory of weaponry, everything from rifles and laser guns and plasma bombs to water lances, temporal whips, weird noodly stingers without apparent handles. Under a whole rack of plasma rifles, on a sphere of rubber molded to resemble a human skull, lay an intricately inscribed puzzle box that looked straight from the workshops of hell itself. Lars, again, saw contraptions and gadgetry he couldn't comprehend, beads and spheres and hollow claw-shaped things that looked more like art than instruments of death.

Jay shoved a couple of top-load duffle bags, military issue, at Frank and Lars.

"Grab everything you can, and hurry," she said, shoving the hell-cube into her pocket. "We don't know how long that shiny motherfucker will be out, and who knows what other puppets he'll throw at us. Cops might be on their way, too. The fish did shoot a hole through the neighborhood."

Stuffing his bag with big-ass blasters, Lars said, "Look at all this shit. Fishman's *Killtoy* Emporium, more like. You could take over a planet with gear like this."

Jay's galaxy eyes reflected in the circuited steel of a long, tech-laced broadsword. "That's the idea."

Frank was moving slowly, sap and splinters stitching back together in his wide trunk wound. The wolf blood had healed Lars' shoulder, protecting itself, but he could still feel the blaster's burn. He filled a bag, found himself a set of spider-silk combat digs in the section of the room dedicated to armor and wearables, then stripped in the middle of the room, down to his skivvies with the big tail hole in the back through which a wedge of hairy asscrack was grossly visible. There was even a pair of boots, big stomping things crisscrossed with tech he couldn't fathom. Dressed in black and cinching the boot straps—the pants, thankfully, button-fly—he called to Fish, who was muttering weakly at the Rubber Room's entrance. "What tricks are these kicks packing, Fishman? Jetpacks? Super-speed?"

"That's just overstock from the emporium," Fish said. "They're foot vibrators. For the podophiles. You click the heels together and get a sensuous little tickle."

Lars tapped his heels like he was wearing ruby slippers, and the boots hummed with vibration. It wasn't unpleasant, but he couldn't see getting off on foot-jiggling. "Fuck it," he said, "they fit."

When they'd filled the bags, the only things left hanging in the Rubber Room were mech armor and water lances. Nobody had any idea how to swing a spear made of hexed H_2O, and anyway, both the armor and the spears were too big for the bags. As they headed for the front door, Jay said, "Bring the amphibian, too. He can show us how this stuff works on the way."

Fish's frog eyes stretched so wide Lars thought they might pop out and roll into the sex toy wreckage in the middle of the floor, to be lost forever among butt plugs. "Me, what, me? That's kidnapping, that's confinement and forced ambulatory locomotion without my express consent on the matter, which I do not give, I have a shop to reassemble. Some of this might still be salvageable. I have my customers to think about. Shipments to be made. Lube fruits to jelly."

"Frank," Jay said, "bring him. If he gives you trouble, put those fuzzy cuffs on him."

The tremuloid, laden with four full bags of stolen weaponry, slid a raw limb over Fish's shoulders. The amphibian drooped, resigned, and gave no reason to bother with the fuzzy cuffs. "I'm taking inventory," he said. "Every broken cock ring, every pilfered laser. I'm sending the invoice to you, Miss Thief. Itemized and alphabetized."

As Frank marched him toward the door, Fish began to list all the broken things in his once-pristine Fucktoy Emporium. The shop was an exercise in chaos now, impressive in its complete and total annihilation. *Hell*, Lars thought, *a fucking hurricane would've left more standing.* Passing Quillian, he marveled at the clean wound the canon had made, as if the gangster had been carved by a giant melon-baller. The silver man's body was solid and sterling all the way through, shiny as the bumper on a brand-new cruiser. Lars suddenly had a deep, resonant urge to be back in *Sheila*'s pilot seat, skiffing the black, stars passing at random in the far-off, just him and the ship and some cranked-to-eleven metal tunes.

When Fish locked up—Jay allowed him that courtesy—they left the KO'ed gangster inside.

51

CHAPTER XI

Night creatures in the canals burped bubbles of gas into the spaces between buildings, the bubbles glowing from some spontaneous luminescence and lighting up the whole city. The soft light reflected on the oil-slick water, and it was almost beautiful enough to forget the stink. Young women passed, bubbles caught under clear umbrellas, their own personal spotlights. Nocturnal birds moved like shadows through the light, snatching mosquitoes and moths the size of Fish's eyeballs from the heavy night air. The boulder-crabs were sluggish, half hidden in gutters, but the citizens of Canal City were out in force, clogging the scaffolded walkways with their drunken selves, every species shouldering, shimmying, or slithering toward their watering hole of choice.

Fish kept up his litany, but he didn't fight or run. He must've realized that if he stayed, Quillian would've put two diamond bullets in his amphibious skull and tossed him into one of the canals for his erroneous canon shot. Lars had seen the gangster do worse, to scarier people, for smaller offenses. Fish had shot him. He was fucked in Canal City, and he knew it.

There were more rivercycles on the canals at this hour, fewer cabs and barges. The cycles' hover-engines added a chugging bassline to the city's cacophony, their paddlewheels kicking up the stagnant water, popping bubbles of light-gas that wafted from the night fauna. Lars kept his eyes on the crowds for animated debris, the lurching of trash-puppets on the hunt. Jay was hauling ass, humping the full bag of weaponry on her back like it was just another limb, a part of her. Frank was trying, but the surprising speed Lars had seen in the tremuloid back on the spinner wasn't there. The tree-man was lumbering. His sallow eyes pleaded for a drink.

When they came to an arched iron footbridge festooned with old padlocks, Lars saw the first golem, another shoddy amalgamation of Fish's battle-damaged sexual appurtenance, this one with a formtex disembodied butt for a head. Lars tried not to laugh. It was on the other side of the canal, behind them, pushing through a gaggle of laughing bridesmaids, their neck gills coiffed and bedazzled for a night out. They shouted epithets at the moving sex toys, too drunk to notice its gaping butt-face or floppy strap-on fists.

"Quillian's awake," Lars said. "We got a dildo-puppet on our ass."

Jay glanced over her shoulder at the butthead golem and glowered. "We should've turned that vulture into powder."

"Maybe," Lars said, moving, "but you don't get to be hot shit in a port town like this without connections, on-world and off. Could be every gangster, senator, and freight tycoon he owes favors would be gunning for us to pay his debts. Better to have one sadist hunting us than a hundred."

"Space is a big place."

"Not big enough."

The crowds were too thick. The golem wasn't making up ground. It tussled with a gang of squid-faced punks in identical plastic jackets, brass rings piercing their tentacled beards. Their brawl knocked a crate of alien saltfish from the branches of a tremuloid stevedore, and the big, chain-laden tree-man joined the melee. Lars smirked. The butthead would have its phallic hands full with that bunch.

54

He turned a corner and was suddenly in the middle of a street market, stalls selling tchotchkes and swill and all manner of grilled critters and sea-flora. Lars realized he was ravenous. Jay and the rest were already ahead, Frank prodding the forlorn Fish along through the crowd. Behind them, a fishmonger began shouting, and Lars saw the tentpoles of her stall fold into themselves, twisting into man-shape, a gutted shark for a head. The shark-golem loomed over the shoppers and revelers, dead slabs of fish entwining with the tentpoles to form a scaly mimicry of musculature. It was pushing through the crowd, tossing shoppers into toppling stalls. Screams. A siren somewhere. Butthead edging in from an alley, punks and tremuloid apparently dispatched. The mood of the crowd began to shift, panic diffusing like a drop of dye in water. It spread subtly, bloomed.

Jay veered toward a canal-access stairway, and the others followed. The wolf writhed inside Lars as he smelled blood and meat and the far-off moons. His blood wanted to let go, to let the animal burst out again and sate itself. It was always like that—the more he turned, the more the animal in him wanted another turning.

"Frank," Jay said, "hail a taxi."

The shark-golem's head appeared over the railing above them, looking down on the small dock with its dead black eyes. Rivercycles splashed by, and the smell was overpowering. Piss and brimstone. Frank shot one of his branches over the water, and a barnacled taxi swerved toward them, exhaust pipes spewing black smoke. The taxi was an open design, barely more than a raft, but the engine looked heavy and powerful, made for speed. The driver, a slug-rat with a thick green beard, yelled for them to board. The golems were climbing over railings now. Falling purposefully into the water. Jay pulled her knife from her boot.

"Sorry," she said. "We need to borrow your ride."

The driver shrugged and dragged a long, chipped cutlass from his dash. "Bitch, you think you're the first jacker I've run through in this rathole city? Dropped a dozen in these waters, gutted, left to bloat."

As he pushed forward with his sword, Frank's tentacle-branch slipped down around his slimy rat arm and threw him, shouting, into the canal. Jay busied herself at the controls, looking for a way to disengage the rat's killswitch. More splashes echoed from the flood walls. Lars looked up, and an army of debris-men stared back. *The fuck?* Quillian could only manipulate two at a time—the gangster had said as much when he'd handed Lars his contract. The limits of golemancy, at least for Quillian's race. How in the cosmic hell was he puppeting an army?

"It was me," Fish said, following his gaze.

"What was you? Are you calling up your own crew of trash-creatures?"

"He wanted more power, you know? More juice." Fish rubbed his wrist nervously, more of the trash creatures splashing into the canal around them. "I'm a businessman. An innovator and entrepreneur. Money is money—in this town, you can't be picky. Just a little rewiring to a pair of anti-grav cuffs and *voila*. If you're familiar with the hex frequencies, it's nothing."

"So?"

"So, uh, well . . . Quillian can puppet a hundred of these things," Fish gulped, "with the power enhancers I sold him. Works with any psychokinetic ability. Ups the voltage fifty-fold."

"Hot Cosmic Christ, Fishman," Lars howled, "you gave that bastard an army."

Silhouettes of junk soldiers marched beneath the water's surface. They were coming, dozens of them, crawling, splashing, sinking. It wasn't about unpaid debts or Guild bounties, Lars knew. It was vengeance. Shoot a piece of a man's arm off and lock him in a sex shop, and suddenly he's not such a cold, calculating bastard. He wanted their heads.

Lars dropped to one knee and threw his bags of guns on the deck. Unzipping one, he called to Jay, "Let's get the hell out of here."

"I'm trying," she rasped back.

Bubbles of gas ballooned beneath the surface, membrane-lanterns growing from the breath-glands of animals, and Lars could see the dark shapes nearing. Close enough now to reach with rubbish hands. A yellow bubble broke the surface, and a fat claw made of mashed-together fish parts reached up. As it did, Jay grabbed the taxi's controls and punched the accelerator.

CHAPTER XII

The engine groaned and the taxi began to skid on the water. Frank looped his branches around the starboard railing, grabbing Fish as the amphibian nearly toppled over. Lars wound one arm through the straps of his gun bags, the weight of them enough to keep him from sliding. "Fish," he yelled over the engines, "which one of these should I bust out for those garbage goons?"

"You thieves," Fish blubbered, "you ruined my shop, you took my stuff, you're kidnapping me—"

"We're gonna save your life," Lars said. "Now tell me what heat to use on these assholes."

Fish frowned and said, "That chrome one. The one with the sight on it. Precision blaster. Try not to shoot any innocent people."

"Just guilty trash," said the wolfman, hefting the blaster. "Got it."

Lars flicked the safety and aimed at the canal behind them. The taxi furrowed the water in its oily wake, and the engine exhaust billowed with long chains of smoke. Rivercycles sloshed in the waves, plowed out of the way by Jay. Their riders shouted from the water until they noticed the army walking beneath them—then they

58

scrambled for docks. Quillian Nine's golems kept dropping into the canal, kept marching for Lars and his crew. Bad fucking luck, this whole stop. They could've gone anywhere in the galaxy for hardware. But Jay had to have Fishman's goods, right in Quillian's back yard.

"Hold on!" Jay called back, and then they weren't in the water anymore, not soaring between canal walls, they were bouncing, crashing, across hard ground. The taxi splintered, and the heavy engine broke from the stern and whipped wildly over Lars' head, taking half the pilot house roof with it as it careened into the outer wall of the shuttle terminal. Lars found himself flat on his chest against the deck, Frank huddled nearby over a rattled but still intact Fish.

Jay came up from some cubicle in the pilot house, a dark scuff of soot across half her face.

"You okay?" Lars said.

Wiping the ash off with the back of her hand, she said, "Grab the shit. We make it to a shuttle, then we're nonstop to the cruiser and off this planet."

Lars shouldered his bag, blaster in hand. From the creaking sound of wood behind him, he knew Frank was following. Then some grating alien voice shouted for them to stop. All around them, flooding out from the terminal, were uniformed officers, Canal City PD and Port Security, all with skinny laser pistols and semi-automatic harpoons. The guns were trained on Lars and crew. Sights speckled them with red dots.

"You want to explain the joy ride?" said one of the nearer cops. "Does that stretch of water look like a fucking highway?"

"Sorry, Officer," Lars said, "I just like to feel the wind in my hair."

Before the officer—or any others—could harpoon his wisecracking wolf ass, someone screamed, and a body in CCPD blue splattered the pavement between them. Golems had trudged up from the canal bottom. Slime-covered and draped in algae, they came. Fists of junk pounded through the ragged line of cops, some species faring better than others. Slug-rats and hominids burst like sacks of meat. Crustaceans and leather-skinned things took punches and unloaded

FRANK

their pistols. Lasers cut empty holes through the animated rubbish. Harpoons bounced or stuck harmlessly.

Jay took off in a dead sprint for the shuttle platforms. "Run!"

Lars was behind her, beside her, wolf blood swelling. He choked back the urge to hulk out. No time to go wolf. Above them, beyond the skylights, the aerodocks—massive cylindrical magnet-islands—hovered high over the coastal ocean, partly blurred by smog and darkness. Dark shapes landed and took off in the commerce of travel, oblivious, and Lars couldn't wait to get his ass in *Sheila*'s pilot seat and shoot off this godforsaken waterpit. Sounds of battle faded behind them, the cops overrun by Quillian's puppet army. Golems entered the terminal. New arrivals from off-world fled for the exits. Armed security fired on the stone men from behind luggage racks and shipping containers. They paid no attention to Lars or the others—the golems were tearing up the terminal, the main hub of Canal City's interplanetary trade.

A shuttle was docked at one of the platforms, doors open. Its passengers still huddled inside, away from gunfire. Lars dove in and held the door for Jay, Fish, and Frank. Everyone inside, he let it go, but the sliding door stayed open.

"What the fuck?" Lars said to no one in particular. "Take *off*, you oversized butt plug!"

"It-it's automated," one of the passengers said from the floor. "It's on a timer."

Marching steadily through the battle of the terminal, algae stuck in its crevices and leather bits burned black by laser fire, was the butthead golem, the gaping anus in its face staring down at them like a cyclopean eye.

"That was one of my best pieces," Fish lamented of the butt. "Based the design on one of the biggest pop stars in the city. He modeled for me personally. A perennial top seller."

Amid the chaos of the terminal, the butthead wrenched its own space-dildo fist from its arm, reached back, and hurled the chrome claw straight for Fish's grief-stricken face. The doors began to close, dildo fist soaring—and then a thunk, and a large phallic dent in the door only inches from the amphibian's wide eyeballs.

"Holy Frog Mother . . ." Fish muttered.

Lars laughed. "I think assface is sweet on you."

The noise of battle raged outside as the shuttle lifted, ascending its prescribed route. Something thudded on the roof. Beating. Punching.

"Hot Cosmic Jeezus," Lars spat, "for real?"

If he saw another sex toy any time in the next century, it would sure as shit be too soon. He'd had it with murderous coital accessories, and with animated junk in general. There was no game in killing something that wasn't alive. Even most robots had an A.I. Quillian's trash soldiers were just marionettes. Across the shuttle, Jay was crouched near Frank, her knife raised and gleaming. The rest of the passengers were frozen in terror. The warm smell of fresh piss spread across the shuttle. Lars couldn't blame them. He didn't say a word.

As the shuttle neared the aerodock, the floppy strap-on hand punched through the roof, its rubbery material shredding as it pried back metal. Wind gusted as the pressure leaked from the shuttle. Lars dropped to his back and took aim. He could see the golem's anal visage through the hole it'd ripped. The shredded strap-ons reached in again, pulling back more of the roof. The shuttle was settling onto its platform now. PortSec on the dock were already firing. Thin laserbeams sliced through its steel and leather torso. Lars steadied the blaster's sight between the head's butt cheeks—and pulled the trigger. Blaster plasma funneled straight up its rubber poop chute. The assface reared back, bursting in a spray of latex confetti, the rest of the body crumpling.

Doors opened. The security team didn't lower their guns, and Lars didn't like what might happen next: another shootout with port guards, more dead cops in their wake. It wasn't that he had any special affinity for cops. But dead cops, especially in a city this big, meant more attention from the Bounty Guild, and a higher price than station security or dead smugglers would garner. A backspace spinner like Victor's Halo was one thing; this was Canal City. Space was a big place, but it wasn't that big. They didn't need this kind of heat trailing them the whole mission.

"Nice shot," called one of the Port Security grunts, holstering her laser. "Blasted his whole face off. What's going on down there? Looks like a war zone."

"It's that little bitch Quillian, isn't it?" said another cop. "Is he fucking rolling on something? Killing cops, fucking up port traffic . . ."

The first cop nodded. "Even he doesn't have the funds to bribe his way out of this shit. The Consortium'll drop him in an ocean trench. Let the Old Ones sort 'im out."

"Nah," said a third. "Exile. Offworld. Knows too many shipper cartels. Can't trench a man with connections."

"Where you going, sharpshooter?" the first PortSec said to Lars.

"A-97," Jay called out. "Cruiser dock."

"Just routine business, man," Lars added. "Shit to haul across the black."

The PortSec jerked back a gloved thumb. "Head left, follow the numbers. Not too far."

O

Sheila rose into the dark sky. Below him, through the side windows in cockpit, Lars could see smoke in Canal City, fires burning around the terminal. Bubbles of light floated among the clouds, small beads of yellow popping in the altitude.

CHAPTER XIII

Rock and roll. Cold beer. The synthetic gravy-sodden goodness of a vat-grown protein MRE. Beasting gave him a hunger like nothing else, and Lars was slurping the only meat he had on hand, chugging the chow straight from the can and wiping the gravy from his lips with his tattooed forearm. They were putting distance between themselves and the water planet, roaring through the black big empty on cruise control. Jay hadn't yet told him the next destination, and Lars hadn't asked. After the clusterfuck in Canal City, he was content to eat, drink, and ride, the piercing silence of space drowned out by the wails of heavy metal.

Once they'd reached open space, Jay had locked herself in his sleeping bunk with one of the weapons bags, hadn't been out since. In the cargo bay, Frank was sitting among his own trash, roots splayed, with his branch in a beer. The tremuloid looked melancholy and brutalized. He sagged a little to the left where the stone golem had beaten his side to splinters. Fish huddled in a far corner of the hold, half hidden by a crate of canned rations. He hiccupped and belched, telltale signs of space sickness or at least indigestion. Amphibian probably'd never been offworld, at least not anytime recent. It was always rough, that first zip into the black, the artificial gravity not quite like the real planet-heavy thing.

"You gotta drink it away, Fishman," Lars said. "Booze through the queasiness. You get drunk enough, you'll forget you're a bazillion miles from solid ground. Frank," the tremuloid raised his myriad eyes, "grab Fish an oat soda before he retches on my trash heap."

Leaves rustled as Frank reached a branch toward the fridge.

"No thanks," Fish said. "Beer is for degenerates and lowlifes. And thieves, apparently."

"Nobody'd planned to bust and plunder your shop, man. Far as I can tell, Jay wanted to *buy* your merch. And not the artisanal anal beads. I don't know her well, but I do know she doesn't like the word 'no.' Isn't that right, Frank?" The tremuloid, taking Fish's beer for himself, seemed to shrug. "Then fucking Quillian shows up? Just a run of bad fortune, that was. Maelstrom of shit luck. You should be toasting we got out with our balls still under our willies."

"You're not familiar with amphibious anatomy, are you, Mr. Breakfast?"

"You saying fish-guys don't have dicks? Tough break." Lars swigged from his bottle. "And it's *Breaks*-face. Lars Breaxface, independent contractor slash adventurer. Breaker of faces. Giving Tree over there is Frank. Chatty Cathy, that one. Never shuts up."

"I've seen his kind before," Fish said. "What are you? Some kind of bear wearing a skin suit?"

"Werewolf."

"Never heard of it."

"One and only in the universe," Lars said, beard framing a big grin.

Fish raised a scaly brow. "Yeah? You have to let me take some casts, couple of pictures. I could sell the heck out of a one-and-only-in-the-universe cock prosthetic. Connoisseurs would go nuts."

"One, no casts of my junk. Wolfman's got nards, but if somebody wants a peek, they come sweet talk the real thing. Two, newsflash, there's no shop to sell it in. No molds, no workshop, no jellied lube. I'm sorry, man. That's the new normal. It's all fucked."

The brief excitement over Lars' werewolf penis faded from Fish's face. The amphibian drooped. "What am I supposed to do? Start over on some other backward nowhere planet? Someplace Quillian can't find me? I don't have anything. I don't even have a change of underwear."

Tears welled in Fish's dinner-plate eyeballs. They rolled big and wet over the scales of his cheeks as he sobbed, and Lars was embarrassed for him. Somewhere in a soft corner of himself, he felt a little guilty, too, for his part in demolishing the shop and stealing the hardware. He rooted around in the stores of MREs and freeze-dried foodstuffs for the bottle of grain alcohol he'd gotten as a bonus on a bootlegging run. The run had been just shy of twelve parsecs, and *Sheila* had made it in under a day. The hooch-sellers had been pleased.

He found it, a brown bottle with a thick cork in its mouth, and handed it to the blubbering amphibian. "Take the medicine, Fishman. Doctor Werewolf's orders."

○

By the time Jay came out of the bunk, they were all piss-drunk. Frank had passed out, his sucking branch still in a can. Lars and Fish were playing a made-up game with the empty cans, throwing them toward an open crate on the far wall and inventing rules as they went along. Fish was telling sex toy stories, the funniest and most horrifying custom jobs he'd fashioned over the years.

"Six feet long," the amphibian was saying, "Like a—like a cat o' nine tails. Gelatinous. I had to rig a secretion feature, make it ooze from its pustule knobs." He gagged, showing his black tongue, and waved the nearly empty brown bottle in the air. "But, baby, what a paycheck. I did it. I made it all work. Because I—I was an artist. Am— an artist."

Lars nodded seriously. He'd been shotgunning MREs, and there were globs of gravy in his beard. "I hear you, man. I fucking hear you. Art. Big oozing dick art, man. Fuckin' A."

At the entrance to the cargo bay, silhouetted in the blue light of the corridor, Jay cleared her throat. "We're going to Cairn. We have someone else to pick up."

"Cairn?" Lars scoffed. "Wasteland. Nothing there but bugs and rocks. Can't get drunk on rocks."

"You kidnapped me," Fish slurred. "Fishnapped." He started laughing, suddenly hiccupped, then laughed again.

"Why Fish, anyway?" Lars said. "Arms dealers all over the whatsit—the galaxy. Secret ones, right? Clandestine outfits, out there on empty moons, orbiting quasars. Why this guy's gun bits? Why me? Why Frank? With that—that nega-stuff, negativium, you could buy a whole army."

Jay made her way to the fridge and popped the tab on the last beer. "An army would be more trouble than it's worth. And anyway, my plan isn't war—it's Ragnarok."

"Ragna-rock-n-roll," Lars cheered. He burped, tossed his empty at the crate. It bounced and rattled. "Fuck yeah."

"I don't need an army. I need a wolf. Apparently, you're the only one in this universe," Jay said. "And I don't need Mr. Fishman's 'gun bits.'"

"But my," Fish hiccupped, "my shop, my life. You took all of my things."

Jay smirked, her amethyst eyes flickering, and pulled a tube of negativium from her pocket. Just like the one she'd flashed back at the cat-infested bar where she'd drafted Lars into her mission of vengeance. The wolfman squinted at the vial.

"Hey now, princess. How do I know that isn't my loot?" he said. "You could be playing us both with the one stash."

From the same pocket, she pulled out a second tube. Both held the substance so dark it was almost shadow—a crystallized absence. "Mr. Fishman, you can get off at the next spinner we come across. We'll leave you with whatever you have in your pockets, and you can hitch a ride back to Canal City and reclaim whatever is left of your obscene little store. Or you can come with us for just a little while and get paid more than your whole shop was ever worth."

"What," hiccup, "do I want with rocket fuel? Some of those pieces were p-priceless. Handmade. I'd been running that store half my life."

"Fishy. F-F-Fishman," Lars said. "You know fences, right? Dealers? Big wigs? Sell that much neg, you could have an emporium franchise in every system. Be the real king of the fucktoys. Emperor, more like. Emperor of the emporium empire."

The amphibian contemplated the empty bottle in his webbed hands. "Emperor of the Fucktoy Empire." He turned his wide eyes to Jay. "Not much choice, is there? If I get off, where would I go?"

Hairy, gravy-stained face grinning, Lars clapped Fish on the back—the amphibian nearly toppling on impact—and said, "All right, Fish! Official member of the team. Oh-*Fish*-al." He laughed too loudly at that, even with the volume of the rock 'n' roll. "Get you the decoder ring and whistle in the morning."

"Lars," Jay said, "head to the cockpit and set course for Cairn. Subspace—we need to make up time. And Mr. Fishman," she added. From some other pocket on her fatigues, she pulled the puzzle box, its esoteric etchings dark and menacing on its gilded surface. "Tell me everything you can about this box."

As horror bulged in the amphibian's eyes, Lars stood up, swaying a little, and said, "One problem with your course, princess." He jerked his chin toward the can in her other hand. "We're out of beer."

CHAPTER XIV

From his stool in the spinner's only pub, Lars could see the flashing neon altar of the Church of the Hot Cosmic Jeezus Christ. A hologram of the Cosmic Messiah gave passersby a beatific smile, a miniature blue galaxy swirling around their third eye. Lars watched the trid flicker and thought of the clapboard church he'd gone to as a kid, balanced on stilts between the twin bell towers of a submerged Spanish cathedral. *She's got the whole world in her hands* and so forth, a bunch of dirty flood-worker families in their shabbiest *shabbos* best singing off-key over the diluvial landscape. Gods had a tendency to spread faster than the clap in the answer-hungry cosmos, half a hundred hollow deities for every charted star in the Universe. A couple of pilgrims with faces painted blue knelt beneath the neon and waved their prayers at the hologram, and Lars chugged the beer in his hand, waving the barkeep for another.

The first spinner they'd come to was a far-flung relay station halfway between Canal City and fuck-all. He'd barely seen it from *Sheila*'s windows: a little steel-plated hemorrhoid donut with a couple of freighters docked on its rim, dim beacon lights blinking yellow in the black Big Empty. Compared to the Victor's Halo, this station was a hole in the wall—a blip in the void—one bar, one church, a fueling station, a couple of poorly stocked duty-free shops. That was the beauty of space: You could set up shop just about anywhere. No running out of real estate in the black. And if you were selling something people wanted—fuel, food, fornication—sooner or later, they'd find you.

By the time they'd docked, Lars had more or less sobered up. Frank was still passed out in the cargo bay, not even a solid kick to the trunk could rouse him. They decided to lock up, let the old tree sleep it off. Lars followed Jay into the station, Fish keeping to the rear, away from the princess. The amphibian still looked sick and skittish, rattled by the puzzle box Jay had waved under his gills. He'd promised to tell her all about it—after the beer run. She'd pressed him, even waved her scary knife a little bit, but by that time, Lars was docking at the little spinner, and the princess had given up, shoved the box into a pocket, figuring—Lars guessed—that she had Fish by the short-and-scalies so what was another hour. She would get what she wanted.

"You religious, Fish?" Lars felt beer foam on his beard and left it there, breathing in the floral bitterness of it.

Fish hunched over an untouched tumbler of fermented tea. Gill flaps quivered around his shirt collar as he sighed. "Holy Frog Mother, from whose pond we all have sprung, in whose mouth we shall all be swallowed."

"That's some dark shit," Lars said. "Getting eaten by your mother."

Jay had stepped away into the station, the stool next to Lars still warm from her ass. He looked for her in the thin crowd—a handful of truckers and freight crew, the pilgrims on their way to distant holy lands. No sign of the purple tendrils. Probably taking a leak. Or woman things. He didn't know jack shit about what those might be.

"It's a metaphor," said Fish, "cycle of life. Birth and death. The Mother is everything, Alpha and Omega. Beginning and end."

"I heard a similar thing. As a kid. The old preacher giving us her best fire and brimstone." The hologram across the way flickered again. Its third eye seemed to look everywhere and nowhere. A clever

71

trick of programming. "That line sort of loses its punch when you're already swimming in the waters of Armageddon. I never had much use."

"You don't believe?"

Lars shrugged. "Believe what? Cosmic Christ, Frog Mother? Throw your lot with one, you're atheist and infidel to the rest of the pantheon. I just take it a step further. Believe in what I see, hear, smell, and fuck." Sipped his beer for dramatic effect. It'd been a while since he waxed philosophic. Too much time cruising alone and beating off. "Fish," he said, "the fuck is that box Jay's carrying around? Some kind of super-nuke? Planet-buster? I'm not so sure I want it bouncing around *Sheila*, getting her all exploded and such."

Scaly eyelids closed over Fish's big eyeballs, opened slowly. "I don't know. A scavenger came around a few years back—maybe a decade, even—mumbling about mining artifacts between universes, negative space. *Pickpocketing the seams of the nether-verses*, he said. He had one of them, said it was a powerful weapon, and he was willing to take trade in dildos. I just liked its look—spooky, right? All those notches and runes? I figured someone would come through and know what to do with it."

"You figured you'd hock it and make a dime."

"I'm a businessman," Fish shrugged. "The look in your friend's eyes, though. She *knows* something. She knows what it does, or where it's from. And if the scav was telling the truth, if it has something to do with realities outside this universe, then I'm terrified, Breaxface. Start messing with the fabric of existence and you could short-circuit the whole thing, unravel space and time. Shove the whole cosmos down the Frog Mother's throat."

Lars started to sing, "*She's got the whole world in her throat . . .*"

"What?"

"Forget it. You said you'd tell her what was what post-beer run. What're you gonna say? That it's a bauble from the seams of the universe? Fuck does that even mean?"

Fish hung his head. "I'll think of something. Maybe she'll forget it by the time we reach Cairn."

"Or she'll have some new enforcer who ain't pleasant like me and Frank to knock you around till you tell her which buttons to press. We don't know what's on Cairn. Could be anything." Lars finished his beer, and the bartender floated over, its cloud language taking a moment to translate.

Another brewski, hair-person? it said.

"Nah," Lars told it, "but I gotta make a to-go order. Ten kegs, all varieties. Surprise me."

The barkeep nodded its appendage and drifted into the pub's back room.

A shape obscured the church's neon, and Lars looked up to see Jay coming out of the azure church, wiping her mouth with shred of blue cloth. She saw the two of them still sitting at the bar and seemed to smile.

"Drink?" Lars said as she made her way across the corridor.

"No, thanks," she said. "I'm good. We ready?"

"Keep's rolling out the keg order now. Should be set till Cairn, at least. Unless Frank gets his noodle plugged into them."

"Don't worry about Frank. He's sober when he needs to be." She took a stool and turned toward Fish. "Now," she said. "about my box."

Of course, Lars had to fucking laugh.

CHAPTER XV

Fish and Jay stared as his giggle fit devolved into beer hiccups.

"Forget it," Lars said, choking back a hiccup. "Lost in translation."

The other two blinked. The brimstone stink of a fart clouded the bar, followed by the return of the bartender. Its appendage was twisted around the handle of a pushcart laden with kegs.

Where you want these? it said.

"Shit, uh," Lars scratched behind his ear, "Give us a minute. We're hashing out the check."

The barkeep's cloud-shoulders gave the distinct impression of a shrug. *It's all good, man-of-the-fur. Pay when you're ready.*

The puzzle box was suddenly in Jay's long, pale fingers, its arcane etchings like the art project of some cubist hellbeast. Jay thrust it toward Fishman. "Tell me how to open it. Where's the lock? The triggering rune?"

The sex-toy salesman shrugged his skinny, scaled shoulders. "I don't know," he said, "I don't know the ins and outs and whats-its of the thing—I'm not versed in esoteric curios. I'm a retailer and an engineer, but my passion is erotics. I sold the hardware to make ends meet. Weapon sales kept the emporium out of the red, okay?"

"What he means is," Lars said, clearing his throat, "is that he's no expert on arcane hoodoo shit. But he's heard stories. He knows things."

Jay raised a scar-perforated brow. "Knows things? I *know* things. What do you *know*, Mr. Fishman?"

"I know—" Fish started, reaching for the box.

Alarms. A lazy klaxon sounded in the corridor, red trid flashing in meandering pixels around the ceiling: *Lockdown.* A pair of lumpy space-trolls in ill-fitting StatSec blues lurched into the saloon, concussion rifles at the ready. *More rent-a-cops,* Lars thought. *Just what we fucking need.*

"Keep calm," the fatter troll said. "Nothing to worry about. Just a little exsanguination over at the chapel." He nodded behind him, helmet flopping between his ear cavities. "Color me surprised, a cult founded on eating bodies and drinking blood has a few nutzos who take the preaching literally."

The other troll waved a blacklight. "We just gotta check everybody for fluids. Mouths or other ingestion orifices-slash-appendages. Painless, unless you're UV sensitive. In which case, lodge an official complaint."

Lars started to stand. The first troll whipped his rifle, sight leveled on the wolfman's chest. "Easy, Tiny," the troll muttered. "Just let us do our job."

Fish was cowering, and beside him, Jay took a sip of the boozy tea. She licked her lips, black tongue snaking around from chin to nose and back again. It wasn't enough. In the blacklight, the spatter glowed white on her face.

The trolls raised their rifles.

"You're under arrest," one said. "We don't countenance murders on this spinner. Not even to quench biological thirsts. It ain't sanitary."

Jay set the drink and the box on the bar. Her long, white thumb rubbed the corner of her lips, and her firework eyes narrowed into a glare Lars had only seen in apex predators. It was the death stare of a hunter. She was going to eat those motherfuckers.

One of the trolls dangled a set of magnetic shackles. "If you could, uh, please put these on."

Sinews tensed under scarred white skin.

"Jay—" Lars started.

Then she pounced.

Concussion slugs thudded against the walls and ceiling. Bar patrons shrieked. One troll tottered backward, shouting for backup. The other couldn't scream—his flabby throat was between Jay's teeth. Rigor mortis had his fat finger squeezing the rifle's trigger, arm bouncing with each burst. More StatSec boots were marching down the corridor, and the living troll was finding his aim. The rifle sight burned red on Jay's cheek—before Lars kicked the gun out of the guard's hands. Another boot to the troll's wobbling face, and he fell back, KO'ed, like a tumorous ragdoll.

"Jay, cosmic fuck, you gave *me* a verbal flogging over blasting that smuggler back at V's Halo. This is a fucking *StatSec* guard! How is *that* laying low? We already have a bounty chasing us from that airlock you burst. You want every bounty hunter in this sector on our asses?"

She looked up, fangs bloodstained and frightening. She wiped the troll's green blood from her mouth with her palm. "I've been holding back for days," she said. "I'm hungry."

"Cosmic fucking Christ." Lars grabbed one of the rifles just as the first of the cops' backup rounded the corner to the saloon. Klaxons blared. The wolfman fired a round into the guard's forehead, just under the helmet, and she fell in a heap beside her bleeding colleague.

"Where's Fishman?" Jay said behind him. "Where's my fucking box?"

Lars turned. Amphibian and devil-box were gone, disappeared into thin air like the barkeep's fart smell. The bartender was hiding behind the cart of kegs. One of its clouded eyes hovered cautiously above the barrels, watching the destruction.

"Can't have gone far," Lars said. "This spinner's the size of rat turd."

Jay's long knife glinted in the flashing lights. "He's fucking sushi."

Another StatSec guard stormed in, frozen for a moment as it realized Jay's blade had severed its head from its body. Then both head and body crumpled, and blood sprayed the ceiling like a garden hose. Jay stepped over the spurting corpse, disappearing into the corridor, the church across the way gone dark. The hologram of the Cosmic Messiah had powered down when the alarms sounded—danger and salvation apparently mutually exclusive.

As he followed Jay's footsteps over the StatSec dead, the bartender's meek cloud-voice came from its hiding place, *Can I still mark your tab for ten kegs?*

○

The corridor was awash with StatSec blood. Body parts littered the steel parquet, each piece bearing some insignia or accoutrement of the rent-a-cop confederation of Station Security. The truckers and travelers had all apparently taken shelter in their ships or behind the merchandise racks of the duty-free. Lars saw no bystander corpses. A few stray station cats lapped at the warm blood, translucent skin flashing red in the lights of the alarms.

As he passed the dim entrance to the Church of the Hot Cosmic Jeezus Christ, he heard the unmistakable click of a gun behind him. Even in the dark, the diamond pistol gleamed.

"Sorry, Lars," came Fish's voice from the shadows. "You're a nice guy, I think. A little lewd for my taste, and kind of stupid. And that hyper-masculine air you put on has to be compensation for—"

"Ain't compensating for anything," Lars growled. "I'm a goddamned werewolf badass. And werewolves are awesome—extremely awesome—as sure as shit stinks and beer is better cold."

"I can't let her do it," the amphibian continued. "I can't let her end the universe. She might be telling the truth about her family, her mission of justice and vengeance, I don't know. But if there's even a chance this box will flip the universe inside out and upside down, I can't let anyone have it." Fish sighed. "Throw your keys in the offering bowl. I need your starship."

Lars snarled. He felt the twitch in his fingerbones.

"Don't," Fish said. "You might. You might take me. But I know this pistol. Hair trigger, laser-accurate. I sold it to Quillian last year. Even odds you end up with a diamond bullet in your wolf brain, and neither of us want that, okay?"

"You can't hold me up and abscond with *Sheila*. I gave you my *booze*, man."

"You also destroyed everything that mattered to me in this universe and delivered weapons of mass destruction to a crazed bloodsucker. Now, please. The keys."

Lars dug the pink rabbit's foot from his fatigues and dropped it into the offering bowl, the key singing as it hit the curve of the brass. "I'm going to have to kill you for this, Fish. If she doesn't get you first. Nobody takes *Sheila* from me."

Fish stepped into the stroboscopic alarm light. The big diamond pistol never wavered in its aim. Lars stared past the barrel, into the amphibian's big, shining eyes. Fish's webbed hand swiped the rabbit's foot from the bowl, and the key—*Sheila*'s key—dangled from his fingers as he walked backward into the flashing darkness of the spinner's main corridor, never turning his back on Lars. The moment Fish disappeared around the curve of the wall, Lars felt the wolf surge in his blood. His bones began to break and reform, growing. It hurt like hell, draining his blood of the last remnants of the water planet's lunar juice. His veins burned. But fuck it. He had to get that key back. Nobody space-jacked *Sheila*. Nobody.

CHAPTER XVI

The wolf stalked the flashing red corridor. No sign of Fish, but Lars could smell him—that polyester-and-clam stink, faint with the musk and ball-sweat of the rabbit's foot. They were circling the spinner opposite Jay's carnage. Pretty soon he'd run into the bloodsucking alien princess—he hoped he found Fish before then.

Every second in his wolf skin this far away from a moon, not even a half-dead lunar battery strapped to his back, burned inside his bones, but the thought of losing *Sheila* burned worse. He thought of the amphibian swaggering into *Sheila* like he owned her. Rummaging through his porn stash. Making off with his lunar batteries. Fucking up the perfect butt-divots in the pilot seat that had taken him years to get exactly, comfortably right. Lars breathed the landscape of scent: Fish, blood, recycled air. He dropped to all fours and galloped, claws scraping the metal floor.

◯

A clattering in one of the duty-frees, and the wolf stopped, sniffed, and snarled. From behind a shelf of brightly foiled snacks, an Y'klarian trucker stumbled out, all four of her furry wings in the air.

"He went that way, man," the trucker stuttered. "Waving his gun around like a magic wand or some shit."

"*Yeah,*" Lars growled, "*he's Mister fucking Wizard.*"

Gunshots. Two. One whizzing over his shoulder, the other biting into the flesh of his thigh. Lars howled. The trucker beat her wings and found cover in the rafters. Shrugging off the pain—it was only a flesh wound—Lars tore down the corridor, zagging wall to wall as bullets ricocheted off the chrome floor. Then the diamond pistol was clicking empty, and Lars stood over the cowering amphibian. Fish had his back to a docking airlock, but the slip was empty—nothing but big fat space beyond its thick porthole. He dropped the pistol, which gleamed and clattered, and raised his webbed hands.

"You got me," he said. "I admit it, bad idea trying to steal your ship, et cetera, but that woman? The so-called princess? She's murderous. She's off her rocker. You'll be complicit in the end of the universe, maybe. Or worse. We don't even know what this thing does."

"*You shot me.*"

"I know, I know. Sorry about that. No hard feelings, right? I mean, it was out of necessity, and maybe a little bit out of fear, too. You are a vicious animal four times my size and you did just threaten to kill me."

"*Keys,*" said the werewolf.

Fish fumbled for the rabbit's foot, which dangled like a charm from his vest. He tossed it underhand, and Lars caught it on one black claw, *Sheila*'s key swinging on its chain.

"*Box.*"

The werewolf could hear the erratic thump of Fish's protean heart. Gills fluttered wildly on the fish-man's neck. From another pocket in his vest, he pulled the ornate box, the still-pulsing alarm lights making it flash red and menacing.

"Would you believe it, I got lost?" Fish said. "Trying to find which dock we were hitched to. I was peeking through the windows, but they all looked the same. Then I figured if I kept going that way, she'd get me first. And she wouldn't hesitate." Fish turned the box over in his fingers. "Just *snikt*, and I'd be the Headless Fishman."

"You're absolutely right."

Fish's eyes ballooned, and in their silvery reflection was Jay, blood-soaked and tendrils wild. She was standing legs spread, shoulders hunched, the knife in her fist dripping gore on the metal floor.

"Throw me the box," she said.

"Jay," Lars muttered, "*what—the fuck. This is a mess.*"

"When I want to hear your tongue, I'll cut it out and listen to it fall on the ground."

The wolf flashed his fangs, and a low growl boiled in his throat. Who the fuck did she think she was? A spinner full of amputated StatSec, blood all over the place. The shootout in Canal City. One snafu after another. Her mission of righteous vengeance had so far been a mission of epic clusterfucks, and Lars was getting tired of having to claw his way out.

Jay stepped forward; Lars blocked her path, filling the whole of the dock-tube with his frame.

"Don't make me cut off something you'd rather keep," she said. Her teeth gritted, blood still oozing from her mouth.

"*Just take it. No need to kill him.*"

From behind him, barely more than a whisper, he heard Fish say, "I'm sorry, Lars." And then the wrenching of the dock's emergency open latch, the alarm lights switching from red to blue, a pre-recorded message blaring *Warning: Depressurized Hull, Warning: Depressurized Hull,* and the airlock was opening, its gears unwinding, its seams screaming with the rush of air surging to fill the vacuum of space.

Lars would have killed him. If he could have caught the amphibian, he would've clawed his heart out as they both choked and froze to death in orbit of the spinner. But Fish was sucked out first and fast—the door buckling under the pressure. Lars braced against the doorframe with his boot, pain screaming through his bones as he put all his weight on his wounded leg. He caught a pipe in the rafters with one hand, and with the other, clutched Jay's ankle as she soared headfirst and determined toward the void.

"Let me go!" she said "I have to get him! *I need the box!*"

"*Fuck the box.*"

Body parts whipped past them, leaving streaks of blood on the floor and walls. In the space beyond the open airlock, Fish tumbled, the box frozen in his fist. From the ragged wounds of hacked-off limbs, long tangles of bloodrope swirled through the black, Jay's magic reaching for the amphibian, failing, dissolving into clouds of gore. Lars felt his leg beginning to buckle, the gunshot burning white-hot, his grip loosening, and Jay kicking, trying to wrench free. Fish was screaming, frog lips mouthing *Oh fuck oh fuck oh fuck*, and with the crackle of burning fire, space itself seemed to rip open, a mist of blue light melting in from some pocket of netherspace, unzippering of *the seams of the universe*, the light circling a portal in the void.

"That's it!" Jay shouted "He opened it! *We have to go!*"

Lars' claws dug into the meat of her ankle as she kicked. "*We're not jumping into fucking space.*"

The princess howled. Another lasso of blood snaked across space, but it still wasn't enough. The blue portal—the throat of the Frog Mother, for all Lars knew—swallowed Fishman and the stray StatSec body parts and the puzzle box. It swallowed the nearest ship that'd docked on the spinner, too, and then, as quickly as it had opened, it swallowed itself, closing up into a pinpoint of light, and then into nothing, with no sign left of anything it had taken. Whole torsos were sucking past them now, trailing guts, thumping into them with lifeless disregard. A steel helmet with a head still in it slammed into Lars' knuckles, and his hand opened reflexively, losing its grip on the pipe, and he knew he was going out—out into the empty, with no hole in the universe to swallow him up and save him.

CHAPTER XVII

Get your head outta the lilacs, Breaxface. Budge was always saying bullshit like that. Lars could hear the old minotaur's voice now, vivid thunder in the clouds of his memory. Hexed tattoos had only been the first step. Without meditation, Lars would've just been a beast with new ink. In the glow of his campfire, the aurochs-headed witch-monk would sit, chanting, preparing the enchanted ink that would save Lars from himself, symbols as fail-safes on the werewolf's scarred skin. Here, floating outside the spinner, the stars weren't much different from those Lars had meditated under in the black mountains; only the patterns were different, the spaces between them seeming further, infinite, like the space between his hand and the open door of the airlock. *Get your head outta the lilacs,* he could hear the monk say again, and somebody was screaming, maybe him, muffled in the vacuum of space. Echoes of Earth's orbit and the capsule and the smiling wolfish skull. He was still gripping Jay's ankle, the two of them about to die in the fading ether of Fish's transdimensional getaway. Ice crystals hardened on Jay's bootlaces, on the fringe of his fur, on his tongue and in his lungs, burning. *Get your head outta the lilacs, Breaxface.* He wondered what Budge would've made of the Frog Mother, of the open maw of the universe swallowing a man.

Shit, Budge, the wolfman thought, gasping, *ain't smelled a lilac in years.*

His wolf-self strained against the ink on his skin, virus fighting the hex to save itself, and Lars reached, expecting to scrape space, and clawed instead at the hard, knotted meat of a tree limb. He jerked to a stop, almost losing his grip on the vampire princess. The rough branch wound itself around the wolfman's fist, and he looked back to see Frank in the doorway, bracing against the frame with every root and limb. The tremuloid pulled, reeling them in with his branches, wood-flesh straining beneath the cracks in his bark. Frank's yellow eyes were all squinted, determined, and Lars almost felt like he wasn't going to die in the next five seconds. He clung to Jay's ankle so hard he thought he might break it, but he didn't care. If she got out of this clusterfuck alive with only a broken bone and some scratches, he figured she was still ahead—and damn lucky. His chest heaved, lungs trying to breathe airless space and his wolf blood repairing fragile tissue even as it froze. No moons for probably light-years, lunar batteries back on *Sheila* in their neat little boxes, and he felt the last dregs of moon energy begin to fade from his body, Jay waving almost weightless in the void, howling, bloody, it'd be easy enough to let her go, climb back into the spinner, and set off in his cruiser for some vacation planet, forget the princess, her mission, the whole goddamn mess.

But if he dropped her, would Frank still yank him back from the black?

Fuck. Lars snarled, at Jay and the disappeared Fish and the whole spastic galaxy. Then he used the last of his strength to pull Jay toward Frank's reaching limbs. The tremuloid wrapped a branch around her boot, and Lars climbed—with the help of Frank's steadying limbs—back to the airlock. When he was behind Frank, the tree-man pulled Jay inside, and a couple of bulky truckers rolled a big steel table in front of the open airlock. Loose body parts vacuum-sealed the seams around the table, making a wet, meaty sound as the universe sucked on them from the outside.

Lars sucked breath. The air was thin, half the spinner's atmosphere reserves lost to the open slip. Jay, cradled in Frank's branches, coughed and heaved, her alien anatomy craving whatever it was she needed from the air.

"What were you sons-of-bitches doing, suicide by airlock?" said one of the truckers.

All the moon gone from his cells, Lars didn't have the energy to quip. His body broke, bent itself back into man-form. The spider-silk fatigues were still intact, if a little stretched around the seams. The boots were fucked. His toes stuck out the front of each like five-pronged tongues. Kicking off the boots, he pulled himself over to lean against the cold corridor wall, under one the flashing alarm lights, its brilliance bathing him in alternating black and blue.

He felt something soft in his hand. The rabbit's foot. Keychain still circling his finger. He said a silent, half-hearted prayer to all the gods of space travel and pulled himself to his feet.

"Hey, Frank," he said, "meet me back at *Sheila*. I need to get some shoes."

○

When he got back to the cruiser, sporting fresh kicks and dragging the cart of kegs, Frank and Jay were in the hold. The tree stood upright and alert, all his eyes cleared of at least some of their fog. The princess hunched against a crate of canned meat. Lars thumped in, his new shoes squeaking slightly, and began to unload the kegs. He'd been lucky. One of the trucker shops kept a stock of top-shelf formtex shitkickers, with a pair in his size. Knee-high and matte black, guaranteed to form to any foot, man or beast.

In the spinner, he'd seen almost no one. The few truckers and pilgrims onboard had fled Jay's rampage and the depressurization, and only the spinner's android skeleton crew was left to clean up, starting with welding a plate over the open airlock. He'd twice slipped in blood. If any StatSec had been left alive, Lars and his two passengers would've been shot to death just to save the hassle of arrest. But Jay had been thorough.

87

As he'd walked back from the boot shop, he passed the cosmic chapel, looking for a moment at the dark altar where the hologram of the god of his youth had projected, the smiling otherworldly woman-god with her third all-seeing eye. It still had the smell of bullshit. But Lars dug a coin from his pocket and tossed it into the donation bowl anyway. With Jay and Fish ripping holes in the universe, he wasn't taking any chances.

When the beer was stacked and strapped in place, Lars shoved the cart back into the slip's antechamber and engaged the airlock. Jay hadn't moved. She seemed to stare beyond the hull, into the stygian void.

"Princess," he said, "I got a fuckton of questions for you." When she started to speak, he stopped her: "Not now. I haven't slept in Jeezus knows how long. I've been shot, strangled, and hung out an airlock. I haven't been fucked in weeks, and the only thing I've eaten since my last job is canned meat in synthetic gravy."

He turned, headed for the corridor toward the bow. "I'm going up to the controls and getting my baby into open space. Then I'm setting auto-course for someplace with a cheap whorehouse and decent food, locking her up with a passcode, and going to sleep."

"We have to stick to the mission," Jay said.

"Yeah? We'll vote on it tomorrow. Goodnight, princess."

CHAPTER XVIII

They were wet and gorgeous and writhing. Three of them, bodies in the dark, drudged up from memory in the stroboscopic reality of his dreams. Tourists on a planet of beautiful ruins, black sandscapes, beanstalk trees with sparse violet canopies. He'd met her/them on a long vacation, splurging on R&R after a shit merc job in the cold crags of some disputed corporate asteroid. She/they were 3Flesh, a race in triplicate, three identical bodies connected by twisted, pulsing umbilici: each cord snaking from the skull of the central Flesh to its stereo-bodies. Their skin was translucent and bioluminesced a faint blue, and Hot Cosmic Jeezus Christ they looked like angels, if angels were triplets connected at the head by fleshy rope. Best sex of his life, and he hadn't even had to pay for it. She/they had wanted him. And he'd wanted them/her, the ephemerality of their connection as intoxicating as any alien hooch he'd ever tried.

Lars woke up with a shudder and warm cum on his sheets. *Finally*, he thought. His fur-covered balls had been begging for relief since the Pickled Quasar. He rustled the spider-silk armor from the floor, rolled on a pair of mismatched socks, and shimmied each foot into a formtex boot. Dressed in yesterday's clothes, he shrugged on a

89

shoulder holster and dropped a thick-muzzled automatic under his left arm. Didn't usually carry onboard, but he had to have a balls-out heart-to-heart with Jay the Ninja Princess. The weight of the gun made him feel better.

○

In the hold, Jay was slouched against some cargo netting, eyes closed. Most of the blood had been cleaned off of her, a smattering of stains on her clothes. A white bandage wrapped the ankle Lars' wolf-claws had mauled to save her. Frank was in sentry mode, his numerous eyes watching Lars and Jay at the same time.

"Don't worry, Frank," Lars said. "She's safe. Unless she tries to drink my neck too. Then I'll unload a clip into her face. But I don't want to. It'd take forever to clean up."

He made his way to the stack of kegs. He unlatched one, tapped it, and poured three mugs, each mostly foam. Fucking spinner bartenders, man. Chiselers, all of them. Lars passed one of the mugs to the tremuloid and sat on a crate. After a long minute of dead silence, he started to laugh.

"Saw this cartoon once when I was a kid. The library, they had all this weird shit. Like some musty old museum, except the shit's just on shelves instead of glass cases. A couple of us, we dug up this real old file, this cartoon cat and dog, gross as hell—gross even by our standards, which in a flood town, where the sewage runoff backs up every other day, are pretty low. One day, the cat squeaks out an epic ass-blast, this airborne toxic event of a fart, so radioactive it's sapient. It starts talking. The cat, he thinks the fart cloud is his son. Names it—names it Stinky." Lars almost spilled his beer he was laughing so hard. That stupid cartoon, hell, he hadn't thought of it in decades. It was nothing, just an afternoon with friends whose names he'd forgotten, wasting time on a day the rains were bad and they couldn't kick mud or swim for the underwater city off the coast. "Stinky runs away. And I was thinking—I was thinking about that bartender. Reminded me of little Stinky. Poor bastard. Him and his whole fart race."

He kept laughing, choking on his beer, then chugging the second, his beard wet with foam. Frank just stared. As Lars went for refills, Jay started to move, her joints cracking as she stretched. Lars offered her a mug. She took it, but she didn't drink.

"Sorry," he said, "fresh out of blood kegs."

Her eyes hardened, and she took a sip, wiping the foam off her nose.

Lars took his spot on the crate. "So. The fuck are you, a vampire? Should we add that to the list? Magic ninja *vampire* space princess. I saw *Wolfman Meets Dracula.* Drac makes Wolfman his man-slave, makes him eat bugs and shit. It's degrading."

"My race requires fresh blood," she said. "Regular feedings. On my world, there's a slave class to feed on. Out here, traveling, it's more difficult."

"So, you murder people." Lars took a gulp, noted the dark malts. It wasn't a bad beer, under all the foam. "Which is cool. Fine. It's a dog-eat-dog universe. But you should've given me a heads up, let me know some regular blood-feeding would be part of the equation. You really fucked it up on that spinner. Low profile that wasn't."

Jay shrugged. "Doesn't fucking matter. That little toad got away with my key. And even if he didn't, I don't know if it would do anything. I don't even know what button to press."

"Me neither. I was always shit at the Rubik's cube."

"The what?"

"Nothing. Homeworld kitsch." Less foam this time, the keg was evening out. He poured a refill for Frank too, who stood mute as a telephone pole on his coiled roots. "Okay, you're an alien vampire ninja space princess. Why did you dive headlong for that space-hole? And what *is* the box? Fishman grumbled about it being a harbinger of end times, ripping up pieces of the universe. Felt so strongly about it he jumped out a fucking airlock. Seems like there's maybe an ounce of truth in that tale."

A half-smile played on Jay's lips. If not for her fangs, it would've looked soft, even flirty. "It's a key," she said. "To a pocket universe. Separate-but-connected existence beyond this dimension.

I've been looking for one all my life. Or something like it—some way home."

"Home?"

"Home is a galaxy in a pocket-verse. When I went into exile, I didn't just leave the kingdom, the planet—I was taken to another plane of existence, another bubble of space-time, your universe. There are dozens of keys, maybe hundreds, across the cosmos. I've found some, but most are too old, too arcane, too specialized to alien epistemology to operate. Some are planet-sized, some aren't even in this dimension. Then I heard about this key, the one traded to that dildo peddler. I knew if I enlisted you first, I'd be more likely to come out of that store with the box. That business with the golemancer—"

"I don't want to say I told you so," Lars interrupted. "But I fucking told you so."

The vampire princess leaned forward, her scarred breasts pressed together in the V of her neckline. She drank her beer empty and handed him the mug. "Anything else you want to know?"

He thought of the 3Flesh, her/their long luminescent tongues, what those identical wet bodies had been able to do. He smiled. That coital sorcery was the high score to beat.

CHAPTER XIX

Lars flexed and went to the keg for refills. His leg still burned a little where Fish had shot him, the wolf blood, low on lunar power, slow to stitch him back together. He'd plugged into a lunar battery while he slept, but it hadn't been enough. The turn back at the spinner, so far from any moon, had drained too much. He handed Jay and Frank their mugs, slurped foam off his.

"Yeah," he said, "one or two more things. What's on Cairn?"

"Someone we need," Jay said. "A hexsmith."

"A witch."

Jay grinned, all those sharp teeth glistening with the wetness of the brew. "She'd hate that word."

First Jay's blood magic, then Fish's enchanted puzzle box. Now a bona fide space witch. What was next, a star-killing unicorn? It was all too much hocus-pocus. Shit didn't mesh with his skeptic worldview. He looked down and caught a glimpse of the hex tattoos on his arms and sighed. Maybe hocus pocus was part of the fabric of the universe. And maybe he had the proof right there on his skin. Didn't mean he had to like it.

"Okay," he said, "a *hexsmith*. Question C: why me?"

A flash in those purple eyes. "You know why."

"Dys-7. You want an atom bomb in wolfskin. But that doesn't compute—we're still a handful of jackasses going up against, if your story checks out, an army of rebels and pretenders to the throne. Why not hire someone like Quillian to conjure you a swarm of trash-soldiers? Or any number of dangerous sons-of-bitches that aren't yours truly?"

Jay settled back against a crate, drank a long gulp with a wry grin wedged in the corners of her lips. "You really want out? We can turn back to Canal City . . ."

"I don't want out," Lars said. "I just want to know why you need a werewolf."

"Spoilers," she said, setting the empty mug on the floor. Frank shuffled toward the stereo and jabbed a couple of buttons with a branch, and suddenly there was raging death metal playing at a polite volume, triple-bass drums a muffled, seizing heartbeat. Jay's smile was still there, and Lars wasn't sure he liked it. He hated surprises.

"I hate surprises," he said.

"You'll just have to trust me. Come with me, let the wolf loose on the people who killed my family, get paid. It's easy."

"Easy," Lars repeated.

Mugs were all empty, and this time Frank poured, managing an expert ratio of foam. Lars looked at the small porthole in the door, stars whizzing by, as if he could tell where they were by a glimpse of constellation.

"I set the nav system for Freewheel when we ditched the spinner. My guess, we're about three hours out. It's a casino planet past the fringe of Federation space. A thousand and one places to get fed, fucked, and drunk, which pretty much covers the sum total of what I need right now. Cairn and the hexsmith can wait."

Jay smiled and moved closer to him, grazing his forearm with an armored breast. "Who says we need Freewheel for all that?"

There was no fighting it. His mouth dried up like the asshole of an old cat, his chest ramped up to match the pounding of the triple bass, and his erection reached omega levels, explosive. He felt Jay's

95

hot breath on his beard hairs, her fingers along his waistline. It was, he had to admit, what he'd been jonesing for since he'd first seen her back at that cat-infested neon saloon. His gaze sank into the shadow between her scarred, pale breasts. Hard to say whether her nethers were humanoid, but he'd blown his juice in stranger. Everybody had some sort of orifice or ovipositor—it was just a matter of creative positioning, sexual imagination. He started to reach for the zipper on her body armor, then heard the click of his thick-barreled revolver even as he felt its nose jab his favorite rib.

"What the hell?" he said. "I thought we were having a moment."

"We don't have a moment," said Jay, pushing the revolver further into his side. "Set course for Cairn, and jump into FTL. I've waited a fucking lifetime for this. I'm not taking a holiday in some neon backwater while you get your rocks off and choke on steak. We go to Cairn and we get on with the mission."

Lars sighed. His erection withered. *Goddamn.*

"Okay," he said, "get the gun out of my rib meat. I'll set for Cairn, futtle and fuck-all. No reason for the hot-and-bother ruse. I'm a professional."

The princess flipped the revolver, shook its six slugs onto his lap, and held it for him to take. He dropped it back into the shoulder holster and scooped the bullets with one hand, shoving them into the pocket of his black dungarees as he stood. The smile was all but gone from Jay's mouth. *Bloodsucking vampire mouth,* he reminded himself. If she didn't shoot him with his own gun, she might just drain him till he was a cold blue corpse. It disturbed him a bit when his dick twitched at the thought. But only a bit.

CHAPTER XX

It was the moons. An early job. He was still fresh to exile and taking any contract with a promise of paycheck. The Federation had been in an expansionist phase, taking planets into the confederate fold—whether they wanted it or not, if they had resources the Fed-Prime thought it needed. Peasant-collective planetoid in the Dys-X system, seventh in orbit of a pair of twin red stars. The population of Dys-7, what there was of it, huddled mostly in a handful of urban clusters, the rest of the surface given to farming and mining collectives, all of it on a rock riddled with rare metals. Fed wanted plausible deniability. Let a couple of free agents wreak some havoc, strongarm the Dys council into annexation. That was the mission.

All those goddamn moons spinning in the red sky. Flooding his blood. When the carrier landed, he let the beast loose—and it swallowed him. He hadn't yet marked his skin with hexed ink or meditated in the black mountains of Nowhere, repeating the mantras that his monk-tattooist Budge had told him. He hadn't learned control. The moons were too much, and he lost himself inside the wolf. He woke stiff in hard-caked gore, blood an inch thick. No one in the city was left alive, not even the other mercenaries. Dogs, miners, councilwomen, children. Their bodies were shredded, bits of vein and tendon still under his fingernails and stuck between his teeth. The rest of the cities were willing to surrender, but Prime didn't want to acknowledge the bloodshed. Brushed the whole fucking thing under the rug, even stiffed him on the paycheck. He hadn't done a government job since—and had spent a long year hiding in the mountains, under Budge's needle. *Deep-fried Hell*, he thought, *a goddamn nightmare.*

For the first time since the Pickled Quasar, Lars wondered why exactly he was on this wild sheep chase. Jay's vial of negativium was a big score—a retirement score. And sure, he'd admit it, he was an adventure junkie, and Jay's vengeance had the sweet tang of epic whup-ass all over it. The vampire princess wanted a massacre. But if she wanted Dys-7, a whole city of usurpers gutted and chewed on, the answer was *hell nah.* No fucking way would he go full-on wolf berserker like that again. Lars looked down at the spirals and runes inked along his arms, hoping he couldn't get lost in the wolf again even if he wanted to.

Streaking past the cockpit's windows was the kaleidoscopic striation of faster-than-light. It was close enough to an acid trip, without the flashbacks and neurological burn, and Lars loved every minute of it, every sizzling color. He sat back in the cushion of the cockpit, pilot seat warm and still molded to his own ass, and watched the underside of space-time fly by, wishing he could hear the tunes playing on the stereo, some righteous metal to drown out his memories, to forget everything but the lights.

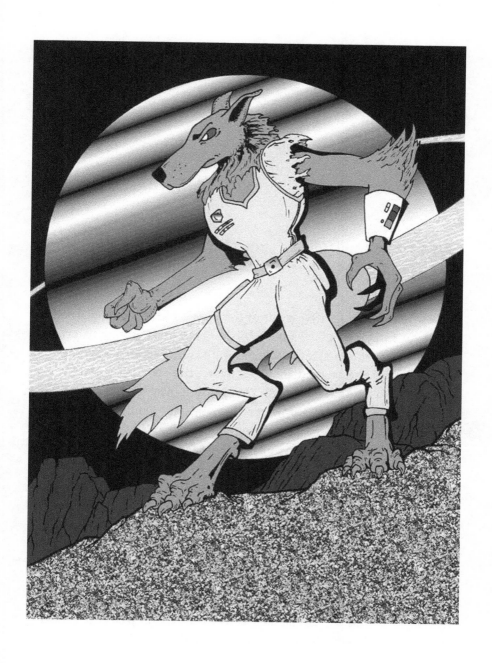

CHAPTER XXI

Somewhere in the relative orbit of the planet Cairn, *Sheila* warped out of the technicolor jetstream of futtle-drive and slowed to cruising speed. Ahead, moon-sized balloons of phosphorescent gas floated, at least a dozen, and beyond them, eclipsing the corona of a white star, was a brown moonless world. The gas bubbles turned toward the sun's light, and as the ship neared them, Lars could see that they weren't gas, they were something living—heaving, semi-corporeal ghost-like things, luminescent glow-organs pulsing inside their twilight skins.

"Star whales," Jay said. She stood behind the pilot's seat, *Sheila*'s array of controls reflecting in her amethyst eyes. "They feed on energy waves. Schools flock to novas, dwarves—big light sources."

"They breathe out there?"

"Who says they breathe?"

For all the alien things he'd seen since leaving Terra in his tachyonic wake, he was awestruck by the sight of the whale. He eased the throttle and let *Sheila* coast toward Cairn, past the glowing leviathan, the heavy ghosts drinking in the blinding light of the star.

○

Jay stayed behind him as they approached the planet. Clouds swirled above its desert surface, white and thin mottled with dark raging patches of gray-black storm. Lars had known, even as they'd come up from subspace, that Cairn was without a moon—he'd felt the lack of lunar energy—but that didn't mean there was nothing in its orbit. A massive hive-station hung in the space beyond Cairn's atmosphere, a shining and light-speckled structure shaped like a giant yam and built of hardened, crystalline slime.

"Dock at the station," Jay said. "The Cairnish have a network of blaster satellites orbiting the entire planet. Any vessel without clearance is vaporized."

"Fuck do they care? Planet's half dead—Cairnish haven't lived on it in what, a millennium?"

The Cairnish were well known in the galaxy, mostly as deep-space pilots, and Cairn a perennial legend in the dark corners of interstellar watering holes. Alien plague had decimated the population, triggering an exodus among the survivors, and what was left of the dryslug race lived in diaspora across the cosmos, a memetic bitterness against all other sapient life ingrained in their collective memory. They were notorious racists and generally unpleasant, but the heavy six-legged slugs, with their gnashing sentient tumors—four-dimensional feelers, time-antennae—could see things in the subspace strata most races couldn't even begin to perceive. The Embassy orbiting Cairn was more a function of nostalgia than anything else—Cairn was home, even if it would kill any Cairnish survivor to breathe its air. Pub gossip also had it that there were treasures galore beneath the planet's surface, left behind in the slugs' haste to evacuate. Lars decided he wouldn't mind checking it out firsthand, nosing through subterranean slug city ruins for priceless kitsch to pawn back at Freewheel or elsewhere.

"They're sentimental," Jay said.

"They're assholes." Docking arms poked from the hive-station's middle like errant hairs. Lars eased *Sheila* into a slip, waited for the airlock to fuse. "What do we say when they ask us our

101

business? That we're looking for a witch to help us on our murder-revenge mission to a vampire-planet pocket universe?"

"We tell them the truth. We're here to see the sights."

"One of those sights being a formidable hexsmith."

"Exactly."

Lars popped the key from the console and stuffed it rabbit's-foot-first into his pocket, heard it clink against the six loose revolver bullets. A message from the hive fed into his stereo system, announcing they were to be boarded by Cairnish officials. When the door began to open, Lars had joined Jay and Frank in the cargo hold, all of them politely bereft of weaponry. He was still wearing the shoulder holster and felt stupid with the empty slot under his arm—he hoped the dryslug wouldn't notice.

The door opened, and the Cairnish official slithered in. It was flanked by two Siskelian lackeys, each outfitted in the black uniform of StatSec and holding chunky laser-sighted rifles. The dryslug wriggled between them, its thin legs helping to skid its thick, segmented body along the floor. It was dressed in a rainbow of elaborately wrapped scarves, each loosely wound around its time-tumors: blind growths of howling teeth. Its face was cracked and speckled, and its wide mouth was set in a vicious frown.

What's your business on Cairn? said the hive official, its translated voice echoing as the facsimile sense-language of the tumors muddled the interpreter sensors.

"Sightseeing," Lars said. "Beautiful landscape, I've heard—"

The slug's tumors hissed. *Princess.*

"Yes," Jay said. "I'm back. I'm here to see the Hand."

The tumors spasmed, and an echoed cry reverberated through the cargo hold. Lars turned to Jay and mouthed *What the fuck?*

The Hand is not a friend of the Cairnish, the official said. The Siskelians' fists tightened on their rifles. They were smaller than the smuggling crew Lars had scuffled with on Victor's Halo, without the fat middles and dull eyes. These blue fuckers had military training. He didn't want to have to rip them to pieces. They'd be trouble.

"I know," said Jay, "That's why I'm here. I want to take the Hand off your planet."

The dryslug's sallow eyes squinted, focused hard on the princess. Tumors bucked on its back and chest, teeth grinding. *You would remove this thorn from the skin of the Hive?*

"I would." The princess sat back on her preferred crate. "But I need something in return."

Another hiss, tumors wild like an orgy of tube worms. *The Ambassador,* said the official.

"I'll talk to her," Jay said.

The official began to turn back to the door, picking at its scarves with a claw. *Very well,* it said, *come with me.*

CHAPTER XXII

Hardslime tunnels curved and crisscrossed throughout the Hive, a labyrinth of petrified ooze that still looked wet and dripping till you got up close. Advanced tech studded the walls, and hidden lights illuminated the walkways, shining off the slime. Siskelian mercs were stationed everywhere—a platoon of them for every scarf-festooned dryslug on the moon-sized station. The slugs might have been in charge, but it was the blue hired guns who were keeping the place running.

Lars followed Jay, Frank, and the slug official through an impossible-to-remember path up the Hive's interior. He wasn't happy about leaving *Sheila* at the dock, but Jay seemed sure his precious cruiser would be unmolested, and the official itself had given its word. The wolfman had locked up, told his baby he'd be right back, and slipped the rabbit-footed keys into the pocket of his armor-laced fatigues. Then the maze of the Hive, the four of them, plus their Siskelian escort, stopping only when they reached a large, locked door with a pair of blue mercenaries in full battle armor at attention on side. As if choreographed, both mercs turned to train their big blaster rifles on the non-slug newcomers as they approached.

The Ambassador, the official said. *We will see her.*

"She hasn't given the order," mumbled one of the guards.

The slug's tumors gnashed at the mercenary, but the armored Siskelian didn't react. Must be used to the things, Lars figured. Even the worst things in the galaxy are easy to get used to, you're around them long enough.

The big door sighed, some hidden hydraulic lock releasing, and slid open. The guards stepped back into position, shouldering the rifles, and the official slithered inside, Lars and crew shuffling in behind.

○

Lars couldn't stop himself from letting out a loud and disbelieving "Jeezus fucking Christ" at the sight of the Cairnish Ambassador. He froze, gawking, till Jay elbowed him to keep walking. The consular slug was huge, a fat mass of peeling leather skin and man-sized tumors, five times the size of the Cairnish he'd seen throughout the Hive, like a truckload of leather couches had been beamed with Gamma rays and fused together into a tumor-riddled monstrosity. Her mouth, and the mouths of the blind tumors, frothed with slime, and around her, amid unintelligible trid displays with holograms overlaying holograms like someone had forgotten to wear their red-and-blue glasses at a 3-D movie, were the rotting husks of other slugs, their tumors slumped over their bellies like dicks after sex. The whole nest stank of sweat and death, and Lars, senses heightened with his wolf blood, choked on the smell. The official who'd met them at the dock bowed to its leader and hissed something that the translators didn't catch. The Ambassador reared her head, and her tumors writhed.

Princess, she said. The alien voice boomed in the confines of the room.

"Ambassador," Jay said. "It's been a long time."

Not long enough. The Ambassador bristled. *Our pestilence halved when you left. I thought I asked you not to return.*

"You did. But I haven't returned to stay. I'm here to take the Hand home."

The big slug shuddered as it laughed. Its tumors shrieked, biting the air. *Home? You have no home, exile. That's why we took you in, allowed you to defile our land.*

"Like you said, Ambassador . . ." Jay smiled—the demure smile of someone skilled in diplomacy. Lars had to give her credit. Even if she'd only been a royal for the first few years of her life, she'd learned a thing or two about leverage. "It has been a long time."

Tumors screeched. The Ambassador lowed her head, coming face to face with the ninja princess. *A disturbance is sensed. A fissure in time. Explain this, Princess. Do you plan to cross the Cairnish? If you do . . .* The slug's wide mouth pulled into a hideous grin, and a claw swept from beneath layers of gilded scarves to gesture toward her nest of corpses. *I will feed you to my children as they hatch.*

"The fissure is the doorway to our universe," said Jay. "That's all your antennae are sensing. Our way home."

For a moment, neither Jay nor the Ambassador moved. Lars felt a fart blossoming in the pit of his bowels, but he decided to hold it in, lest the squeak send the tumors into a frenzy. Finally, the Ambassador lifted her head, settling back into her perch among the dead.

As you wish, Princess. You will descend to the surface and take the Hand home. Cut the cancer from our planet. Tumors wailed at the mention of Hand's name. *Is there anything else you wish to ask of the Cairnish?*

CHAPTER XXIII

Drag burned harmlessly along *Sheila*'s armored nose as the cruiser slanted into Cairn's atmosphere. Lars eased the throttle, slowed the descent to an easy speed.

"A knife?" he said again. "We traipse all through that wretched hive of scum and villainy to hold court with the Queen Slug, and your one request for helping them get this witch off world was a fucking knife?"

Jay was stationed in her annoying new perch right behind the pilot seat, gripping the pleather as the ship bucked with turbulence. In the distance, sprite lightning crackled in the sky, and clouds obscured most of the brown and beige landscape.

"It's not just a knife." The knife was in her boot sheath, ornate pommel level with her knee. She pulled it out, admired it as if checking her reflection in the blade. "It's a Cairnish ceremonial dirk. A holy relic. Forged through arcane metallurgy the slugs lost in the exodus."

Lars glanced over his shoulder. "It looks just like your other knife."

"It is just like my other knife," she said. "It's exactly like my other knife. Lost the other one when that toad jumped the airlock with my key."

Land was rising in front of them now, wide wastelands sliced through with blood-red rivers and boils of old mountains. Patches of black hair on the skin of the planet turned out to be trees, gnarled blackroots with slim yellow leaves. Lars tried to focus on the landing. Jay had given him exact coordinates, as sure of the numbers as if she'd been rattling off her birthday. He cut *Sheila* up over a knob of mountain peaks, bringing her low over a river valley, scattering a herd of hard-shelled beasts.

"Whole bags of swords and sorcery back there that we stole from Fishman," Lars said. "You couldn't pick out a good blade from that heap? What about that broadsword you were sweet on?"

He could almost hear her shrug. "I'm particular," she said, "about some things. Maybe I'm just sentimental too."

"Gift from a boyfriend," Lars muttered. "I get it."

"Not really," she said. She thrust her face forward over his shoulder, edging him sideways in his seat. Ahead, the stretch of wasteland narrowed into the fork of a red river, and at its apex sat a small silver dome glinting in the sunlight. "Set it down. We're here."

○

Rocks, brush, and random junk littered the wasteland around the dome, forcing Lars to park *Sheila* several shiplengths away. As the landing gear thudded against the desiccated earth, the whole cruiser shuddered, and a cloud of dust spread around it like a dense fart. Watching the dust settle made the wolfman's stomach rumble—that gas from back at the Ambassador's nest had gone shy, giving his guts a wicked ache. He needed to blast off some butt thunder pronto. And after that, he needed a long deuce and a hot breakfast, some moist little alien beauty in his bunk with her hindquarters poised at the ready. Instead, he was following a shifty murder princess into the desert den of a mysterious space witch. So much for luck.

Keys safely jangling in his pocket, Lars bee-lined through the cargo hold to his lunar battery stash. He could feel it, his blood—tapped of lunar energy like an engine running on fumes. It'd been reckless to change on that spinner, no moons in range to siphon, to recharge. He powered up two of the batteries and strapped them to his back. The packs' white lights pulsed as he felt the surge of lunar juice diffuse into his wolf blood. It would be a little while before he could turn again, but with this moonless rock, he didn't have much of a choice—it was battery power or zip. He rooted through one of the weapons bags from Fish's emporium and grabbed a bunch of shit he liked—combat knives he strapped to his arms and legs, a couple of plasma-cell revolvers. Locked and loaded, he rested the barrel of a laser cannon on his shoulder and grinned at Jay and Frank, who were watching irritably from the door.

"Ready?" he said.

Jay glowered. "We've been ready for ten minutes."

"Fuckin' A, then. Let's rock 'n' roll."

◯

Outside was hot and desolate and bone-dry. The air smelled of rust and sulfur, with an extremely faint undercurrent of patchouli oil that made Lars' stomach turn. As they headed for the dome—a silver thumbnail on the bleak horizon—the wolfman noticed that most of what he'd thought was junk was in fact a wind farm: a whole haphazard field of makeshift windmills cobbled together from blackwood, animal bones, scraps of steel, old hardened dryslug slime. Sun-bleached skulls from alien animals smiled from their rotor hubs, a kind of grim welcome, as the blades moved slowly around them, squeaking in the breeze.

"Love the arts and crafts," Lars said, tightening his grip on the cannon.

"You should see her macramé."

A grin spread across Lars's face—Jay was always so damn serious, it was a relief to know she could speak smartass when the occasion called—then faded just as quickly. Something changed in the scent of the wind. An animal smell. Bitter, acerbic. Venom and chitin. From nowhere, some unseen dimension, a crustacean claw as long as Jay's leg slipped into reality and clipped a whole branch from Frank's topiary crown. The tremuloid reeled, spraying hot sap.

Lars wheeled and started blasting the shimmering air with laserfire. "Fucking *Christ*. Jay—what was *that?*"

Jay was in full ninja crouch, eyes glittering. The Cairnish dagger in her fist caught sunlight: bright and menacing. "Chronoscorp," she called back. "Four-D predator. Why do you think the Cairnish evolved those tumors?"

"Figured they were chainsmokers."

Another claw burst into the third dimension, barely missing Jay as she leapt acrobatically from crouch to kick. Her boot landed on some random bit of the beast's obscured anatomy, shell cracking under impact, and the time-scorpion screeched.

Lars blasted again, hitting nothing but air. "I can't even see the fucker!"

Jay landed on dusty earth and rolled, dodging long, dripping stingers that breached time, stuck in rock, disappeared. With her ridged blade, she lashed out at nothing, and a stinger thudded wetly on the ground, severed from a chitin tentacle. It bled green into the dust. The monster screamed again.

"It's not in our dimension," Jay said, shaking scorp blood from her knife. "Not all of it."

More stingers in and out of ripples in time. Still a fountain of sap-blood, Frank hefted his own severed limb and swung, cracking one of the scorpion's lethal claws. Lars' cannon clicked empty, and he chucked it, double-fisting the plasma revolvers. Jay whirled and jived through the onslaught of barbed tentacles. Ducking behind one of the skull-topped windmills, the princess ensorcelled Frank's spraying sap, twisting it into ropes she wound around the monster's flashing limbs. The green blood oozing from the severed stinger she formed into a shield, and charged forward, the sap-ropes a web, the chronoscorp writhing with anger. Slowed, it was an easier target, and the revolvers tore through its carapace, brain already burned through with plasma holes as Frank brought his branch-arm down for the final blow, shattering the tentacled time-scorpion's nightmare face.

They were all heaving, out of breath, covered in green blood.

"What is this, planet of the time monsters?" Lars gasped. He felt his guts jag, and the deadly Embassy fart finally squeaked between his cheeks. At least that was a relief.

Frank threw down his lost limb and sat on a rock, depleted. Sap oozed down his trunk, over some of his eyes even, and he looked like he needed to get good and drunk. Lars couldn't blame him—he felt like emptying a keg himself. From the direction of the dome, he heard the clunking of metal and then he saw them, just barely, making their way through the field of windmills: a tall robot and a small old woman wrapped in robes. Even with the distance, he could tell she was the same vampire species as Jay, the purple tendril-hair and pale skin dead giveaways. As they neared, the woman shouted something that sounded like a snake gargling the words *Jade-Caesura-R'lyeh*. He tapped the language sensor on his collar.

"Sensors must've gotten fucked up in the fight," he said. "She's talking gibberish."

"It isn't gibberish," Jay said, watching the witch approach. "That's my name."

CHAPTER XXIV

The witch was quick for an old broad. She walked with a hunch, occasionally leaning on her android, but in no time at all they were standing next to the dead chronoscorp, a hard frown carved into the woman's mummified face. She nudged the scorp's cracked claw with a bare foot.

"Goddamn bugs," she said. "Desert's lousy with them."

She turned her gaze to Jay, squinting through thick red-quartz lenses. The witch was smaller than the princess, shriveled and bent by age. Her purple hair-tendrils were faded almost lavender, her skin yellowed and thin like the pages of an old book—arms and face marked with the same ritualistic scars. Her dusty robes hung low enough to make out a faded brand under her gaunt clavicle: a smaller, simpler knot than the one burned into Jay's chest. She pulled the glasses from her face and blinked sand from her eyes, darker and redder than Jay's amethyst, and Lars noticed that her left hand, holding the wire frames, was a prosthesis—a mechanical claw of bone-dry wood and copper wire, fastened with leather to the stump, which whirred with clockwork as it moved. The woman replaced her glasses and sniffed in disgust. Beneath her arched, scarred nose,

"AuntieHand" —mggln✱

yellow lips puckered over a mouthful of fangs, her whole face sharp and carved like a well-used ax.

"I'm home, Auntie," Jay said.

"This isn't your home. Remember that," the witch snapped. She eyed the princess's sheathed dagger. "Still playing nice with that grub bitch, I see." Then she seemed to notice Frank, the tremuloid nursing his scorpion wounds. "You've been watering your houseplant. What'd you do, run him through a wood chipper?"

Jay started to speak, but the witch held up her wooden hand.

"No excuses. If you'd stayed, you would know this arcana." She motioned for her robot, a seven-foot Frankenstein of bolts and steel. Each of the android's parts was mismatched and cobbled together, a motley of metal right down to the screws. Its left arm was painted in red camouflage and blossomed into a hefty concussion cannon at the elbow; the right was candy-striped black and yellow, the six-fingered gripper of a loader bot, Federation insignia still on the shoulder. The thick, rusted trunk of it had been hollowed out, and black liquid sloshed inside behind a pane of warped glass. On its bucket face, above two red slits of eye, was its callsign in faded block letters: BOR15.

The android grabbed Frank's chopped limb with its grip-arm and held it against the sap-seeping wound in the tremuloid's upper foliage. Frank didn't move, but his eyes took on a shade of embarrassment, and Lars felt sorry for the arboreal bastard. Frank kept getting the worst of the battle damage, and the big guy never even complained. No wonder he drank so much.

"Steady it, Boris," the witch said. "Can't see as well as I used to."

The wooden hand twitched, fingers moving like insects as the gears buzzed. Sap crawled up Frank's bark-skin. It sucked into the wound and wrapped around the area of cleavage like a poultice, hardened, the severed branch re-attached where the time-scorpion had cut it, the scar almost invisible. The witch moved her magic hand down the length of Frank's trunk, and as she did, the scorpion's green blood dissipated and the tremuloid's wounds and scars dissolved. Even his eyes looked less yellow.

"Jay," Lars whispered, "the fuck is all this? This witch your granny?"

"My teacher," Jay said. "The one who saved me."

It was only then that either the witch or the robot seemed to notice him. The robot's eyes flashed, and its cannon charged audibly, the wide barrel aimed at the wolfman's face.

"Pathogen detected," the bot said. "Recommend immediate termination."

Lars spat in the dust. Robots, man. They all had that stupid robot voice, like some ancient recording played through static on a shortwave radio. A concussion blast was swelling inside the barrel— he could hear the contralto thrum of it. He raised the revolvers, one each for the robot's eyes.

"Check again, Iron Giant," Lars said. "It's not fucking contagious."

The old witch was doing her squint thing, looking him up and down. She walked close to him; small pieces of bone and burnished coins hanging from her robes rattled as she moved. Lars swung one of the revolvers to meet her. The android twitched.

"Lars, don't," Jay muttered.

"Don't what? Piss off the Tin Man and the Wicked Witch? I don't much care for blasters getting waved in my mug."

As he spoke, the witch waved her hand like she was swatting a fly, and he felt his heart slow, blood thicken inside his veins. He felt suddenly heavy, as if the gravity had shifted, the planet ballooning beneath him. He dropped the guns.

"It's all right, Boris," the witch said. "Our princess has herself a pet."

She leaned closer, and he could smell her worse than he could before—dried blood, dust, dead animal, the overwhelming reek of patchouli. Some things were constant no matter what corner of the universe. The witch parted her parched lips, and a long black tongue stretched over her fangs—licking his cheek. He couldn't move. The scorpion's blood was drying on his skin and it started to itch. The old woman's eyes shimmered beneath her lenses. *Dirty old bag*, he thought, *at least buy me a drink first.*

116

He felt the weight in his veins deflate—back to normal, more or less.

The witch's face cracked into a reptile grin. "The beast."

"He's what you said we needed. A wolf," Jay said. "We can finally go home. Crush the rebellion."

"Always with crushing the rebellion, my little bug." The old woman shook her head and began walking toward the hut. She held up her clockwork hand, and the scorpion blood on Jay and Lars fell away like dust. "Come on. Bring your pets. This heat is making my tits sweat."

Lars shook the last of the green blood-dust from his beard. The android—Boris—was already following its master. "Charming old bitch."

"You don't know that half of it." Jay kept her eyes on the receding figures, tall and hunched. Frank stood at her shoulder. He seemed in good spirits, ready to party. Lars wouldn't have minded heading back to the cruiser and toasting Frank's health with a pint or two, but he could tell that wasn't on the docket—they were on the mission, and the witch was part of it. She and her weird junkyard robot.

Jay started for the silver dome, Frank following lockstep. Lars pocketed his revolvers and hauled ass to catch up, the dead husk of the scorpion behind them beginning to stink in the heat.

CHAPTER XXV

Auntie Hand had been old since before Jay was born. Last scion of an ancient family of conjurers and hexsmiths, court witch and arcane advisor since the alien princess's great-grandmother's reign. Not even royals called her by the name on her skin. She was the Hand, as much in name as in practice: The Left Hand of the Throne. She was also the royal preceptor of blood magic and hex arts—and the one who'd saved Jay from the execution squad the rebellion had sent for her family, finding a whole new macrocosmos in which to hide the young sovereign.

Jay spat into the dust as they walked through the stick-forest of windmills. "She's all I have left," the princess added. "The only person from my world in this entire universe. And you're exactly right—she's a raging bitch."

If Auntie Hand, shuffling ahead with her Franken-bot, heard Jay's whisper, the old woman made no sign. She didn't lose a step. The silver hut was further than it looked, and bigger. Once they passed into the rocky clearing beyond the witch's windmills, Lars saw that the hut rose out of the cracked earth like liquid, a mound of mercury molded roughly into building shape almost twice the size of *Sheila*.

Walls shifted texture and shade, liquid and stirring. Windows swallowed themselves and opened again in random blooms of light.

"Quicksilver ants," Hand said by way of explanation. "Domesticated, with a little drone spell to keep them sedate. Not much timber on this rock to go building cabins and cathedrals."

"Why not go down into the ruins? Dryslug cities? I thought they were a billion strong before the blight. Could live in castles down there." Lars pictured epic underground cities of hardened slime, decaying metropolises choked with the bones of the blighted Cairnish—and packed to the stalactites with black-market valuables and museum-quality trash. Jay's mission promised a fat paycheck, but she hadn't paid up yet, and Lars was getting antsy for some scrip. The buried Cairnish treasure got him jonesing to channel his inner Indiana.

"Too dark," said the witch. "Those filthy grubs look like they enjoy suntans? I like it up here, out in the open, you can see what's coming. You have to watch, in open desert though. Crust of this planet is a hollowed out, tunnels everywhere. Bugs don't get you, cave-ins will. Fall so far into the planet nobody'd hear you splat."

When they reached the hut, Boris turned, taking a sentry post, its red eyes scanning the desert behind them. Auntie Hand waved her wooden appendage, and a large hole opened up in the hut's outer wall. The old woman led them into the main room, which was cluttered with scavenged junk: bones and black stumps and bleached, smiling skulls. Chrono-carapaces, scraped clean, forming bowls for everything from rusted bolts to slime shards. Broken machinery from a dozen different planets stacked shoulder high, wires and tubes and semi-organic arteries hanging loose from their panels like trophy scalps. The witch nodded to a table—a big, burnished slab of Cairnish hardslime—at the far end of the room. Beside it was an electric stove, wires snaking directly into the churning liquid wall.

Robes rattling, the witch busied herself with a percolator near the stove. "Generator's out back. All those mills—plenty of power, especially when the westerly kicks up. Not like it used to be, when we were huddling around hex fires in a river cave, eh, little bug?"

"No," Jay said, looking away. "It isn't."

The princess sat at the hardslime table, taking the seat nearest the witch's stove. Frank hunched in the closed-in space of the hut, foliage curled down as much as possible. Even then, the tremuloid's uppermost branches scraped ants and ceiling, dropping bits of liquid silver to the swept dirt floor. Lars looked around for a wineskin or a beer fridge. A fight always made him thirsty—hell, everything did. And hungry. In every corner of the hut, all he saw was junk and bone. The whole scene creeped him out a little. Like some mad scientist's lab.

"Sorry, uh, Auntie," Lars called to the witch, "you got any chow? Fresh meat? I been eating canned for weeks."

Auntie Hand turned, her face flaming orange in the glow of the stove coils. A window opened, spotlighting the table and throwing the witch into shadow. "Fresh kill outside, I believe," she said with a razor-toothed grin. "Go crack yourself off a claw."

Some fucking host.

On the stove, the percolator whistled steam. Hand quieted it with her wood claw, bringing it—and a rattling tray of hollowed-out hardslime cups—to the slab of table. "We don't need food here. Boris doesn't eat. Me—I find what I need. And I need it rarely. Not like little bug." With a wooden finger, the witch pushed her glasses up to the bridge of her nose. "She's thirsty. I can see it in her eyes."

"I drink when I have to," said Jay.

"A queen drinks when she *wants* to."

"I don't plan to be that kind of queen."

The Hand let out a laugh, a dark, ugly sound, like scraping barbed wire over hollow teeth. "My little bug. Bleeding heart as ever." Hand lifted herself onto the slime bench and sipped at her tea.

"Auntie . . ." Jay began.

"Yes, bug, I know. It is time to go back." The cup shook a little in the old woman's hand. "I knew as soon as I saw you. You said you wouldn't come back—not until you'd found what we needed. The key, the beast. And now you're here, and that fat worm above us is cheering in her hideous nest at the thought of poor little me finally leaving this forsaken planet."

"Auntie . . . I lost the key."

The witch slammed her cup on the table, hissing Jay's real name. A flash of blood-red light burned in the old woman's eyes. Jay shrank from the glare—then gritted her teeth and stared back.

"I'll find another one," said the princess. "I found that one, didn't I?"

A hole widened near the entryway, and Auntie Hand's gaze shifted to the junk robot outside. Lars saw her face soften, a small smile tug at her pale lips. The kind of smile that made him wish he still had those revolvers in hand, and maybe a slug or two already brain-deep in the witch's skull. The lady was bad news—you didn't need hocus pocus to divine that.

"Listen, Mizz Hand," Lars said, "it wasn't Jay's fault. This skeezy little dildo salesman jumped out of an airlock with it and got himself portaled out of existence."

"A queen takes responsibility for her own mistakes," said the Hand. "And a court witch always has a Plan B."

"A lot of royal folks raw-dog it, huh?" Lars asked.

"Raw . . . dog?"

"Lars," Jay snapped, "shut up." The princess stood up, hand on the pommel of her slug knife. "I'm going for some air. Auntie, we are leaving. We have to. We've already been here too long."

The Hand coughed, gripping the table with both hands. The kettle rattled. "Yes, bug. Perhaps you're right."

Jay nodded and headed for an opening in the hut wall, disappearing into the desert sun. The witch watched her go then turned to Lars. "Tea?"

"Nothing harder? Stone cold bitch like you, I'd wager you keep a decanter around."

At that, Frank seemed to perk up from his perch near the junk piles.

The witch poured three cups of a thick blue-black tea. A thin eyelid slid over one of her cloudy eyes—a wink. "This'll knock you on your ass, beast."

Lars took a cup. The dark liquid bubbled, and he thought of the fairytales his mother had told him when he was just a flood town urchin back on Terra, when witches were nothing but myths and nightmares. Those witches, you never ate or drank their shit— whether it was an apple, a house of candy, or a mug of grog, it was all potion and poison. Best case scenario, you'd wind up comatose till your true love date-raped you in your sleep. More likely, you were chopped, ziplocked, and stashed in the freezer next to the last jackass who drank the witch's tea. Lars shot a glance at Frank, who was studying his own cup with every one of his yellow eyes. The wolfman pushed the tea aside.

"No thanks, lady. My ass has been knocked enough."

"Suit yourself." Hand downed her cup, then reached for Lars' and downed that too, both still boiling hot.

Lars stretched, joints cracking. He hadn't had enough rest in weeks, not even with the post-spinner sleep and 3Flesh dreams. It was all right in the witch's hut, hot but dry, and he didn't mind sparring with the old bag. She reminded him of his own grandmother, another stone cold bitch in her own right, hardened by the heavy fists of two now-dead husbands and a lifetime of watching the world go to shit. Jay needed a minute, so he figured he'd buy her one, get the Hand yarning. "What'd you do to the Cairnish, they want you out of here so badly? Put curses on all their grandfathers? Make their dicks turn blue and crawl away?"

"This," she waved the wooden hand toward the stacks of junk, "it's all holy relics to them. Right down to the ice trays and nipple clamps." Another razor smile as she poured a third cup of the black tea. "Grubs can't abide anyone setting foot on their Motherworld. It's sacred, yadda-yadda, but more than that, they're jealous—they can't come down here, so why should we?"

"Then why let you scuttle down here? Sweet talk?"

"For all their posturing, grubs are a primitive lot. Not a hex-savvy worm in the brood. I had a little princess with me, remember. Wanted dead or alive across galaxies. What better place to keep her safe than the most jealously guarded planet in the universe? I made a deal with the Ambassador to get some things they wanted very badly. So, they've tolerated me. In their own way, I like to think they want me here. A custodian for this old rock. I keep it tidy."

"Yeah, real safe and tidy." Lars sniffed. Goddamn he needed a beer. His stomach was lurching. His tongue felt like the floor. "Satellite-mounted lasers circling twenty-four-seven, monsters ambushing you from other dimensions. Fucking paradise. Can't see why Jay would ever want to leave."

"Little bug . . ." The old witch seemed wistful, for a moment. Then she spat onto the stove coils, watched the black mucous sizzle. "She failed. She wouldn't have lost that key if she'd continued training. Impatient, petulant. It's the royal blood—royals never have patience for anything. All the spoiled princess knows are parlor tricks. If she didn't have you, her rabid dog, the rebellion would eat her alive."

Blood ropes, blood walls, that sick shit she'd managed as they battled Quillian's stone men—that all seemed like more than parlor tricks to Lars. But what did he know? The old woman could freeze his blood with a flick of a finger. Maybe if Jay had stayed to finish training with Witch-Yoda Hand, she'd be an unstoppable Blood Jedi.

"I've been hearing all about this whole trip," Lars said. "You don't need an army, just yours truly, werewolf in space. And I have to tell you, it sounds like thirty-one flavors of bullshit. Nobody's taking back a whole planet with just me, some blood magic, and that sober bastard over there from the Forest of Doom."

"If it were open battle," the witch admitted, "you're right. But that isn't the plan."

Lars leaned back. "Then tell old Lars the plan. I'm all ears."

Auntie Hand snapped the fingers, and immediately Boris the junk-bot thumped into the hut. Jay crept in beside the mech, her purple tendril-hair tussled and dusty, in her hand a growler of ale from the *Sheila*'s hold. Lars felt himself salivate at the thought of a sudsy brew.

"First," said the witch, "we go home."

She held out her wooden prosthesis, and the black liquid in Boris's glass chest began to bubble and part. A hole opened up in the ceiling of the hut, and a shaft of light slanted to illuminate what had been obscured in the black: another of the rune-riddled puzzle boxes. A hellion key identical to the one with which Fish absconded.

124

"Auntie . . ." Jay sputtered. "What the fuck?"

The old witch touched the old knot of scars on her chest and flashed a shark-toothed grin. Bowing slightly to her young monarch, she said, "Plan B."

CHAPTER XXVI

The beer was piss-warm, but Lars didn't care. After time scorpions and the old witch's tea fumes and the concussive desert heat, it was nectar of the gods, and he savored every foamy mouthful before gulping it down. The sun was setting beyond the fork of the river, cooling the landscape and making thin silhouettes out of the field of windmills. The wolfman sat on an old chunk of hardslime and watched, tipping the growler occasionally to Frank's sucking appendage. Frank seemed distressed in the presence of the witch, eyes spying every which way, foliage aflutter, and Lars couldn't blame him. Hand gave him the heebie-jeebies too. The old lady had power—too much power. Especially over the ninja princess. Lars spat into the dust. Mommy issues, he figured. Some dangerous combo of guilt and loyalty. Old wise Auntie had Jay by the short-and-curlies.

The robot, Boris, came stomping by, patrolling perimeter. Its red LED eyes burned above its fat bolted jaw. Lars jerked the growler away from Frank and offered it to the motley 'droid.

"Hey, bolts," he said, "brewski?"

The robot halted. "Term not defined in any known galactic dictionaries."

"Beer, Frankenstein. You want a sip?"

Red eyes flashed. "Mark-III android models do not require fermented grain beverages."

"Me either, bolts. It's a want not a need." Lars swallowed another mouthful of the ale. It was going flat, but he still loved it. Who was he kidding? Mark-I werewolves *did* require fermented grain beverages. A whole fucking lot of them. He held the growler out for Frank, unwilling to let go of it. Yeah, he was bogarting the jug. So what? "Tell me a few things, huh? What are you and Broom-Hilda doing on this rock? Setting up a flea market for foxes?"

That static-fuzzed voice welled up from the robot's steel throat. "We are waiting."

"Okay," Lars said. "Waiting." He took one last pull off the jug, down to the bitter dregs, and pitched it into the dust. Above them, in the purpling sky, the pale outline of the Embassy was barely visible, making him nostalgic for a good old-fashioned moon. The lunar batteries were doing their trick—he felt the energy in his blood and bones, the power to wolf out returning. He wasn't running on empty anymore. "Waiting on what, death by slug laser? Bet those Embassy fuckers are getting pretty antsy up there. They want you gone yesterday. You and the wicked witch."

"Mother can handle the Embassy," Boris said. "She always has. They are afraid."

A few meters away, a fox crept up from some subterranean den, rippled its armored coat, and sniffed at the empty growler. A low percussive revving, then a flash of blue light, and the fox exploded into ash and cinders. Lars jumped, and his bladder threatened mutiny, sloshing and swollen from all that ale. Boris's gun-arm dropped, the mouth of the barrel still glowing white-hot.

"Cosmic *Christ*, bolts. That could've been dinner."

The robot turned, continuing its patrol, not even bothering to shrug. Frank took a cue from the iron giant, lurching the opposite way into darkness, and Lars unzipped, pissing into the dust as the sun disappeared and the ashes of the fox grew cold.

O

The stench of witch's brew in the dome had gone beyond suffocating as the so-called tea burned to a tar on the stove coils. Lars slunk amid the hut's array of knickknacks and slug junk, hazy from the beer. Finally, after bumping into a shelf or two and getting dizzy on the turbulent blooms of the quicksilver walls, he found Jay and the Hand. The space vamps sat on opposing sides of the hardslime slab, fangs clenched.

"The Library," Jay said. "You want to go back to the *Library*."

"Se'grob and his gaggle of dusty old corpses," the Hand spat. "Holier than thou in their castle of books. No, I don't want to go back there. But the key—"

"You have the key. You've had it this whole time and you didn't tell me. Why send me halfway across this universe searching for something you already had swimming in your robot's guts?"

"I didn't trust it," said the witch. "I still don't. It was damaged in our transit across the breach. And even if it hadn't been—all these years, I don't remember the sequence. I only used it that once, little bug, to save you."

"But," Jay scratched at a crack in the hardslime, "it's in the book. And the Librarians have the book."

"I'll make a queen of you yet," Auntie Hand grinned. She turned to Lars, who was picking through a bin of old bones. "Don't touch that."

Lars held one up—a long, curved tooth or claw, patinaed with age. "What's all this for? Just jangles for your dresses?"

"Those are the remains of a slug's time antennae," Hand replied. "Tumor teeth. Invaluable for divination and chronometric echo-location."

The wolfman tossed the tooth back into the bin. "Whatever, lady. You guys ready to split? All this dust is starting to make my dick chafe."

Auntie Hand stood, fixed her red glasses, and leaned on her twisted cane. "Let me get a few things."

The witch turned, but before she could even switch off the flame on the boiling stove, gunfire erupted outside the hut. Glowing bursts of plasma tore through the hut's canopy, raining red-hot globs of quicksilver ants. In a flash, black blood ballooned from the witch's good hand, forming a shield to protect herself and the princess. Lars ducked behind a half-toppled stack of shelves as tumor teeth clattered around him. Somewhere beyond the walls, an alert blaring from Boris the android stated the obvious—they were under attack.

CHAPTER XXVII

Galaxy light illuminated the edges of the night, and the hardslime Embassy shone in the darkness like an irradiated space yam. It would've been pretty except for the chrome-plated starjet strafing the desert in an effort to turn Lars and crew into plasma-scorched corpses. From the doorway of the hut, Lars could see Boris and Frank taking cover in the field of windmills. The robot was letting loose burst after burst from its gun-arm, while the tremuloid tottered beside it, hurling rocks.

"Jeezus, Frank," Lars muttered, "at least grab a blaster or something." Then he turned to Jay and the Hand. "I thought you said this rock was locked down. 'Vessels without clearance are vaporized,' I think were the exact words. How is it this joker's raining gunfire on us right now? He get his passport punched?"

"I–I don't know," Jay stuttered.

Auntie Hand scowled. "Slugs are getting lazy."

"We're sitting ducks out here in the dust. Let's haul ass to *Sheila* and burn atmosphere," Lars said. "A lot more firepower on the cruiser than what we're packing in our pockets."

A volley of plasma bounced and sizzled across *Sheila*'s shields, and Lars gasped—it was one thing to shoot at him or one of these other meat bags. It was another to shoot his baby. That bastard was gonna scuff his paintjob. The wolfman tore off running toward the ship, pulling his revolver from its holster, and felt infinitely stupid wearing his two dozen knives. He never liked being the asshole who brings a knife to a laser fight. The chrome jet made another pass over *Sheila*, her shields still holding, Boris shooting so much at the incoming ship that the barrel of his arm glowed red. But it was a well-placed rock that knocked the jet's stabilizer loose. The attacking craft's wings wobbled. It turned, heading into a tailspin. *Just fucking explode*, Lars thought, *save us all the hassle*. The jet didn't explode—not even a little fire on the wings for effect. It pulled its nose up just enough to crash-land on its belly in a stretch of desert between the windmills and the red river, throwing up a thick cloud of dust in its wake.

"Jeezus, Frank," Lars said, catching up to the old tree. "Nice aim."

Boris's gun-arm was still smoking. "Target neutralized."

"Doubt it, bolts. Simple airbag could've saved that dude from mega-death." Lars cracked his knuckles, the tattooed letters BADD WOLF stretching across his fingers. He kissed one fist, then the other. "Time to blow this piggy's house in."

"Lars, stop." It was Jay, with the witch hobbling right behind her.

"Motherfucker tried to blast up *Sheila*. He's losing a couple teeth, maybe an arm or two. End of story."

"We need to go. Whoever it is, leave him for the scorpions. We've got bigger problems."

The wolfman clenched, head to asshole. He didn't like leaving chins unpunched. It went against his whole code of justice. Eye for an eye, chin for a chin. Fuck with me and you get fucked. But the princess was boss—and following her gaze up to the night sky, he knew she was right. Streaks of fire were raining down from the Hive. Embassy dropships inbound, heading right for them.

CHAPTER XXVIII

Sheila was close but not close enough. In seconds, they'd have a whole army of Siskelian mercenaries up their asses. Even with the witch and her war droid, Lars didn't like the odds. Not on a planet without a moon.

"I'll deal with this," Auntie Hand grumbled. "Just stay out of my way."

"Those are whole dropships," Lars said. "What are you gonna do, serve them some of your black-tar brew?"

The Hand stepped out of the field of windmills and dropped her cane. With her wood-and-wire hand raised high, she said, "Watch and learn, beast." She brought her other hand up and bit into the palm like Jay had back in Canal City and Victor's Halo, black blood oozing from the wound. She threw the bitten hand skyward, and blood sprayed.

Lars turned to Jay. "Is she serious? She thinks she's gonna bloodwall these fuckers?"

The princess's white, scarred hand clenched around her dryslug dagger. The Embassy, the stars, and the streaks of dropships

132

dragging through the atmosphere reflected in her eyes, and it was pretty, sort of. Minus the chemtrails from the descending merc army.

"Just shut up, Lars. Let her do this."

Blood bloomed from the witch's hand. It stretched, a black sheet, razor-thin and pushing starward. Hand's scarred brow creased with effort. Her skin, even paler than its usual paper-white, sucked at her bones. The dropships were more than streaks in the sky now. They were heavy things, three of them: Hardslime cocoons festooned with spotlights and growing quickly as they descended to the surface. Beside Lars, Jay unsheathed the Cairnish dagger—and slashed her own palm.

"Jay, what—" Lars started, but she was already a step ahead.

"Auntie!" Jay called, throwing the whip of blood she'd woven. It exploded into droplets, combining with Hand's blood, each drop miniscule but calculated, a matrix of bloodhex casting toward space like a net.

Hex like that was myth—intergalactic fairytale. If the witch could hold back three ships dropping full-speed from orbit with her bloodwall, then it was magic nobody in the Federation or otherwise had seen in generations. Sure as fuck it'd never been seen on Terra, except on the library's old TV. It might have saved the planet, held back the oceans, cleared away the black clouds of orbiting debris. The bloodnet disappeared into the darkness, and Lars thought of his mother, caked in dirt from double shifts in the floodyards, and the bullshit cosmic roulette that gave some people, whole races, hex and hocus-pocus while others were left to drown and rot. Lars gritted his teeth, pointed the revolver at an incoming dropship, and squeezed the trigger, blasting plasma till the power cell beeped empty.

"Take *that*, motherfuckers," he spat at the sky. Frank was looking at him with half his yellow eyes, looking as concerned as a mute tree could look. "Just getting into the spirit, Frank. Doing my part in the war for the wasteland."

He threw the empty pistol to the dirt and turned to Jay. She stood with her hands out, feeding blood into Auntie Hand's spell, eyes starting to take on a grayish haze.

"Jay," he said, "Hot Cosmic Christ, put a band-aid on that—"

A crash. The princess wavered, but her blood kept pouring. Out in the desert, one of the dropships lay wrecked and burning, its flickering spotlights illuminating black bloodspatter across its hull. But there were still two more ships, and both Jay and the Hand already looked half dead.

"Jay," Lars said, "Jay!"

Her blood laced with the witch's. Another net was forming. *They're gonna bloodhex themselves to death*, Lars thought. No time for diplomacy. They had to get to *Sheila* and split.

"Frank, a little help?" he said, nodding toward the princess. Frank's sallow eyes widened when he saw her, and the branch that knocked her out was so fast Lars thought the old tree might've killed her. But when the tremuloid's limbs cradled her, she was still breathing, the wound on her palm barely dripping black.

Next to the Hand, Boris's disconcerting robot voice repeated "Mother? Mother?" The Hand was a powerful hexsmith—might've been the premier hemomancer in this universe or any other. But she'd shed too much blood taking one ship down. Before the net could wrap around the next incoming slug vessel, the witch fainted, and the un-enchanted blood of the net splashed across rows of bone windmills.

Boris caught her in the crook of its gun-arm, its candy-striped gripper reaching to pick up her cane.

Lars nodded to Frank. "Can you run?"

Some combination of branch and foliage gave an affirmative reply. The tremuloid took off in lumbering jog through the windmills, Jay dropping in his branches, and behind him the robot Boris, pistons wheezing as it sprinted mechanically for the cruiser. With the batteries on his back, Lars felt currents of moonpower in his veins and fought the urge to wolf out and race to the head of the pack. In wolf form, he could've lapped them twice, but what was the point? Waste of good moon juice. And anyway, nobody was going anywhere without him. He was the one with the keys.

CHAPTER XXIX

By the time they reached her, *Sheila* was under an inch of dirt. You could hardly see the pinup girl or the yellow flames beneath the grime. The dropships were landing, sending clouds of dust in all directions. Lars fumbled in his pocket for the keys, smiling as he touched the lucky rabbit's foot. Unlocking the door, the wolfman ducked into the cruiser, kicking cans and rubbish out of the way to make a path for guests.

Boris clumped in with the knocked-out Hand, then Frank with the knocked-out Jay. The princess was already starting to stir.

"Throw them on that pile of cargo netting," Lars said. "That's where I sleep it off when the bunk's a million miles away."

The robot and the tree plunked their vampire cargo onto the nets, then stood side by side like soldiers awaiting orders. *Sheeeit*, Lars thought. He wasn't a fucking commandant. He didn't give orders, he took them—begrudgingly, and only for a paycheck.

"You two keep an eye on our bloodsucking Sleeping Beauties. I'm gonna haul my ass to the pilot seat and blast us off this shithole planet."

The planet shook—the Embassy dropships making their landing, he figured. The vamp women flopped a little, and empty cans rattled across the floor. Frank wrapped his branches protectively over the pallet of kegs.

"Pour me one, Frank. I'll be back for it when we're spacebound."

○

Two inches of dust caked in the windshield, but there were no cracks or beeping alarms, and all the gadgets and gizmos of the pilot deck looked to be in working order. Lars plugged the key into the ignition and revved up the engines to the tune of that old muscle car. In a minute, they'd be jetting past the Embassy and futtling off to wherever the fuck and it wouldn't matter if there were ten Siskelians or two hundred marching across the desert. It wouldn't matter who the asshole in the chrome wreck was either. They could all circle jerk onto a time scorpion for all he cared. Engines ready. Zoom zoom.

The speakers around him—normally reserved for crunching heavy metal tunes—crackled to life and issued a warning: "*We have our satellites locked onto your location. If you attempt to escape, we will be forced to fire.*"

Some Embassy lackey. Probably a slimy Siskelian twerp picking his nose in front a trid display. Lars smacked the switch on the interstellar comms. "Bullshit. If you wanted to roast us, we'd be fifty shades of ash already."

A pause. Then another voice, hissing and strained. "*You have destroyed our ship and further defiled our sacred home. The deal is no more. The Ambassador desires the Hand. Release her to the hirelings surrounding your vehicle.*"

He couldn't be sure, but he figured it was the same slug that'd met them at the docking port. He imagined what the thing's tumors were doing just then, biting at the air like hungry worms. Lars scratched the back of his neck and grumbled. "Wait a minute. Defiled, huh? You sluggos watching me piss from up there?"

"*The intruder. You have brought another trespasser to our lands. It tracks you. It follows you.*"

Cosmic fucking Christ. The slugs were in a tizzy over the cocksucker in the starjet, and throwing blame on Lars and crew. Weren't they supposed to be the ones with the space guns? Pew-pew and down comes anything inching into orbit? Way Lars figured it, the mercs should've been poking at the jet crash and burning laser holes through any survivors, instead of circling *Sheila*. Captain Chrome wasn't his problem.

"Listen, we don't know that pilot from fuck-all. We just want to blast off. We can still do the deal as planned—no more Hand on your planet, no worries. Call off your dogs and we'll mosey."

"*The Hand destroyed our ship, killed our hirelings. Intruder or no intruder, the deal is rescinded. Release the Hand,*" the slug hissed. "*The hirelings are waiting.*"

On the cam system, he could see the ring of mercs lined up around *Sheila*'s back door, rifles all nasty-looking and ready to fire. The goddamn witch. He knew she was trouble, and tossing that dropship had done zero except piss off the slugs. What'd they need her for anyway? Jay had him, and with Boris aboard she had a puzzle box. Instruction booklet waiting on some Library someplace. Sounded like the princess knew all about it. No blood witch required. Why not hand her over, let the Cairnish do their thing? The old bag could take care of herself. Choke the whole slug lot with a couple of bloodropes. He checked the gauges on his lunar batteries. Still up and running, maybe half strength with the recharge they'd had to give him after the incident with Fish on that backwater spinner. He still felt the lingering drain of turning wolf in the chapel of the Cosmic Christ. That had been fucking stupid, he knew, wolfing out so far from lunar recharge. The batteries had filled him back up, but it was a weaker sauce. Still, it would have to do. He ducked out of the cockpit toward the cargo hold, and left the engines running.

○

In the hold, Jay was awake and already lifting the tech-laced sword from one of Fish's Rubber Room sacks. She smiled, testing the weight of it in her scarred hands. Auntie Hand was still KO'ed, the 'droid in sentry mode beside her. Frank was in his corner spot sucking beer from three cups.

"One of those is mine, Frank," Lars said. To Jay, he added, "Slugs want your Auntie. Got a platoon of blue-skinned sellswords knocking at our door to deliver. They say we fouled the deal by crashing that dropship."

"I heard."

"So? Must've gotten their sats back online after the jet got by—they've got sights on us. Space lasers pointed right at my baby." Lars swiped a cup from Frank and guzzled. "I say we make the trade. Show the slugs we wanna play nice. What's one old lady against the whole mission of righteous vengeance, right?"

Jay whirled the broadsword around in some fancy one-handed ninja move, its blade sizzling with lightning while her other hand unsheathed the slug dagger and kept it low and close. The gray static was gone from her eyes—they burned purple, deep and endless.

"Yeah," Lars said, kicking up a big gun from another one of Fish's sacks. "Figured it'd be the hard way. What about old Auntie? Can't she bloodwall these fuckers and give *Sheila* a bubble to shield us from the sats? Maybe we can still make a run for it."

Jay looked down at the old witch, her face softening. "She thinks she's invincible. Being the most powerful hexsmith in the world—in your whole universe—you start to think you can do anything." The princess knelt and tucked the Hand's rattling robes over her exposed hands. The witch didn't stir. "Even a super witch only has so much blood to hex. Her cells need to regenerate. She barely has enough to keep her heart pumping."

Standing over a weapons sack, arms loaded with blaster-guns, the wolfman grunted. "So, what's the plan? Gunfight, then run like hell anyway?"

The vampire princess stood, blue lightning shimmering down the wide blade of her new techno-glaive. "Swordfight," she said. "Then run like hell."

CHAPTER XXX

The door was still closed, locked. Lars stood in front of it with every scary-looking gun he could find holstered, strapped, or zip-tied to his arms, legs, and torso. In his hands, he had Fish's big plasma cannon, its wide barrel aimed straight at the hatch. On his right, Frank creaked and groaned like an old sailing ship, and on his left, Jay stood ready with the broadsword crackling electric. Boris had its gun-arm up, red LED eyes sharp and scanning. Auntie Hand just kept snoring.

Lars tapped the cannon's trigger guard and sniffed. The Cairnish double-cross made his nerves raw, the same feeling he got any time a client tried to back out of a deal. He was hot and sober and undersexed and tired and in need of some quality time with good old-fashioned moonbeams. Instead, he had his half-empty lunar batteries, a bullshit holdup with a bunch of shifty slugs, and a few dozen mercs right outside his ship with a whole lot of firepower trained on his baby, which—between the yeasty stink of empty bottles and cans in the cargo hold, the sap leaking from Frank, and the essential-oil marinade Auntie Hand had been pickled in—smelled increasingly like a hippie's unwashed grundle. Not to mention an as-yet-unidentified mystery man rattling around in that crashed jet. Yet more hitches in

Jay's mission. The whole damn job was too many snags, too little beer and pussy. And it stank.

"Lars," Jay was saying, "can you hear me?"

She was still holding her tricked-out sword, its pommel sizzling with puzzling gizmos. Lars wondered what exactly those upgrades could do—open up a shotgun inside the blade? Zap an opponent with electric blue fireworks? Play your favorite rock-n-roll tunes frontwards and back? Whatever it was, he hoped it'd take out a dozen or two Siskelians in one go.

"Yeah, I heard you," he said.

"We can't just stand here all night."

"Just one more beer. To steady the nerves"

Jay hissed, showing her fangs. "Frank," she ordered, "open the door."

"Don't do it, Frank. I'm captain of this cruiser. One more before shit hits the fan."

A branch slapped the airlock, and the door began to move, half a hundred mercenary soldiers somewhere beyond it in the desert night. *Ah, fuck.* Lars readied the plasma cannon.

"All right, you Siskelian screwheads, listen up. *This* is my—" *Boom.* A blast of neon green plasma tore through the open hatch, and from the dust and the dark came screams. A body ablaze in green fire stumbled out of the darkness, flesh already melting off its bones. As it lumbered closer to the hatch, Lars froze. It was like he'd opened the Lost Ark. The burning Siskelian fell to his knees as muscle and bone sloughed from its legs. In seconds, the merc was nothing but a puddle of charred armor and wet fat slightly sizzling in the dust.

"Target eliminated," announced Boris's robo-voice.

"No shit, bolts," Lars muttered. "Target supernova'ed."

Jay hissed, "Listen," both hands clenching the broadsword's long hilt.

Lars listened. Even with the engines rumbling, he should've heard it before the vampire. The shuffling of things in the desert, the occasional odd squeak of an unoiled wheel.

The broadsword drooped an inch as Jay turned, still listening. "Why aren't they shooting at us?"

More shuffling. More dust clouds and darkness. A burst of gunfire, brief, in the distance. Lars loosened his grip on the cannon and sniffed again. He couldn't smell anything over the stink of the ship. Patchouli and trash. Priority number one after they hit open space: Dump the garbage. How the hell was a wolf supposed to operate without his super-sniff?

"Time scorpion?" Lars ventured. He didn't relish the idea of another one of those interdimensional bastards crawling about, but enemy of my enemy and all that. Let the 4-D arachnid thin the platoon, werewolf and crew could mop up the rest. Then another thought unnerved him: "Those fuckers ever rove in packs?"

"Solitary," Jay whispered. "I don't think it's a chronoscorp. Too quiet."

Frank creaked in his corner. His eyes looked worried. Lars couldn't blame him. The old tree had already lost one limb to a scorpion—and this time the witch wasn't waiting in the wings to piece him back together.

Around the ship, silence congealed, broken only by Frank's creaking and the hum of the air recycler, the farty *fwah* of O2 pumping back into the hold. Then a squawk from Boris's voice box broke the quiet: "Multiple targets incoming."

As the robot's blaster revved, Lars squinted into the darkness. "Can't see anything out there, Johnny 5. Just a burnt merc and a whole lotta dust."

The robot fired, and something splintered in the dark. Lars waited for a scream, or the shriek of a scorpion, anything, but no sound came except the scattering of debris.

"They are Mother's," the bot said.

Jay stepped back, uneasy, and glanced at the sleeping witch. "What does that mean?"

"They are Mother's," Boris repeated. "They are her creations."

The plasma cannon nestled against Lars' shoulder. He sighted on the empty dust cloud and figured, hell, he got lucky the first time. "Whatever they are, they're fucked."

143

As he touched the trigger, a voice sounded in the ether, reverberating from nowhere in particular. Sense-language. Booming and familiar. "Lars Breaxface . . . and his motley crew of nobodies. This is going to be fun."

Quillian Nine. That was who'd been in the chrome jet—the silver gangster, on the run from whatever price Canal City's Consortium had put on his shiny head. Chased them across the black all the way to fucking Cairn, and managed not to get his ass blasted out of the sky when he broke atmosphere. However he'd tracked them, Lars was going to make damn sure he couldn't do it again. Quillian's sense-language had diffused through the hull, unhindered by shield and steel—which meant he was close. Somewhere just out of sight. Captain at the head of his troops. He wondered how the gangster's chin would break—whether it would crack like marble or burst into silver dust.

"Lars," whispered Jay, "look."

Out of the dust clouds, thin shapes began to emerge. White skulls smiled the grins of the dead as halos of blades turned lazily around their heads. The rest of their makeshift bodies were scraps of wood and metal and hardslime. They lurched forward on legs of junk. The witch's windmills. A hundred of them, like the brooms in that Mickey Mouse cartoon, marching and marching from the dust toward the cruiser's open door.

CHAPTER XXXI

Fox skulls. Chronoscorp mandibles. The skinny bone faces of stranger creatures, glowing faintly in the moonless night. Lars remembered what Fish had told him back at the fart-alien's saloon: As long as Quillian wore the enhancer cuffs, he wasn't limited to two aces—he could play the whole deck, and all they had was a couple of jokers.

The windmill army advanced slowly, skeletal smiles eerie in the gloom. As they marched, they pulled blades from their necks with fingers of hexed bone. Black and blue blood was spattered across most of them, and some were missing teeth and limbs. Lars held back a shudder. One sextoy golem had nearly choked the life out of him back at Fish's emporium—now Quillian had a whole new army, one that could snuff a platoon of well-trained mercenaries almost without a shot fired. As long as the gangster had his puppet frequency on broadband and the slugs had their lock on from space, there was no way to fight and no way to run. Lars and crew were ten ways to fucked.

The wolfman brought the cannon back to his shoulder and took aim at the oncoming skull golems. "Hasta la vista, skull-fuckers." His thick finger pressed the trigger. And the cannon beeped impotently. No hot neon plasma burst, no boom. He wiggled the trigger, slapped the barrel a couple of times. It beeped again, angrily, a red light pulsing on the stock, its whole wad blown on his big Siskelian surprise.

Beside him, Boris's gun-arm powered up, and Jay's sword sizzled.

"We should have killed him in Canal City," Jay spat. "You should've let me carve him into jewelry."

Lars chucked the dead cannon into the trash pile and pulled two blasters from his belt. "You're right, princess. Any amount of heat from the Consortium would be better than this bullshit. Let's not make that mistake a second time."

Boris popped a pulse-burst through the open door, and one of the skull puppets crumbled. But behind it, there were dozens more—Jeezus, had there really been so many in the field? Skulls, dust, menacing blades. All of it coming closer to *Sheila*. Lars holstered his blasters.

"Aw, hell naw. Frank, close it up. We're jetting—I'd rather take my chances with space guns."

The tremuloid hesitated—till Jay gave a nod, and a creaking branch poked the toggle, the door to the hold closing with a hiss.

Jay's sword tip scraped the dirty floor, knocking an empty can across the room. "What are you doing?"

Heading for the corridor, Lars called over his shoulder: "Getting off this rock."

◖

Keys jangling from the steering column. A stale brew in the cup holder. Six-legged hula girl shimmying on the dash. Lars revved *Sheila*'s tachyon drive and flipped the burners on the wings for takeoff. Through the windows, he saw nothing but howling dirt. Even on the infrared, all that showed were the flames of the crashed dropship and the cooling bodies of the Siskelian mercs. Quillian and his army were invisible. He tapped the holo-display to funnel more power to the cruiser's defenses. If Quillian's puppets got through, game over. At least in Canal City, Lars had been channeling the ocean planet's double moons. Here, he had only his half-charged batteries. *Sheila* was a coffin, and if they didn't jet, they were all dead already.

He smelled Jay behind him before he felt her, the princess huffing and puffing with her broadsword in hand.

"The fuck, Jay? I'm trying to drive."

The ninja princess was flushed, little roses of lavender on her pale cheekbones. "You frivolous mutant. The slugs were caught with their defenses down once—they won't make that mistake again. They're watching us. They'll blow us out of the fucking sky."

"They could try," Lars said. "*Sheila*'s a Class-V speedcruiser—nothing faster than my baby. We get clear of ozone, I'm futtling subspace for the nearest frontier brothel. You and the rest of the Funky Bunch can sit on the witch's wooden hand."

"Hail the Cairnish. Maybe they'll help us."

"Are you kidding? The slugs hate you and your witch. Why would they help us?"

"Revenge. Quillian just slaughtered the rest of their ground forces."

Lars leaned back in the pilot seat and handed Jay the radio. "Well, give the slugs a ring then. We've got the witch, right? Deal's sealed. They zap Quillian, we jet, and everyone's happy."

"Yeah," said Jay. "Everyone's happy." She tapped a couple of keys on the holo-dash, just below the hula girl, and held the radio mic to her lips. "Hailing Cairnish Embassy, this is Cruiser 62815."

From the radio, the slug voice hissed: "*Princess . . . We are losing patience. Our hirelings . . .*"

"The other intruder—he killed your mercenaries. He's making a mockery of your sanctuary, flooding it with blood."

"*Do not try to fool us, Princess.*"

"We had a deal. The Ambassador gave us her word—we remove the Hand and the Embassy allows us safe passage offworld. We can still honor that deal, if the Cairnish will target the intruder—"

The slug broke in, "*We do not fire on our home. That is why we sent the hirelings.*" The radio crackled as the dryslug paused. "*Destroy*

147

the intruder yourselves. If you do, the Cairnish will honor your agreement—you will be allowed to leave the planet."

"But he's got a fucking *bone army*," Lars blurted.

Jay bared her fangs. "Shut up," she whispered. To the radio, she said, "We'll kill him."

A sound from the speakers sounded almost like a laugh, and then the transmission cut.

Lars tapped the hula girl, and she swayed robotically, reminding him of someone he used to know. "Quillian'll send everything he has at us. Guaranteed he lost his whole operation in Canal City, all that ruckus at the port. Blames you, me, and the erstwhile amphibian. And he's a sick son of a bitch. I say we throw bolts out there and let him thin the herd. He's just a bot—who gives a shit if the puppets smack him with their blades?"

"Yeah," Jay said, "Maybe." Then her eyes widened, and she took off into the corridor, muttering obscenities in her vampire tongue.

Lars called her name, but she didn't turn, and in a second, she was in the hold, heading for the hatch. "Jay, don't," he shouted. "Keep it closed—we need the chokepoint. Send the android out, we can sit tight and have a beer with Frank while he does the hard work!"

But she was already gone, the hatch left open like a wound. Next to his face, a red and yellow blob streaked across the infrared screen, and then he knew why she was running. The blob was tree-shaped, and whipping wildly. Frank was taking on Quillian's skull army all on his own. Muttering his own four-letter litany Lars popped the blasters from their holster and followed Jay's path. Deal or no deal with the space slugs, they were going to battle Quillian and his windmills, and save Frank from getting chopped to bits.

CHAPTER XXXII

There are gladiator pits in Freewheel, big radiant stadiums swimming with corporate holograms and overpriced booze and grilled critters sold out of handcarts, where oily, rippled warriors face off against the beasts of the cosmos. There's the gladiator flexing in the middle of the ring, and on either side there's a big ass door. Door Number One is electrified bars—you can see right in to the monster snarling, stalking, or spidering, taking in the warrior-meat and the bloodthirsty crowds. But Door Number Two—Door Two is an opaque black slab. You can't see shit behind Door Number Two. While the doors are closed, you place your bets on which monster will eat the gladiator first. Lars had won a few bucks on those fights, and lost a small fortune, and that's exactly what this felt like—betting on the glad pits, deciding which was the bigger threat: the swarm of skull-and-steel puppets or Quillian himself. Lars didn't have enough lunar juice to last long in his werewolf skin. In *Sheila*'s dingy hold, staring down teeth of a hundred haunted windmills, Lars calculated the odds. Wolf out now, try to take the skull-fuckers before they killed Frank and Jay, or swallow it, stick to the old-fashioned shoot-em-up, save the beast for the silver bastard.

149

He looked over his shoulder. Boris hadn't moved. "Bolts, you coming?"

"I must protect Mother."

"Protect her by demolishing these pricks. We perish them, we're home free."

The 'droid was rooted in place. Only the LED scanners in its eye-slits moved. "I must stay at Mother's side."

Lars kicked some trash and watched it scuttle across the floor. "You're useless, you know that?"

"I have many uses," the robot said.

"Why don't you rattle them off to my asshole," Lars muttered. "I've got a tree to save."

The wolfman charged out of the hatch with blasters blazing. The skull golems were everywhere. Even with *Sheila*'s meager spotlights, it was all darkness and chaos. In the dust, Jay whirled like a god of chaos, her techno-glaive flashing with electricity as she executed her own broadsword ballet. Skull golems clamored and fell, sliced to splinters, only to reform again and swing their rusty blades. When they got too close, a bloodshield would bloom, and the skull-fucker's blade would stick harmlessly in blood. But they were relentless. Sooner or later, the princess would slip. As he surveyed the area, Lars kept blasting, bolts of black energy chipping away at wood and bone. No sign of Frank or Quillian. No Siskelian stragglers either. Behind him, over the pow and clatter of swordplay and blasters, the wolfman heard scratching. He wheeled on his bootheel, and there they were: a gaggle of skull puppets hacking away at *Sheila*'s hull, definitely scuffing the paint.

"You boney sons of bitches!" he shouted as the pair of blasters clicked empty. Lars dropped the blasters, swung a darklight shotgun from his back, and fired two bursts, each one shattering a puppet's skull to splinters. Their rubbish bodies rattled down the hull. Another two bursts, two more skulls in pieces. The last two turned to Lars with their vacant, hellion smiles and leapt, flecks of *Sheila*'s paintjob on their turbine-blades. The wolfman swung the shotgun and blasted one out of the air, missed the other by an inch. Before he could ready his fist for a good chin punch, it was on him, slicing at his flesh like a trash-puppet sushi chef. He dropped the shotgun, both hands wrenching at its wood-and-wire frame. Its patinaed skull—the long-dead remains of a slug tumor, judging from its lack of eyes and horrible teeth—gnashed at his beard, clipping a bit from the right side. If the scratches in his ship's paint hadn't pissed him off enough, now they'd gone and unbalanced his facial hair. Fending off the golem's mouth with a forearm on its neck, Lars scrounged his weapon-laden body for a knife, found one, and unsheathed it, bringing its pommel down hard on the skull's solid forehead. The skull split, and the windmill's frame fell limp. Lars touched the bitten side of his beard. Un-fucking-balanced. Quillian was going to pay for that.

Lars tried to smell the gangster, that clean gunpowder smell of him, the factory-new stench of his silk suit. All he could scent was the sour meat of the dead mercenaries and the smoke of burning bone. Not far away, surrounded by a ring of dead and living puppets, Jay continued her sword dance. She was bleeding now, from more than just her palm. Fresh black cuts crisscrossed her name scars. Lars picked up the shotgun and aimed for the nearest skull-fucker, one with an armored fox's fleshless face. The puppet juked his first shot, and Lars blasted again. The fox was quick. Its wire joints moved with magic locomotion, the puppet almost flattening itself as it readied itself to leap.

"That's enough," came Quillian's voice from the dark.

The windmills froze, blades outstretched toward their targets.

From the haze smoke and dust came a familiar creaking of old wood, and Frank lumbered out, foliage dropped in surrender, a dozen skull puppets in his branches with something dark in their hands. As if choreographed, each puppet jerked its hexed hands, and torches bloomed with flame. Quillian stepped out from behind the tremuloid hostage, flames reflecting red on his silver face. He wasn't in his gangster glad rags anymore—the puppeteer had opted for full spider-weave body armor and a stupid-looking beret in place of his trademark fedora. Lars saw Jay twitch with her sword, but she knew just as well as he did that any wrong move and Frank would be firewood.

"Congratulations, you Destro-knockoff piss weasel," Lars said. "You managed to slime your tin-can ass out of Canal City before they trenched you. Want a cookie?"

"No cookies, Breaxface. I want you—one piece at a time," said Quillian. "You and this hot little number with the knife. And the tree. And, of course, Mr. Fishman. I'm looking forward to a reunion with the former emporium proprietor. In fact, this whole affair has been elevated to extremely fucking personal. If it were business, Breaxface, I'd let you bribe your way out—maybe just take the woman, as a good-faith gift. But that little amphibious shit shot me, and you let him tag along into the black like he was your kid brother. You should've left him where he was. Now we have a debt to square."

"You're too late. Fish fucked off transdimensionally," Lars called. "Sloughed this whole plane of existence."

"That's too bad." Quillian looked up as if pondering the stars and the universe and existence and shit. Maybe he was, or maybe he just wanted Lars to sweat a little. The wolfman's trigger finger was starting to itch. Quillian would've looked a whole lot better with a burning hole in his face. But Lars knew he wasn't the fastest gun in the west. Sure as shit not faster than the puppeteer's thoughtwaves. Even if he did drop dead, Frank would be toast too. "That is really too bad. But it doesn't matter. You *owe* me, Breaxface. You and your whole crew. And I'm going to collect."

Lars snorted and spat, the loogie landing a centimeter from the gangster's gold-plated loafers. He wiped his mouth with the back of his hand. "Shit, Quillian, if that's all you want, a little reimbursement, I can write you an IOU. Good as cash, anywhere in the universe."

"Just listen, you cave-beast. Let me tell you how this is going to go," Quillian continued. "Since this primordial shrub tossed a rock at my ride and caused it to run aground, I'm going to take your ship. Now, I can see your engines are running so I know I don't need any keys. You can put down your weapons right now and tell me about whatever killswitches and boobytraps you've got set up in there, and I'll let you live. The slugs can figure out what to do with you. Or you can put up a fight—in which case, your tree friend becomes your funeral pyre and I take the ship anyway."

Lars growled, mitts tensing around the darklight shotgun. "You think I'm gonna let you fucking ship-jack my *Sheila*? Already had one ship-napper this week—that motherfucker went out an airlock."

"Easy, Breaxface," Quillian sang. To make his point, the skull-golems in Frank's branches waved their torches. Bark and sap sizzled under the proximity of the flames. Another inch and the old tree would burn.

Surrounded by puppet debris, Jay sheathed her sword and shoved her dagger in her belt. "Wait," she said. "The Cairnish made us a deal. We kill you, we go free. If we don't signal them that you're dead, they'll blast that ship right out of orbit."

"They missed me once."

"They won't miss again."

The silver gangster's face pinched into an invisible smile. "Looks like we're all stuck here then, eh? Might as well make a fire and get cozy." The puppets began to lower their torches again.

"We'll take you," Jay said. Over the smoke of the torches, Lars could smell her sweat, her fear. The puppets stopped, reflections of flames dancing on their corroded turbines.

"You know," said Quillian, cocking his fingers into the shape of a gun, "I miss my old pistol. Big sucker, diamond studded. A bit showy, it's true, but I've always skewed toward the ostentatious. In situations like this, I'd pull out that gleaming gun and I'd point it at your pretty face and with all those diamonds gleaming in the light of these torches, I'd ask you exactly what the fuck do you mean, take me with you?"

"What the hell are you doing, Jay?" Lars hissed.

Jay ignored him. She stepped toward Quillian, and the skull puppets around her bristled their blades. "You stowaway on the cruiser. We hail the Embassy that we left you dead here in the desert. Once we're past the hive's defenses, we'll figure out the next move. Maybe we just get off at the next inhabited planet and you go on your way."

The puppets parted as Quillian walked toward the vampire princess. "What's the double-cross?"

"No double-cross. We want to get off this rock same as you."

Cosmic Christ. Lars had to hand it to her—she was rough around the edges, a trait he found more than a little arousing, but she could play the royal diplomat when she needed to. The only problem: She was bargaining his baby to a sadist. Quillian was close enough to her that the princess's reflection rippled on his mirror face. The wolfman could've reached out, put a darklight slug through that silver skull, and Christ, he wanted to, wanted it more than a free fuck or a cold beer. But it'd be signing Frank's death warrant. And after all the booze he'd shared with the grizzled tremuloid, Lars just didn't have it in him to let the old shrub die.

"Okay," said the gangster. "Deal."

CHAPTER XXXIII

Jay led the way, Frank and Lars behind her, Quillian at the rear with what was left of his windmill army marching lockstep, a grinning swarm. On the way back, among the debris of shattered skull puppets, Lars saw the bodies of the slaughtered mercs, each one barely more than a pile of body parts. He almost felt sorry for the blue bastards. Just doing their job, same as he was. To be hacked to death by an old lady's wind turbines was a hell of a way to go.

As Lars stepped into *Sheila*'s cargo hold, he was already forming a plan. Mostly it consisted of wolfing out and clawing through Quillian's solid metal face. It wasn't his best plan, but he wasn't about to let the gangster make off with his ship, no matter what deal Jay had made. He felt a hand on his arm and suddenly he was pushed hard to the side, almost sprawling in one of the piles of trash, and then the revving of a gun powering up—Boris's arm. Quillian stood halfway through the hatch, one boot still on the dry desert ground, when the robot fired. The blast hit the gangster square in his armored chest, and Quillian sailed back half a dozen feet into the dust, knocking into his line of puppets like a bowling ball, his stupid beret flinging into the darkness.

Before Lars could slap the hatch closed, Jay was through it, both blades out and gleaming. The dagger came in low, but Quillian was fast—he grabbed the blade with his gloved hand and held it. As it bit into his mineral flesh and Lars fumbled for his shotgun, Jay brought the sword down from above. The gangster raised his forearm to block, and on his wrist the metal band of Fish's power enhancer flashed with hex-amplifying circuitry. Lightning sizzled down Jay's blade, and even Quillian's blank face managed to show surprise. Blade cut through arm like it was chrome-plated Jell-O. As the half arm fell to the dirt, everything else seemed to slow. Skull puppets, advancing, wavered. Quillian was as petrified as a statue, a monument to his own stupidity. Jay crouched as if in prayer, head down and tendrils hanging. Lars found a gun, not the shotgun but some other mystery piece of ordinance he'd tucked away, and for a hundred years the snub-nosed barrel inched upward.

Then, with his good hand, Quillian reached for his amputated limb. In one smooth motion, Jay brought the broadsword up through his shoulder, lopping off the whole second arm, and embedded the slug dagger in his back. Without a mouth, in his ethereal broadcast, his sense-language soundsphere, Quillian screamed.

"You *fuckers*. You pieces of *meat-bag shit*. You have no idea what you've done. Who you've fucking fucked with." The gangster was on his knees, armless, hunched with the knife between his shoulders. A silent shockwave radiated from the armless Quillian, and any puppet still standing toppled and broke, skull faces no longer menacing, now only so much desert debris.

"Can't hear you, Quillian," Lars said. "Try sign language."

The gangster roared. Lars stepped up and aimed the snub pistol. Execution wasn't his style—he was a brawler at heart—but Quillian had been a special pain in his ass for entirely too long. The wolfman wasn't taking any more chances.

"Don't shoot." It was Jay. She was unclasping the enhancers from Quillian's dead arms, her broadsword sheathed behind her back. "Leave him. The scorpions will take care of him."

"What about all that 'carve him into jewelry' bullshit?" Lars said. "You said it yourself. Left him alive in Canal City and look what happened."

Pocketing the power cuffs, she stepped behind the deflated gangster and, pressing her boot to his back for leverage, wrenched her dagger from his flesh. "Executing a cripple. Doesn't seem right."

Quillian fell to the dirt, heaving with the rhythm of a being that breathes. "You let me live," he seethed, "and I'll haunt you for the rest of your days."

The vampire princess turned toward the ship. "No," she said simply, "you won't."

Lars shrugged and holstered his pistol. What a disappointment. He was really hoping to see what the little thing could do.

They left the gangster on the ground shouting insults in every language in the galaxy.

○

Back in the hold, Lars relaxed. The hatch hissed closed, its airlock clamping shut. The beer was safe, and so was *Sheila*, minus a few scratches. Nothing he couldn't buff out.

"How'd you know that bucket of bolts would know to blast Chrome Dome?" Lars said, wading through the trash piles toward the kegs.

"Autotargeting, threat assessment," replied the princess. "Boris wouldn't let him anywhere near Auntie. I just had to get him within range."

"Cheers to that."

As Lars grabbed a plastic cup to pour a brew, something brushed against his leg. He kicked it away, and it bounced against the wall—an empty beer bottle, singing hollow on impact. Then a crusty meat can, wound with spare wire and old condom wrappers, knocked his boot heel. A chunk of fox skull wedged into it, and more loose wire stretched from the can's bottom, wriggling like fingers.

159

"Aw hell," he moaned, "Jay, fucker's turning the trash villainous!"

All over the hold, detritus was knitting together in the vague shapes of appendages—garbage hands, trash legs, refuse ribcages. Lars stomped the can-and-wire hand to bits then got to work kicking whatever moving debris he could. Jay hacked at it with her sword, Frank twisted it apart in his branches, Boris squashed it with his clamp-hand. Nothing larger than a leg and a torso made it together, one last sad and desperate move from a sad and desperate Quillian Nine, turning the werewolf's own trash against him. A man's trash is sacred. You don't fuck with trash.

Lars punched the hatch toggle, and out in the desert night Quillian was standing, barely. Armless and angry, the gangster lowed and made a run for the open door. The wolfman raised his mystery pistol.

"Nine," he said, "your number's up."

He pressed the trigger, and a nothing fired, no spiral of negasonic whizbang or hail of old-fashioned lead—nothing but a singing sound, a rising chorus like a hundred angels queeving at the same time. Quillian kept coming. Lars squeezed the trigger a couple more times, slapped the casing and shook it to see if any parts were loose. Nothing but the vulgar angel music. Then he saw the change in the gangster's face: Quillian's pyrite brow was arched with surprise. His carved chin quivered. Drops of mercury liquid slithered from the corners of his smooth silver eyes. The whole face rippled, the funhouse-mirror reflection of Lars—of the hold, of the crew, the whole scene—roiled as Quillian Nine's face began to melt. The gangster's momentum was too much, and Lars couldn't shut the door fast enough. As Quillian convulsed and dissolved on melting legs, he fell into the wolfman, bursting in splash of silver all over Lars and the whole damn cargo hold.

Lars stood gawking as bits of Quillian pooled around his boots. He felt a poke on his right shoulder, and Frank, still sporting burn marks from the puppets' torches, was holding out a ratty mop.

"Shit, Frank," Lars said, "Do I look like Susie Housekeeper?" He kicked a pile of de-puppeted trash to make his point and threw the mop back into its corner, then made his way to the beer. It'd been a long night, and they still weren't offworld yet. The witch was snoring. Jay was inspecting the puppeteer's power enhancers. Frank slumped in his corner, nursing his burns. Boris hadn't moved an inch.

"Hey, bolts," Lars offered, shaking off melted bits of Quillian. "Nice shot, blasting that fucker out the hatch."

"I was protecting Mother."

"You sound like the bastard child of HAL 9000 and Norman Bates."

"I am not a child, I am a Mark-III security android." Boris cocked its head at its clamp-arm. "Mostly."

Lars just sighed. It was brew o'clock, and some double-fisting was in order. Then sayonara Cairn, so long slugs, and a jaunt across the black to the almighty Library, and the fancy-shmancy spellbook that waited in its stacks.

CHAPTER XXXIV

In the pilot seat, Lars took a long swig from the flat beer in the cup holder. The brew tasted ancient, a film of dust floating on top, but whatever, it was booze—the two back in the hold hadn't been enough. For a long minute, he'd sat on a crate with a beer in one hand the little angel-music pistol in the other, aimed at the puddle of Quillian. He'd worried the gangster might T-1000 himself back into humanoid shape and start another trash-golem battle royale, but the silver puppeteer stayed liquid, like somebody'd broken a giant thermometer and dumped it all over the floor.

Outside, the dust storm was starting to subside. Finishing the dusty beer, Lars looked up at the night sky, barely making out the distant shape of the hive-station, and whispered silent, profane prayers to the totem of the dashboard hula girl. It was over. All he had to do was tell the Embassy they'd done the deed. He tapped the comm controls on the trid display and hailed the hive. "Intruder terminated. Dude's a stain on my rug. We clear for takeoff?"

For a moment, no reply came. Then the radio crackled. "*You may leave the planet.*"

"Yippee ki-yay." Lars jerked the cruiser skyward. Over the howl of the wind, Lars heard the intakes wheeze, and the boosters spat blue fire into the dust storm. Clogged exhaust. Not something you have to worry about in open space—which is exactly where he wanted to be, hopping whorehouse to whorehouse across the backspace frontier. A couple of jerks on the fan toggle, and the wheezing stopped, the boosters sneezing out the last of the dust storm's grime.

Sheila lifted and shuddered. Lars punched a big red button, and speed metal began to blare from speakers mounted overhead. Squealing guitar raced like an electric flood through the cockpit, drowning out every damn thing. As he pulled the controls, the cruiser's nose tilted, and the wolfman jacked the throttle, zooming jaggedly through the opaque sky.

○

As the cruiser rocketed from the planet's surface, dust clouds dissolved and atmosphere faded, giving way to the fuzzy black of space and a wide, nasty view of the Embassy. Beyond it, bobbing like interstellar balloons, he saw something else: the huge ghost-shapes of the star whales floating toward Cairn's white-hot star. Lars took that as a good omen. He popped the cover off the FTL ignition and winked at the Cairnish hive.

"So long, slug turds."

He jammed the ignition, pushed the throttle, and waited for the psychedelics of faster-than-light to assault his senses.

Nothing happened.

"Hot Cosmic Jeezus Christ on sixteen crutches and a golden goose." Lars poked the FTL button a couple more times, but the same result: *Sheila* floated in orbit, staring down the moon-sized hive of hardslime. Turning the rock tunes down to a whisper, he called back into the corridor for Jay. "Something's wrong. Futtle drive isn't powering up."

In seconds, the princess was behind him, muttering obscenities faster than the decoders could translate. "The Embassy's got subspace dampeners," she said. Lars fought the urge to call them *futtle befuddlers*—Jay wouldn't have found it funny. "We're trapped in slow-motion till they say it's okay."

"Well, give the slugs a ring then. We killed Quillian, the Hand is offworld—deal's a deal, right? They said safe passage."

"You don't know the Cairnish," Jay replied.

The radio buzzed over the metal music, and a slimy Siskelian voice droned, *"Cruiser 62815, proceed to Embassy docking."*

Lars craned toward the princess. "What the fuck?"

"Cruiser 62815, proceed to docking," the Siskelian voice repeated. *"For exchange of package. The Ambassador has changed her mind. She wants the Hand herself."*

Jay spat another string of profanity at the radio—a sequence of growls and hisses that would make an alligator blush. In the long moment before the Cairnish replied, music hummed and needled at the weight of the silence. Lars could feel Jay breathing, smell the animal scents of her breath and sweat. There was fear in her glands.

Static. Then: *"Your transport is in range of three of our satellites. Proceed to docking or be terminated."*

"That ain't the deal, you blue-blooded fuck," Lars barked into the radio. "Deal is we leave, end of story."

"The deal was for safe passage off the planet upon removal of the intruder. There was no agreement regarding your ship's departure from orbit. That is yet to be negotiated."

Cursing like a sailor, the wolfman turned the cruiser's wheel and set course for the Embassy, wondering where exactly the dryslugs' chins were located—and whether he'd have to punch each and every gnashing tumor too. He was sick of double-crosses. Sick of the slugs and this whole damn region of the universe. He looked out the window at the looming hive and slammed on the brakes. "Jay, I've got an idea. It's maybe the most brilliant idea I've ever had in my life."

"Good," she said, "because I'm seconds away from jumping into space and cutting my way through the hive's hull just to eat the Ambassador's heart out."

"Easy, tiger. We could just dock if you want to run an assassination."

Jay flashed a shark smile. "What's the fun in that?"

"Save the space jumps for another time, princess," Lars said, turning the death metal up to eleven. Music crunched through the mounted speakers. "We're blowing this popsicle stand."

Sheila's boosters charged, and Lars jerked the wheel toward the giant, luminescent star whales. Warnings flashed red across the control panel. The Cairnish space-guns were locking on, charging their laser torpedoes. The FTL-drive dampeners were still in effect— no subspace access—but shit, *Sheila* still had her nitro. Lars cranked the turbo boost and felt the G-force shove him deep into his seat as the cruiser took off for the pod of whales. *Sheila* shook with speed and the all-too-close explosions of plasma torpedoes. Thirty seconds. That's all they needed. Thirty seconds and they'd be among the whales, and home-fucking-free. The gaseous giants loomed ahead, rising in the window like planets. Explosions burst on either side. *Sheila* jerked, hula girl spasming and Jay falling hard against a control panel. Metal crashed in the cargo hold. Green sparks splashed across the cruiser's flame-painted nose. Warnings scrolled across the holographic HUD too fast to read. And then they were surrounded— phantom whale skin all around them, soaking in the energy of the Cairnish ordinance, absorbing it, the plasma of the torpedoes feeding the cosmic beasts.

Lars laughed and hallelujahed and flipped the bird to the hive behind him. Fuck the slugs. Fuck Cairn. Fuck the Ambassador. They'd float with the whales until they were beyond the reach of the futtle befuddlers. Then it'd be back to hypertravel, the wormhole highway, to wherever Jay wanted. Library, another universe, whatever. As long as there was hooch and cooch, he'd be all right. In fact, he'd be just fine.

PART II

RAGNAROK N ROLL

CHAPTER XXXV

Whatever robo-drones, fighter wings, or battle grubs the slugs managed to scramble were too slow out of the docks. As soon as *Sheila* coasted out of jammer range, she'd slipped into the stroboscopic colon of subspace like an overlubed space dildo, leaving the pod of space whales bobbing in the black. Lars didn't take his hand off the controls till they were zooming through a faraway patch of wormhole geography, light-years from the Cairnish, Fed Prime, and any other evil empire, bounty hunter, or hooker with a paternity test who got a bug up their ass to chase his cruiser. Then he switched the ship to autopilot and ducked into the hallway to the cargo hold.

The hold was a wreck. Trash had been rattled from crevices, unstuck from old growths of this or that fungus. One of his crates of canned meat had broken open, and everywhere there were loose weapons and stray shotgun shells and iridescent globs of what used to be Quillian Nine.

Jay and Frank sat in the far corner beneath the cargo nets. Both nursed a beer and a wound—Jay a bruised shoulder, Frank a dozen splintered cuts. Boris stood at attention as if waiting for the dead puppeteer to gloop himself back to life. Lars didn't blame the bot—anything could happen in space, even silver alien gangster zombies.

"You were right, Breaxface," Jay said. "That was the best idea you've ever had in your life."

Lars grabbed a cup, wiped some of Quillian off the rim, and poured himself a brew—then downed it and poured another. "Fucking star whales, man. Beautiful creatures."

"What're we going to do about the mess?"

Frank's eyes glanced nervously at the old mop. His limbs huddled inward.

Lars shrugged. "Seal it off, open the hatch. Shit'll all rush out to fill the Big Empty. Easiest cleanup in the 'verse."

They drank. They looked at the mess. They drank some more.

Looking at her empty cup, Jay coughed. "Seriously, Breaxface," she said. "Thanks. You saved our asses. Mine, Frank's . . . Auntie's. Might be room for somebody like you, you know. When I retake the throne."

"Don't get too attached," he said, scratching at a scar on his arm. "My first family I discarded like an old boot. Second family I tore to shreds in orbit when I first went beast mode. I ain't looking for another one. Universe's ultimate lone wolf, right? Safer for everyone that way."

"My family was murdered by a horde of rioters," Jay said. "I don't need another one. I just want my revenge."

Lars tossed his empty onto the trash pile and fumbled with some junk in the cargo hold. This talk was giving him a weird feeling, something close to the sensation he had when he first met Budge, the minotaur monk, Lars barely more than an animal then—raw, flayed, exposed. The wolfman coughed. "Yeah, well, then we're square. No strings. Just a ragtag crew of badasses on a mission."

The princess chewed her lip, fangs drawing a bead of blood. She used her wrist to wipe it away. "You're right, Breaxface. That's it," she said finally, standing up. "Just the mission." She nodded toward the corridor that led to the bunk, head, and pilot house. "I need to pee."

As the vampire princess headed for the corridor, Lars noticed the witch wasn't in her bed of cargo nets. "Hey, where is Auntie, by the way? Old lady missed the whole party. Didn't fall out the back door, did she?"

Jay paused, gave Boris a look. The robot betrayed nothing.

"What's with the secret agent act?" the wolfman said, his eyes scanning the hold's bulkheads. "She turn into a bat and go roost in the rafters?"

"She's in your bunk," Jay said, leaning against the corridor doorway. A dark look fell across her face as she continued. "Back when we first fled across the breach from my home world, when we were looking for somewhere safe to hide, Auntie could do anything. She could've split the Embassy in half with a glance. Ripped the blood out of every merc in the hive. She picked Cairn because it was empty and protected, and everything the Cairnish had thrown at us to keep us off planet, she'd waved back—time after time till they gave up, let us stay, begrudgingly, a weed taking root on their holy world." The princess's eyes swarmed with starlight and amethyst, and Lars didn't mind so much that she was going on and on about the old lady. "It's this universe. It's, I don't know, the frequency of matter and energy, the vibrations. Things are almost the same, but not quite. Auntie's dying." A hard purple gaze. "And so am I. The longer we're here, away from our world, the more we—come apart, break down. It's slow, takes years, like a river eating through a mountain. But I knew she was running out of time. Older, her body more attuned to home. That's why it has to be now. We have to avenge my family now. We have to cross the breach. She won't last much longer here."

Lars whistled. "Shit. That's heavy."

Boris's gears whirred. "Mother is ill." It was almost a question.

"Yeah, bolts, sounds like." No wonder the witch hadn't deigned to help battle back Quillian's forces. She was a black-magic hospice patient. He hoped she didn't die on his sheets. He only had the one set.

Tossing her empty cup, Jay reached into her hair as she'd done in the lounge with the translucent cats—a moment that now seemed like a million years ago but which had only been a handful of days. She pulled out the vial of negativium, Lars' big fat payment for a job well done, and opened it. Looking right at him, she drew a small shiv from her boot, shaved a sliver of the black shape onto the blade's tip, rolled out her dark tongue, and set the sliver in the center. Then she closed her lips and swallowed millions of credits worth of one of the rarest substances in the universe.

"Well, that was fucking dramatic."

"Holds the sickness off," said Jay. "For a little while."

The wolfman looked at the vial in her long fingers. He wasn't pissed. The space princess had just ripped him off for millions of due wages, and he didn't even give a shit. He *wanted* her to take it. He swirled his beer, watching the last pale traces of foam circle the cup. He wondered again what he actual fuck he was up to, sidekicking Jay's mission of vengeance for a tube of space fuel. He was supposed to be on leave, getting fucked ten ways to Pluto and drinking too much to remember any of it. And afterward, he was supposed to board *Sheila* alone, skip alone across the black, and take whatever muscle or shoot-em-up gig he came across, never making friends, never bullshitting about anything more than the job or the weather. Drink alone in his cruiser, or with whatever lonely barflies were buzzing the saloons. Pay to fuck a nameless body, not even human—and hell, he was never more alone than in those moments, those brittle seconds when connection was supposed to exist, when the physical bits conjoined and there was nothing but business staring back in those eyes/light receptors/optical orifices. For all the near-death and nonsense of Jay's mission, it was something to do. And for the first time since his exile, he wasn't alone doing it.

Lars stopped swirling the beer and chugged it. He stood, crushing the cup and tossing it into the trash pile. "Let's blow this mess into space and get on with the mission. Tie down all the shit we need—starting with the beer."

CHAPTER XXXVI

Garbage jettisoned, *Sheila*'s cargo hold looked cleaner than it'd been in years—minus a few stray streaks and skids of silver puppeteer. Nothing a little Windex wouldn't fix. The hold's iconic piles of rubbish—the rattling empties, the crusty meat cans, sticky nudie mags and greasy takeout buckets, even the film of dust and grime—were all gone, the floor suddenly visible and stark. They'd need some mats or something, Lars thought, maybe a shag rug or some alien beast's skin with the head still attached. The floor was blinding.

Lars had popped the cruiser out of subspace just long enough to open the hatch—everybody crammed single-file in the hallway while the suction of space did its work—then jumped back into the wormhole matrix with autopilot steering his baby straight toward the Library. In the hold, he poured a brew for Frank and himself, then called up some victorious fucking death metal on the hi-fi. Muffled shouts made their way through the tunes—Jay and Boris in the bunk trying to rouse the sleeping Hand. The wolfman sipped his beer and considered his crew: Jay the blood-magic alien vampire ninja princess from another dimension; Frank the drunk, mute, and half-blind ambling oak tree; Boris the bastard android pieced together from robot trash and powered by magic; Auntie the cosmically ill space witch; and of course himself, Lars motherfucking Breaxface, the werewolf in space, the lonest wolf in the universe. It was a strange gang, but strange had lost all meaning back when he'd inhaled a skinchanger virus from a hundred-year-old space capsule. Even time and matter didn't play straight anymore, and a sentient fart or a laser ghost could be ahead of you in line for a bucket of fried cats at the next food court. He sat on the too-clean floor, back against a crate. The beer was dark and cold and damn good. Alien strains of hops and malts—you never knew what you'd get. A saison that tasted like bleached fish, a black lager swimming with fermented egg sacs. This one was deep, like drinking the darkness from a cave. He savored it and closed his eyes, listening to Jay's shouts and Frank's flies buzzing close and that low, hellish guitar, that thudding animal bass drum, that music, Cosmic Christ that music, beating away at the infinite silence beyond the hull.

Frank's limbs creaked, and Lars was aware again of the tremuloid nearby. The old tree slouched against the wall, foliage hanging ragged over half his trunk-face. One branch dipped lazily into his beer cup.

"Hey, Frank," Lars said, tapping the stereo volume to a hum, "how'd you lose those eyes?"

Frank reached up and, with a thin limb, traced one of the gray, empty sockets. The remaining eyes flashed with a remembered anger. The tree tensed. Flies scattered in a tizzy.

"I feel you." Lars extended his forearm, face up. It was hard to see beneath the hair and tattoos, but the flash was laced with scars. Hell, everybody in his crew was scarred up—Frank, the two transdimensional vampires, even the metal body of the android. "This long one here, that's from salvage. Big piece of scrap with a jagged edge. Over here, that round one—engine leech. Greasy bastard was sucking energy from *Sheila*'s core, had to beat the hell out of it with a wrench. Had a mouth like a tube of needles."

Branches snaked down from Frank's canopy and pointed to long gashes in his trunk, cuts like axe marks and pocks from insect ravaging. The tree-man turned and showed a grisly chunk taken from

174

behind his leftmost eye. Auntie Hand's magic had healed over his chronoscorp wounds, but Frank still wore the scars he'd been carrying a long time. Lars wondered how many of them the tree had taken protecting Jay. More than a few, he figured. Frank was more loyal than a kicked dog.

"Probably a few more on us both by the time this shit's over." Lars finished his beer and tossed the cup at the wall. It bounced hollowly and rolled across the floor—the start of a whole new mountain of trash. The mess made him feel better, more at home.

The bunk door hissed open, and Boris carried the old witch into the hold. Jay skulked behind, a nervous look on her face. The robot set the Hand on one of the crates, steadying her with its clamp hand when she seemed to wobble.

"I'm fine, Boris," the witch spat. "I'm the arch-hexsmith of the royal court—not a fucking china doll." Auntie Hand's crimson eyes surveyed the room. "Hope you didn't tidy up for me."

"Nah," said Lars, "it was trash day."

"The slugs," Hand said. "I'd embarrassed them. They're a prideful race. Of course they wouldn't just let us leave."

"We did leave, Auntie," Jay said.

"You ran," said the witch. "That's all we do. That's all we've done is run. I'm tired of it." The witch snorted and spat on a silver streak on the floor. "I should've ripped their blood through their pores and broken that hive into splinters. Watched that bloated Ambassador choke in the vacuum."

Jay leaned against the skid of kegs. "They were protecting us. Involuntarily, but still."

"I've done everything wrong, little bug. I should have protected you myself. We should have raised an army years ago, when I was stronger."

"We didn't know."

"I knew." The witch closed her eyes. "I felt it. The leeching. I knew."

Beeping wailed over the speakers, cutting off the Hand and the whisper of death metal.

"We're here," Lars said. Space and time uncoiled and then congealed around them as *Sheila* surfaced from the wormhole into the here-and-now universe. It felt a little like a helium high, a little like getting gut-punched.

Everyone's eyes turned to the porthole. The witch smiled, her stained fangs turning her grin wicked. "The Library."

CHAPTER XXXVII

The Library was a planet-sized cube, built around a singularity that powered the entire world from its core. Its stacks were cities, its catalogs a map, and even its quietest corners thrummed with the energy of living knowledge. Wizards, scholars, and bored teenagers from a thousand solar systems trekked space-time to viddy the Library's book stash. Most of the Library's catalog had been transferred to digital in the last thousand years, able to be read or heard or traveled holographically, but the Library was centuries ancient and many of the texts impossible to digitize. There were bone books and skin scrolls, books inked along the veins of moth wings and giant stone tomes of glyph-spells. Pickled mind-encyclopedias in cloudy jars. Books with pages conjured and hexed from light and smell and sound. Living books asleep with the braille of their knowledge on their tongues. Lars couldn't have cared less. He hadn't read a book since his tour in the asteroid mines, and even then it was just porno forums and poker how-to's.

Sheila eased toward the square planet, with Lars at her controls. Death metal was still pumping through the speakers in a whisper, as if abiding the Laws of Silence he imagined the Librarians enforced like bespectacled fascists. Jay had told him to head straight for the Librarian capital, an eruption of haphazard tower-stacks, all dark angular wood and slithering marble, among the unbroken city of books. Beacons guided the cruiser to a landing port, and the wolfman was surprised to see the vulgar flashing of aerial adverts flying on either side of the descent path, beckoning him to check out the latest war novels, alien sex manuals, and salacious intergalactic memoirs. Even in a place as ancient and holy as the Library, the neon seeds of marketing had taken root and bloomed. For a moment, he almost wished he was back on Cairn, in the middle of that scorpion-infested wasteland. At least the scorp didn't try to sell him bullshit in thirty-two flavors.

The port reminded him of Canal City, not so much in design as in bustle. There were bioforms from a million systems lugging bags and books and reading tools. It smelled, too, of travel sweat and mildewed pulp, and of the street food itinerant vendors were grilling along the walkways. Nobody hassled the crew as they made their way from the port into the teeming city—no PortSec, no customs. Seemed to Lars that any son of a bitch could walk into the Library with an anti-planetary nuke and good-bye to all the knowledge in the known universe.

He turned to Jay: "They just let us walk in willy-nilly? No pat-downs or rectal checks?"

She nodded toward the steel dome bolted to the wall. "Bots. They're watching us, scanning us—if anything we do threatens the books, we'll have a swarm of nanobots on us."

"You sound like you've seen them."

Auntie Hand, walking point in her quick-hobbling fashion, called back, "Yeah, we've seen them. They've still got my hexbook on their filthy shelves. A sacrifice upon the altar of posterity, they said. I tried to get it back once—their bots asked me to put it back."

"And you didn't blood-magic their shiny metal asses?" Lars didn't figure the fiery old witch for surrender.

"They were persuasive. Agreed to find us somewhere safe to hide if I gave them the book," she said. "And anyway, I know where it is—whenever I need it."

Steadying herself against Boris, the Hand walked on, into the city of knowledge, the City of Books.

○

Dark shapes flew tower to tower, stack to stack, filling the streets with their shadows the whole way to the central temple. Lars hadn't paid much attention. Birds were birds on any planet, whether feathered, armored, or bits of rubber tube. The streets were immaculately clean—another function of the Librarians' bots—but the birds could've been hunting the city's infestation of cats, circling prey. The cats, which boiled out of vents and tunnels between the stacks, were a cousin species to the station breeds: solid black eyes, thin writhing tails, the jade and white of their meat and bone turning thickly beneath sticky, translucent skin. Lars could smell them over the smoking grease of the street food and couldn't decide which he'd rather nosh. He'd downed a couple of cans of mystery meat back on the cruiser, but it hadn't been enough. Never was.

It wasn't until they reached the steps of the temple that Lars realized the shapes hadn't been birds. They were the Librarians.

Several of the winged stewards glided from an arabesque perch to land squarely between Auntie Hand and the temple's entrance. The Librarians, the Priests of Books, were barely more than mummified corpses, each with cybernetic implants jutting through brown, brittle skin. Joints hissed with hydraulic pistons. Holographic monocles projected over sallow, deep-set eyes. Sun-bleached reptilian wings fanned out from their hunched and knobby spines, long strings of words tattooed across them in stark black ink. Their gangly humanoid bodies were wound with papery wrappings printed with symbols, each Librarian their own scroll of knowledge, their own walking book.

"Bat-winged cyber-mummies?" Lars said, gawking. "Expected something more in a cardigan and blouse."

One of the Librarians, a tall one with clockwork arms and mouth set like an ill-tempered trout's, crossed his arms. His wings fluttered. "We told you, Hand."

179

"You are not welcome," said another.

A third joining chorus: "Privileges revoked."

They all smelled of dust. Lars snorted, the Librarian stink invading the delicious scent of grilled meat and stray cat.

The witch stared up at them through her red bottle-cap lenses. The gears in her prosthetic hand whirred—not much different from the arms the first Librarian sported.

"*Auntie*," Jay snapped, moving forward. She turned toward the flock of Librarians perched on the temple's techno-marble steps. "We need the book. Only for a moment. "

"The card catalog," said the first Librarian. He snapped his metal fingers, and a holo-kiosk materialized like the ghost of an arcade game. "In the arcana and sorcery section, I believe."

"Maybe you didn't hear the lady," Lars growled. He was too hungry for this shit. "No time. She tells you what she needs. One of you flying monkeys go fetch."

"Se'grob," Auntie Hand said, addressing the Librarian. "Bring us the book. I only need one page. After that, you can keep it. Shelve it in your bone-dry asshole. We're going *home*."

Se'grob, the Librarian with cyborg arms, sighed and shook his long, desiccated head, wisps of white hair shedding dust with the movement. A dark curve of metal on the book-priest's face projected a visor of holo-screen, small flickers of light playing across its display, and behind it the Librarian's eyes were creased and tired. "Which key?"

The witch's arcane hand scratched the air, and Boris's glass thorax gurgled. Behind the thick, cloudy pane, black blood swirled and parted, revealing the puzzle box. It gleamed in the light of the Library's golden sky. Se'grob and his Librarians gasped.

"You still have it," he said. "It can't be. Too dangerous."

"That's why I need the instruction manual," said the Hand.

Lars felt a tug on his leg. One of the see-through cats was nuzzling his boot, purring like a vibrator on full speed. All of its green meat was on full display with that skin, and the wolfman started to reach for its tail. Wouldn't take more than one whack against the steps to render it dinner.

"Lars?"

Jay was looking at him. The Librarians had dispersed. Hand, Frank, and Boris were following Se'grob up the steps to the temple's open archway.

"They're getting it," Jay went on. "The book. It's on the East Face, will take some time to relay back, even flying. They said we could wait in the temple. They've got food."

Lars shook away the idiot cat. "Those zombies eat?"

"Everything eats."

That seemed true. Hell, it seemed like one of the Prime Directives of the Universe. *Everything eats.* He hoped it was grilled cat. He had a wicked craving.

CHAPTER XXXVIII

The food was shit. Five colors of paste, a black flavorless bread, and two yellowed jars of pickled fruits. From the temple entrance, a retinue of Librarians had led Lars and crew through a shadowy wooden maze of vaulted hallways lined with display cases and ceiling-high shelving—prize books everywhere, collecting dust behind matrices of security lasers—to a small reading alcove. Reading lamps snaked from the ceiling on bendable necks, making the whole scene look like the nest of some glow-eyed library beast, and in the center of a mass of giant, shaggy pillows was a stone table laid out with a spread of what passed for lunch to the mummified book-priests. Lars tried the paste and spat it in a spray of gray all over a pillow. Nobody else touched it. The wolfman could smell the sticky see-through cats threading through the corners of the temple, wondered if anybody would notice one missing.

In the alcove, Lars slumped on one of the big pillows, smelling the dead skin of a hundred mummies in its fibers. Almost enough to take a werewolf's appetite away. He picked again at the weird bread, spotted something crawling out of a cranny, and tossed it back on the table. Beside him, Frank, branches bumping into the snake lights, huddled where he could. Jay paced the ends of the room and eyed the doorway, waiting for the sound of beating batwings. Not far from the door's arch, Auntie Hand coughed and beckoned for her robot. The jars of pickles rattled as Boris stomped toward its master.

"No time to do this right, little bug," she said to Jay, raising her steampunk prosthetic. The clockwork fingers jerked, and the cloudy glass in the droid's core burst, glass spraying the shaggy pillows and a coil of black blood carrying the puzzle box into the witch's waiting hand.

Wiping glass off his pants, Lars muttered, "The *fuck*, lady? In case of emergency, break glass, huh? You didn't bother to build a door in that fucking thing?"

As the gleaming box settled into Auntie Hand's palm, the black blood fell away, splashing the dark marble floor like the remnants of some gruesome death. Boris, chest an empty, shattered jar, seemed unfazed. The robot swiveled and aimed its gun-arm at the doorway, eyes scanning. The witch gripped the box. Its golden shell caught the light of the snake lamps and glistened, its etchings and runes even darker than the pool of blood on the floor. The witch looked at it with a wide shark grin. Lars could see Jay staring at the box, too, entranced. She'd lost one of those fancy gizmos already, and had killed half the folks on a spinner to get it back. Hell, she'd even jumped into open space. Now here was another, the promise of a way back home, the key to the princess's mission of righteous vengeance.

"Careful with that key, Gwildor," Lars said, eying the witch. "Play the wrong tune, it's liable to beam us butt-first to Eternia without my cruiser or any of our sweet rebel-bashing supplies. I'm not going to any universe without *Sheila*."

The witch ignored him. The silence was making him itch. He didn't like the way the two vamps were looking at the old box. Hungry for it, like it was pulsing with virgin blood. He had a bad feeling shit was about to go not at all according to plan.

"Jay," he said finally, "we take it back to the cruiser, yeah? Tap up-down-up-down-left-right-left on the golden gadget and ride *Sheila* through, no problems. That *is* the plan, right?"

Without taking her eyes from the box, Jay whispered: "We need to open it."

"I thought that's what the fancy book is for," Lars said. "Why we're here on the holy planet of nerds and dweebs. Get the cheat code, head back to the ship, then pop open the doorway to Dimension X."

"It is," she said. "But—"

"Quiet," Auntie cut in, handing the puzzle box to Jay. "We need the book to open the key. Se'grob won't let us leave the planet with it."

"Borrowing privileges revoked," said the princess, echoing the Librarians. She held the box with both hands, reading it.

Lars hunched on the edge of his big pillow, all nerves. He wanted to stick to the plan. *Sheila*, the beer he'd stocked up on, all those big bad weapons from Fish's secret room. They needed all that to take on the evil vampire rebels, didn't they? Nearby, in the shadows, one of the cats skulked, sniffing in the direction of the spilled pickles. With one fluid motion, the wolfman grabbed the beast by the scruff and dug his teeth into its flank. It mewled for a long minute, back legs scratching his shoulder as warm blood bathed his chin. He'd have preferred it grilled and kabobbed, maybe with a couple of ketchup packets, but beggars and choosers and all that shit. He was hungry.

On the second bite, it stopped squirming. Neither Jay nor the Hand batted an eye.

Lars wiped his mouth and shrugged. "Just take the book, Jay. We've been stealing shit this whole journey. We have Frank, the witch's 'droid, and a lot of very big guns. Steal it and stick to the plan."

Before she could answer, they heard the wings. A shadow fell over the doorway, and Se'grob hunched beyond it, wings furled, a gold cylinder glinting in his robotic hands. The cylinder was etched with runic markings like those on the puzzle box. The witch's book. As the Librarian entered, Boris made no move to stop him.

"Stealing," Se'grob said finally, "is grounds for having one's borrowing privileges revoked."

"Librarians, man," Lars mumbled, munching another mouthful of raw cat. "Fucking sticklers."

The Hand lurched toward the Librarian, diviner outstretched. "Let me see it."

Se'grob swiped it from her reach. "The *princess* made the request." The tall, winged creature slunk toward Jay almost reverently and held out the cylinder. "Your grace."

Jay took the book, ran her long, pale fingers across its runes. It was old, and powerful—even Lars could see that. There were things in this universe that radiated history, things that were old before the birth of his home planet and the sun it orbited. Things that preempted time. His collection of metal tunes and porno mags seemed so eminently foolish then, ephemeral, against the presence of the ancient object. He was at once awed and annoyed; he wasn't a big fan of existential bullshit.

As Jay touched one end of the cylinder, a hidden latched unlocked, and the book turned and opened, holding itself aloft in the space between her hands, its pieces moving like clockwork, runes lighting across the room like holograms. The book was reading itself. It was telling Jay its secrets.

The whole room was transfixed on the moving book, all eyes reflecting runes of light. Even Se'grob seemed surprised. Lars snacked on cat till there was nothing left but see-through skin full of slimy bones. The book shut itself, the room once again overtaken by shadows without the light of the text, and Jay grabbed the cylinder out of the air.

"What did it say?" Se'grob asked.

Jay held up the golden puzzle box and looked at the Librarian with her galaxy eyes.

"This," she said. And the box opened.

CHAPTER XXXIX

A thunderclap like a rip in the pants of the universe, and the room broke, walls cracking and folding in on themselves, blue light seeping in from nowhere and swirling, a whirlpool of netherlightning with Jay and the cube at its nexus.

"*What have you done?*" Se'grob shouted, and over the crackle of the widening portal, Lars heard the flapping of a thousand leather wings, the angry buzz of microbots swarming. He tossed the empty cat skin, burped, and shook his head. She'd fucking done it. Jay had opened a gateway to another dimension—just like Fish had done in the space outside that spinner. Same light, same crackling fission as universes ground together like slipped gears. The plan was out the window, and all their shit would be left behind in the Library's parking lot. He thanked the Hot Cosmic Jeezus and every faceless deity of the stars that he'd strapped on a set of lunar batteries before setting foot in the City of Books. Whatever was next, he figured his best bet was to take it in wolf form.

The batteries flooded his blood with lunar juice, and the change began. As Lars broke and stretched into hulking werewolf, Frank moved to shield Jay from falling chunks of ceiling. Marble shattered and sprayed as the tremuloid's big branches swatted them away. Laser light flashed as Boris's gun-arm unloaded into the hallway, bombarding enemies unseen. Se'grob, tattooed wings wide and long cybernetic claws outstretched, rushed for the princess. Lars crouched to leap and meet him midair, but the witch was already on the old Librarian, her diviner-hand blazing with blue light, channeling the breach's energy. The old space-vampire thrust her magic hand into the skeletal chest of the Librarian, and Se'grob screamed an inhuman scream, breach energy shooting up through his throat, pouring out of his mouth and eyes in blue-white beams. As the Librarian fell, the Hand tangled with him, perched herself between the twitching wings on his back, and buried her teeth in his skinny neck. Her eyes flashed crimson, and around her hungry mouth poured the dust of the ancient being's veins.

Behind Jay, the room was darkening and falling away—a void opening, ringed in hot blue lightning and the crumbling debris of the temple. Cats were pulled from their hiding places, fighting the gravity of the light, and burnt black in the orbit of the breach. Librarians were at the room's entrance now, crawling over a pile of their dead. Boris's gun pumped concussion rounds into the swarm of bots, the android's claw arm twisting the necks and wings of pissed-off Librarians. The broken glass in his chest didn't seem to bother the old bot. Just a flesh wound. Lars moved to help the robot beat back the mummified horde, but Jay was shouting, her voice fading to an echo.

"*Come on,*" she said, "*it's closing.*"

He turned to see the warrior princess sucked into the darkness, Frank with her, and the witch, mouth full of dust, crawling toward them. Then Auntie Hand looked back, face creased with determination. Her cracked lips formed the robot's name—*Boris*—as the swarm of microbots overtook her creation, the thing that called her *Mother*, filling the cavities of its junkyard body. Boris's eyes turned to the witch, flickering as the nanobots churned through it. As it read the old woman's lips, its eyes flashed red, and its bucket jaw fell open, shouting a countdown in its dumb canned voice—*Ten, nine, eight . . .* As the swarm moved, the android toppled, a heap of warped metal, but the countdown continued, echoing over the roar of the portal. Librarians were over the mound of winged corpses now, the pistons in their bodies hissing, gaunt faces set with hatred, and the robotic swarm was reforming, searching out its next victim.

Lars heard the countdown, saw the black swarm rear up and lock onto him, the next target. Maybe his wolf blood would save him from getting eaten alive from tiny robots. Maybe not. He didn't want to find out. He turned to see the Hand crawling into the shrinking breach and he leapt—knocking witch and wolf into the hot blackness of netherspace, the hole between universes, as Boris's tin voice reached *one*, and the portal closed behind them.

189

CHAPTER XL

The world between worlds was black. Hot and sticky, like the belly of a giant beast. Dense odors cloyed so thick in the darkness Lars thought he'd choke. Under the smell of his own singed fur, he smelled smoke, ash, opened bowels, dead things—smells of slaughterhouse and fire. He closed his eyes. Closed, open—it didn't matter. He couldn't see anything, even his own hands. He was still in wolf mode, though; that much he knew. He felt the hackles raised on his neck, the twitching in his claws, the saliva dripping from his fangs. No sign of Auntie Hand. The witch vanished as soon as the breach had closed. Lars' wolf feet trudged ankle-deep in muck, his formtex boots still holding together even stretched around fat wolf paws. He sniffed, gagging, for information: for Jay or the witch, for Frank's sick-sweet sap-stench, for the wind to tell him where he was and which was out.

"*Fuck*," he said aloud—why not? No one else was there in the blackness. No one alive. He smelled the putrid air again and didn't have to see to know where he was, what the swamp sucking at his feet was made of. He'd relived that nightmare enough times to recognize the reek. It was a swamp of gore: blood and bile, shredded flesh, gnawed organs, splinters of bone. Here and there, tatters of uniforms with Dys-7 patches on their sleeves. He held his breath and kept trudging, no particular direction, the darkness flattened by the overwhelming rot.

Where the fuck was Jay? Frank? Was this the pocket universe they were bouncing all over outer space to unlock? Some bullshit fucking 'verse it was. Maybe he was in hell. Real, legit hell. He didn't believe in hell, hadn't since he was eight years old and the foreman of the flood crew raped Jenny Song and hid her body in the bogs and came to the church, high on its stilts overlooking the flood plains and the green storms, and praised Jeezus and asked forgiveness and the preacher gave it, she gave him absolution, and told the congregation he was saved from hell because he'd said he was oh so sorry to the Cosmic Christ, whose third eye saw all and knew his heart was true. Lars remembered Jenny's laugh, when they'd sneak into the darker corners of the library to find things the town had forgotten, how she'd stutter and snort, and he'd liked that.

The wolfman growled a string of half-audible obscenities, shrugging off the memory. That was what coming face-to-face with your sins did to you—made you think too fucking much. Hell was a heady place. Like some cold Tibetan mountain in reverse: a hot, dark cave in the middle of nothing.

Lars kicked through meat and bone, heading whichever way was forward. He should've walked into one of the city's clawed walls by now, or at least a busted-up vehicle. The landscape of carnage was burned into his dream-memory; he knew it intuitively. *I did this.* He felt the stew of the dead slosh around his legs. *I did this. And this is what Jay wants on her home planet—a massacre-swamp dressed up as retribution.* Lars spat into the darkness, tasting vomit. *If this is hell, I deserve it. I deserve all of it.*

The wolfman stopped, breathed. The smell wasn't so bad now. It almost smelled like dinner. If he got hungry. If he stayed there long enough. Eyes closed, he exhaled long and deep, the way you'd let go of a bong hit, and when he opened his eyes again, he was looking at a wall. A flat, steel wall—embedded with the standard blade-sphincter doorway they had on all those backspace spinners. Soft blue light emanated from divots in the wall, and, looking down, he saw he was

192

standing only in mud, the regular marshland muck of the floodyards, splashed black and brown all the way up to his furry knees. The smell of death lingered, more like a memory than something rotting real-time.

"*Note to self,*" he said through gritted teeth, "*no more transdimensional polka.*"

The door dilated open, and Lars stepped out of the swamp onto the side of a mountain. Black snowcapped crags rose like monster teeth in the distance; stars peppered the whole bowl of sky as bright and diamond-like as if he were sailing space in *Sheila's* pilot seat. He shook his big canine head, knowing exactly what forest moon the magic door had sent him to, exactly which mountain, and exactly whose campfire he was smelling, with the bitter zest of roasted vegetables in the smoke. Never any meat—Budge wasn't the carnivorous type.

Lars stalked the trail, legs still covered in swamp shmutz and starting to itch. The fire wasn't far. Budge's mat was laid out beside it, and the old aurochs-headed witch-monk sat cross-legged on its frayed embroidery looking at the stars.

"Budge," Lars called. The minotaur turned. "Are you real?"

"Real as a solid gold asshole."

Sounded real enough. Sure as shit seemed real—the monk's heart was beating, stomachs gurgling. A familiar smell clung to his inked skin: barnyard and sandalwood. Budge was there all right, in the flesh, on that magic moon mountain, just like Lars had found him years ago, meditating as spiders wove webs between his horns. The hulking monk's gray-blue skin was covered every inch with black tattoos, binding designs that matched those he'd woven into Lars, but whatever inner beast the old shaman was holding back, he never said.

"Is this—?" Lars stumbled; his voice wasn't its ragged werewolf croak. It was human. He looked at his hands—still wolf claws.

"Get your head outta the lilacs, Breaxface," Budge said, shifting on his mat. "Usual laws of what's what don't apply in this place."

"This isn't Jay's pocket vampire universe," Lars said. "It ain't hell either."

The big ox-headed monk flipped the yams and rockbeets burning on the fire's coals. "Sure as shit is not. This is somewhere else."

"Where's Jay? Rest of the crew, the Library, my ship? Puzzle box busts out a laser light show, not even a little Pink Floyd to go along with the pyrotechnics, and I end up slogging pitch-black and taking a doorway to Nowhere. Did I miss the detour to the vamp dimension? That shit under construction?"

The monk speared a beet and inspected its center. He shrugged and left it burning. "There's this legend—this shit goes back a dozen ages, before your species even got the idea to stand up straight, but a version of it cropped up on your planet, too, eventually. Every system's got a take—in space, gods spread faster than the clap."

"That's my line."

"You stole it from me," Budge said. He started moving the veggies from the fire, one by one, to a terra cotta plate. "Legend goes, when a world is at its end, the stars will disappear from the sky and the Big Bad Wolf will come along and huff and puff and open his snout far as his jaws will crank it and swallow the sun and moon. Trees will burst, mountains will melt, and all binds will snap. *All* binds, wolfman. The wolf will stalk forth all the way to grandma's house with his mouth open wide, his upper jaw tearing the sky and his lower jaw the earth, and flames will burn from his eyes. The Big Bad Wolf will pluck the gods from their nosebleed seats and eat them too, and great serpents will chow down on the rest until nothing's left but darkness."

The monk sat dead-still with his bull eyes on Lars. Then, with a fat hand, he swiped a beet from the plate and began to chew.

"What the hell's that mean?" Lars said. "I'm gonna fucking eat the moon?"

"Means that vampire princess of yours thinks she's just unleashing vengeance. She isn't. This will be the end of that world and of you, wolfman. Everything will perish but the beast, and eventually that tiny bubble of universe will pop and cease to be, its energy the catalyst for another universe and another."

"Cosmic Christ, Budge," Lars said, offering his arms, "give me better tats. Hyper-hoodoo legend-proof ink. Bind me."

Budge snacked on another beet and talked with his mouth full. "You already got my best work."

Lars watched the old monk nosh his charred dinner. *Swallow the sun and moon, eat the gods . . .* The fuck? He put as much stock in ancient prophecy as he did the various pantheons of the cosmos, which is to say nearly zero. Nearly. There was always that niggling suspicion, that thorny superstitious *what if.* Well, not *super*stitious. Just a littlestitious.

"Budge," he said to the minotaur, "how the hell do I get out of this place? Legend or no, I got shit to do."

The old monk dropped a yam rind and stood. His bull-headed shadow fell on Lars as he rose. Budge was massive, and all power inside that tattooed flesh. Pale horns carved with intricate runes curled a full head above Lars' twitching wolf ears, and the ornate silver ring in the monk's nostrils shook as he said, "It's just a jump to the left."

Lars looked left; over the cliffside, there was nothing but a dense, empty darkness. "Budge—"

"And then a step to the right."

"A spinner door, another portal, whatever it is—"

The minotaur's arms flexed as he rested his giant hands on his belt. "With your hands on your hips . . ."

The campfire crackled, burning brighter, a little blue.

" . . . You bring your knees in tight."

Then the monk pelvic-thrusted with so much force, a supersonic wave of bull-penis witch mojo sent the werewolf reeling over the cliff's edge, scraping at sheer rock with his claws, Budge's great bull head craning over the edge, above him, growing smaller as Lars tumbled into the void below.

CHAPTER XLI

Netherspace shat them out, with all the cyanoscopic pyrotechnics and transdimensional whizbang of departure, onto a cold blue beach. Sand sprayed as Lars landed shoulder-first, rolling into a thatch of black seaweed. He heard the witch nearby, coughing and rasping obscenities that would've made a Nevada floodworker blush, but he didn't care, couldn't care, too far down the rabbit hole of space-time mindfuckery. He lay face down on the cobalt sand, shrinking and cracking back to his human self. He'd trudged the genocide of Dys-7, Budge had launched him off a cliff, and now he was—where? Jay's homeworld?—as if all that shit was just a bad acid trip.

The sky was dark, the shore drenched in moonlight. Above the water, three white moons hung in different phases—the smallest a full disc, the largest just a sliver—and beyond them, he saw the system's sun burning purple-black, a negastar, creator and catalyzer of negativium. So that was where Jay had gotten her precious stash—her planet revolved around negative energy. Unlight gave her world life. Then he noticed the rest of the sky: black, blank. Not a single star or constellation, nothing at all beyond the dark sun and its satellites—a darkness not even seen at the furthest frontier edges of backspace.

The negastar system whirled in a bubble that grew like a Cairnish tumor from the body of the universe, empty save for Jay's world.

Lars got to his feet. Around him, pieces of the Library scattered the beach: chunks of wall and ceiling, charred bits of cat, both halves of the stone table. The desiccated corpse of the Librarian Se'grob lay crumpled like a dead angel, his gnawed throat still leaking dust. Lars grabbed a blackened bit of cat and started munching. He looked around for any sign of Jay, of Frank—nothing. Hand rummaged through the weeds, cursing. Black waves lapped at the shoreline, where red bioluminescent tangles pulsed in the wet sand at the water's edge; along the intestinal strands, nodes of tentacles swirled around cloudy white eyeballs. The look of them made almost made him sick.

"Maybe I made it to hell after all, Budge," he muttered.

Auntie Hand stumbled in the seaweed, and Lars reached to help the witch get her footing. She slapped his hand away. "You think I made it this far in my life by relying on men to steady me? Fuck off. And get your head out of the sand. Up and start walking. City's over the wall."

She scowled at him, then past him, blinking behind her quartz eyeglasses, and gasped. "That's new."

Lars turned. Behind him, the beach ended at the foot of a massive black wall, skyscraper-high and perforated with wide, dripping drainpipes.

"How can that be new?" he said. "You guys have only been gone, what, a couple decades?" The wall stretched both ways down the beach for as far as the wolfman could see. At its top, the lights of a city glowed through the fog. "This must've taken a hundred years to build."

"It's just higher is all. A lot higher," Hand scoffed. Her eyes searched the upper reaches of the wall. "Decades . . ." she muttered. "Time doesn't tick the same way this side of the breach. We're not in your universe anymore."

"Speaking of 'we,'" Lars said, "where is everyone else? Frank, Jay? And Jeezus, bolts going nova in the middle of a flock of Librarians. You set that rusty bastard to self-destruct. Why?"

197

The witch shrugged and picked up a long piece of driftwood, leaning on it to test it with her weight. "Boris was a means to an end. Do you get weepy when your toaster breaks?"

Then, as if just noticing the eyeball node near her feet, the witch stabbed the end of the wood into its milky iris, grinding until it popped. Tentacles twitched and fell limp. White slime oozed onto the wet sand.

"Cosmic Christ," Lars muttered. "That's disgusting."

"Lookingweed," said Hand. "It's watching us."

"What's it gonna do, stare us to death?"

Lars scanned the beach. More of the creepy red eye-weed, still no trace of princess or tremuloid. Beyond the ring of Library debris, the sand was smooth. No prints, barely a splinter of driftwood. He sniffed—even with his wolf senses, he could smell nothing but himself, the witch, and the sea.

"Look," Lars said. "I just got knocked into oblivion by some inter-universe big dick energy. I want a couple of answers. Where are we? What the shit is lookingweed and what the fuck are we even doing here if we aren't helping our vengeful warrior princess?"

"Jay can handle herself," said the Hand. "I've made sure of that." She glanced at the black sea, then started to shuffle toward the high wall with her driftwood as an ersatz cane. "We arrived at low tide. The moons here wreak havoc on our oceans. We don't have a lot of time to get past that tidal wall."

"Why don't you just magic us over it?" Lars said, following her up the dunes. "Cast some flying hex or something. Float us up in a fart bubble."

The witch sighed. "There was a time, beast, that I could have pulled your blood through your eyes until you were a hollow bag of flesh and ridden that blood like a liquid dragon over the highest towers of the city. But I'm an old woman, and the sickness of your cancerous universe has yet to leave my guts. So, shut your fat stupid mouth and start walking."

"Lady, let me tell you stupid: Opening a dimensional breach in the middle of a fucking library. I told you and the princess to stick with the plan. Now we've got no cruiser, no weapons, no third key, no

MREs. My beer *and* my ship are back on that spinning nerd cube. Every mouth-breather in the stacks is probably doing keg stands in my cargo hold. We ran around like assholes grabbing up gear, and for what? So, Jay could blast us to Vampire Planet without so much as a laser pocketknife?"

He could see it now, all those winged sons of bitches drinking his booze and scratching *Sheila*'s paint and sitting in his fucking seat. The whole mission of vengeance had been one clusterfuck after another. Now the avenging prodigal daughter had disappeared, apparently spat into some other corner of the world by the hocus pocus of dimensional travel. He needed to see her, to tell her he was done. He'd be wingman to the vengeance part, help her kill her family's killers. But that was it. No massacre, no counter-revolution. Then he'd take the first portal back to Universe Prime and get drunk enough to piss straight lager.

Auntie Hand kept on hobbling. "We won't need knives," she said. "We just need the beast."

"The Big Bad Wolf," Lars muttered, and aped sucking in a big breath. "Here to huff and puff and blow the house down."

"Something like that," the witch said, as the black wall loomed larger with each step.

CHAPTER XLII

More tangles of lookingweed stretched in a red web across the wet face of the wall. A hundred milk-white eyes stared down from the black stone, tentacles flaring around them like breathing gills. The wall was punctuated by runoff pipes large enough to fly *Sheila* through with room to spare. Lars wished again that he had his cruiser and a cold beer, and while he was wishing, he figured it couldn't hurt to add a hot lunch and a couple of young and willing bodies with tits like full moons. He smelled the salt of the sea and rot and slime in the drainpipes and the sweat and patchouli of the old witch and the dust of the Librarian's corpse. He could smell the lookingweed, too, something completely alien, like burnt aluminum and wet wax and not really at all like either of those things. Fuck, Lars thought, just . . . fuck. He was down the fucking rabbit hole now. In Twilight Oz, Bloodsucker Wonderland, following an alien witch to the foot of an unscalable wall.

Hand turned and rested on her driftwood cane, her prosthesis whirring.

"What is that, anyway?" Lars said, nodding at the wood and metal hand. "Plenty of flesh-sculptors back in my 'verse. Why bumblefuck around with a subpar appendage? Sentimental value?"

A bolt of black blood arced between Auntie's fake fingers. "It's a diviner," she said. "Got rid of the old one a long time ago."

"You fucking cut off your own hand?"

"Without sacrifice," said the witch, "there can be nothing gained. We all give a little something to get what we want." Her crimson galaxy eyes darted toward the shore, widening. Something screeched in the distance. "Tide's rising."

Lars looked back. The water had reached the debris they'd brought with them through the breach. Se'grob's body had already washed away. In the purple half-light, he saw shapes breaking the waves further off the coast. Long, dark bodies coiling across the surface and slipping back into black water. Sharp silhouettes of fins.

"Fuck was that?" Lars said. "Vampire sharks?"

"Serpents," Hand said.

"Get the fuck out."

The witch blinked, her red lenses magnifying the gesture.

Lars shook his hairy head. "That's what he said. 'Serpents will chow down on the rest.' Figured it was fucking metaphor. Or nonsense."

Auntie Hand leaned forward on her cane. "What who said?"

"Nobody," he shrugged. "You see any weird shit in the breach? Sins come back to haunt you? My tumble down the rabbit hole got a little existential."

"I made my peace with sin a long time ago," said Hand.

"Some things there's no peace to be made." He looked at his arms, rubbed blue sand from his tattoos. "I got a visitation and a prophecy—another old witch saying I'd bring the Wolfpocalypse. That 'swallow the sun and moon' bit. He said serpents would finish the job."

Auntie Hand's wooden claw whirred as it reached for the wolfman's arm. A smooth, cold finger ran along the lines of a binding tattoo. Lars' hackles raised; he felt the wolf snarl inside him. He ripped his arm away.

"Buy me a drink first."

The witch's fangs showed. "I wouldn't pay much attention to hallucinations in the armpit of space-time, beast. A lot of nonsense and hoodoo in there. Nothing but a bad dream."

"This," Lars muttered, "coming from a vampire space witch from another dimension."

"I'm an arch-hexsmith," she said, raising her scarred arm to her mouth. "I don't dither in nonsense."

When the arm met her lips, she bared rows of razor teeth and bit deep into the flesh. Black blood bubbled at the corners of her mouth. Lars was horrified—the witch had finally snapped, like a coyote in a bear trap. She spat into the sand and held her bleeding arm toward the wall. Blood coiled out of the wound, rising as rope, up and up to the lowest drainpipe. As the bloodrope drained her veins, the witch faltered, and Lars had to grab her shoulder to keep her from toppling into the dunes. This time she didn't protest. The rope was almost up to the leaking pipe, and Hand's galaxy eyes were dimming, rolling back.

"Stop," he said. "You're gonna drain out like a tapped keg."

"If we're here when the tide comes," she said weakly, "the serpents—" A cough interrupted her thought. As the fit subsided, she growled, "I've come too far and lived too long to be lunch for some pond snake."

The bloodrope latched to the mouth of the pipe, and Auntie Hand gripped it with her clockwork hand. "Hold on," she said. Around her feet, in the sand, a circle of blood pooled and congealed, then began to lift from the ground, dripping sand and blood while holding the witch in the air.

"Didn't know you vamps could do that," Lars said. "Woulda been useful for Jay to pop us on one of these back in Canal City."

"Little bug still has a lot to learn," the witch said. "She's too focused on kicking and swinging knives around like some circus performer." She paused, breathing deeply. "Well, step on, I can't hold this all night."

Lars grabbed the witch's clockwork hand and stepped onto the disc. It was weird, the weight of him sinking slightly into the surface of blood. Witch blood. Steadying himself, he expected a jolt from the old prosthesis but it only felt like wood, a slight vibration in the fingers as the sprockets whirred. The disc lifted, and Lars felt the ground fall away beneath them, the wall rising, the white eyes of lookingweed following their ascent, tentacles seeming to reach, Auntie Hand sucking the rope of blood back into her arm as it pulled them closer and closer to the dark and waiting drain.

CHAPTER XLIII

Lars stood at the edge of the wide pipe, feet ankle deep in stagnant water. Below, black ocean crawled across the beach, washing over the red web of lookingweed. The sea was lousy with serpents—a whole legion of them, he could see now. Writhing through each other, on top of themselves, as much a part of the tide as the water itself.

"You said the weed was watching us," Lars said finally. "What's that mean?"

Auntie Hand was leaning against the pipe's wall, breathing heavily. The wound on her arm was already closing, the last of her blood sucking back into her veins, roiling out of the much.

"There's so much of it now," she said. "I used to use it in the castle gardens. An eye or two near each entrance, to keep them safe. You can see through it if you know the hex. Eyes everywhere." She moved the fingers of her wooden hand, watching the brass gears turn. "Didn't help much, of course. When the revolution swept through. They knew about the weed, and you saw—a pointed stick, a well-placed boot, and no more looking. But I saw them. I knew they were coming, the peasant army, legion of slaves. Nothing in this world or any other had blood enough to stop them. After the guards were slaughtered, they broke through my bloodwalls. Slashed my ropes. They were swimming in blood by the time they reached the princess. And as I broke the breach and pushed her through, I made sure they choked on it."

"Jeezus . . ." Lars said. "So it's like a security camera?"

Hand sighed—sounding a little like a growl. "It's not here by accident. The city is watching. Someone knows we're here. If they know that hex, they might know others. I wasn't the only hexsmith on this world."

The water had reached the foot of the wall. It rose steadily, waves and serpents crashing against the stone.

"You ready to websling to the next pipe up?" Lars asked. "In five minutes, we're gonna be ass-deep in sea monster."

The witch struggled to her feet. She leaned too hard on the driftwood. Even if she could manage another blood disc and rope, Lars thought, who's to say she wouldn't drop dead in the middle of the climb and drop them both into the infested sea? He dropped to his stomach and leaned over the edge of the pipe. Wind whipped at his beard, howled in his ears. A node of lookingweed clung to a patch of wall just below. Its eye was watching the tide.

He held out his hand in a gesture of fuckoffitude. The clouded eye glanced up through its ring of tentacles. Creepy fucking eyeballs, and somebody spying on them via botanical witchcraft, about to watch them die? That annoyed him more than the death tide.

The water was halfway up to the drainpipe. He could make out the razor scales on the skins of the serpents, the batwing fins. As they writhed, their heads stayed hidden in the dark surf. He could only imagine how many teeth were in those mouths.

Lars saw Auntie Hand lean again on her cane, turned to look at the trio of moons hanging over the black sea. He was beat and ravenous and his bones ached from his last wolf-out. But the lunar light felt like the kiss of the gods, and he felt his veins surging. Fuck it, what choice did he have? The tunnel was all darkness—no telling how far they'd wander blind before they found safety. Guaranteed the tide would get them first. Auntie Hand was all out of hex juice. The wolf was their only hope. Maybe he could claw his way up the wall,

Hand lashed to his back. It was a shitty plan, but he couldn't think of another one. As his hands began to twitch, he heard the hissing of serpents growing louder beneath them, the crashing of waves. No way was Lars Breaxface, Werewolf in Space, going down without swinging. A high wave crashed below, spraying into the tunnel. The dark, skeletal fins were close enough to spit on. And he did—hulking, growling, the beast in gray fur, he spat on the nearest serpent just to show them that he could.

Well, Budge, he thought, readying his claws, looks like your prophecy is bullshit. Bullshit . . . from a minotaur. He had to laugh.

CHAPTER XLIV

The sea broke beneath him, and up out of the black water snaked the face of nightmares. Its great circular maw twisted open, teeth upon razor teeth in infinite peristaltic intervals down the holes of their throats. From mouth to asshole, the serpents were meat grinders. The mouth, big enough to swallow a bus, bore toward him in a spray of brine. His right claw clenched into a beast-fist. The serpent's shadow over him, long and writhing. Teeth reaching for him like each one was hungry. Too bad the snake had no eyes—motherfucker didn't even see it coming:

Full-bore wolfman uppercut, straight to the serpent's chin.

The meat-grinder mouth kicked back, an alien shriek piercing the hollow of the drainage pipe. Its echo rang in Lars' super-hearing ears, but he didn't care—he'd just sucker-punched a sea monster. Achievement unlocked. His hand throbbed, but only for a moment. Pale goop oozed from a crack in the serpent's hard skin, splashing all over the drainpipe as it whipped its head and shrieked again. The froth of waves lapped at the tunnel's edge. Behind the wailing serpent, two more, mouths churning. The tunnel darkened with their shadows. Lars hunched on his haunches, ready to spring. Seawater boiled. All three serpents lunged.

Lars leapt. He stepped on the cracked lip of the snake he'd punched, kicked off over the gaping grind-mouth, and dug both claws into its blind face. The other two snakes twisted and gnashed at their brother. Pale ooze rained as their teeth tore snakeflesh. Too quickly—they were cutting through to where Lars was swinging from his claw-grip, slipping on serpent blood. He hadn't thought of Step Two in his Punch a Monster plan—he didn't think he'd make it that far. He could see the ocean beyond the tail of the dying serpent, and in its dark waters more fins, more teeth. The two mouths were drilling closer, the dying serpent disappearing into their throats. Then suddenly they weren't. More snake shrieks, echoes. The dead serpent fell, Lars stuck to its face with both claws, and there in the stinking water stood Auntie Hand with both fists around bloodropes pulling straight from their wounds, and the serpents wailing and writhing as they choked on their own blood. Lars pulled his claws from the dead snake's flesh and gave the witch two big, bloody thumbs up.

Three dead serpents. Water up to the witch's knees. More monsters gnashing at the tails of their fallen brothers.

"*Round two?*" Lars croaked. The witch's eyes flashed, and she managed a sneer—but she still looked faded, drained. Blood leaked lazily from her wrinkled arms. Over the noise and violence of the monsters and the tide, Lars heard something mechanical. The rumble and whoosh of an engine—and then a shadow fell over the tails of the dead serpents.

As it grew, the shadow took the shape of a very large tree.

Hot Cosmic Christ, Lars thought. *Old Frank to the rescue.*

Frank was hanging by a couple of nylon cables from the belly of an aircraft that looked like the bastard child of a scarab beetle and a Cylon. Lars turned, full wolf and covered in goop, to the old witch. "*Our ride's here.*"

Frank swung toward the pipe, the wind in his foliage shaking loose leaves into the rising waves. His smattering of eyes, bloodshot and sallow, lost all of the dullness they had when the tremuloid was boozing—Frank was stone sober and determined. The tree reached

209

with several branches, but he was too far out. The aircraft hovered as near to the wall as it dared. Serpents, bursting from surf, gnashed at Frank and fell again.

Lars had an idea. He gripped the fin of the chin-punched snake and shouted down to the Hand, "*Come on.*" They didn't have much time. Tide was rising; the witch had to swim. Lars wrenched the big fin from the serpent's back with a sound like leather pants ripping in the ass, and pale blood sprayed. He ran the length of the serpentine corpse, Auntie Hand somewhere behind him, but she was on her own. He'd saved her ass enough already. Far as he could tell, Jay's mission of vengeance didn't require a half-dead witch, and he wasn't about to die without getting paid. When he reached the tail, Lars held the fin high—and lunged.

The fin caught the sea wind. The werewolf was up, gliding. Over the infested waters, wide mouths and frothing surf. Then he was choking—wet rope around his face, in his mouth like a bridle, tasting of brine and death and still smelling of the insides of serpents' veins. He felt the witch's knees on his back and hard, wooden fingers grip the fur at his nape. On the fin, they glided, Frank's branches reaching, serpents rising for the airborne prey. It was only their idiot bloodlust that saved Lars and Hand from getting chomped, ground, and swallowed—serpent wrestled upon serpent, each dragging the others back down into the waves. Lars caught one of Frank's limbs, dropped the fin, and dug in with both claws. He'd apologize for it later, with a whole keg. He wasn't about to take any chances now. The scarab aircraft jerked skyward, and Lars held on as the ocean dropped away until all he could make out was its darkness—and then they were over the wall, the city sprawling lambent and baroque and alive for as far as he could see.

CHAPTER XLV

The city was a neon Mordor. Ornate, jagged towers twisted up from the streets like stalagmites, lights flashing red, purple, blue, the skyline broken randomly with garish mirrored pyramids and the occasional belching smokestack. The sky buzzed with the movement of scarab craft, graffiti-marred zeppelins, and quick winged creatures. Clouds of white lightning danced in the air, electric, changing shape to mimic everything that passed by. Below, the avenues and alleyways bent and re-met according to alien logic—not a single roadway in the city seemed straight—and on the streets, in swarms, were people. Jay's people. The alien vampires of the Negaverse. The masses she wanted the werewolf to massacre.

The scarab hovered over a platform jutting from one of the stalagmite towers, allowing Frank, Lars, and the Hand to disentangle from its belly before setting down on the concrete pad. Wind whipped at the trio, high up as they were, and over the smog stink of the engine, the air was still coastal—sticky, briny—but beyond that the smells were urban and grit, industry and living things clustered dense in the city's sprawl. Lars bent on all fours and shook snake blood off him like a wet dog. Nearby, one of the lightning clouds floated, zapped itself vaguely into werewolf shape. Lars couldn't tell whether the cloud was sentient or just some bizarre weather phenomenon, but it felt like mocking just the same. He shook his head, and his body, still feasting on the planet's triple moonlight, began grudgingly to snap back into human form.

Auntie Hand looked half zombie, unsteady without her scavenged bit of driftwood. Serpent blood clung to her robes, and the wounds on her arms were slow to heal. Frank eyed her nervously, a branch never far from the old witch. The tremuloid had fresh wounds on his trunk, and not just the claw marks from Lars. Frank, too, had seen battle since falling through the breach.

"Frank," Lars said, "where's Jay?" If Frank had been with her, the smell of her had already washed away. Still, he had to ask. Their fearless princess was AWOL.

The big tree did his best approximation of a shrug. His eyes burned fierce and melancholy.

A hydraulic whoosh emanated from the scarab's cockpit, and the pilot climbed out with gusto. He unsnapped a helmet that looked like some ancient gasmask, and beneath he was smiling.

"Holy Devil's Tits," he shouted, "fucking *aliens*, man! Fighting fucking *sea serpents!*" The pilot was, of course, Jay's species, and his fangs glowed white when he smiled. Where Jay's head-tendrils hung over her shoulder like dreads, his were mohawked and tattooed with intricate designs. His eyes were hidden behind circular brass-rimmed pilot goggles, and his body was long and sinewy under a set of fitted black coveralls. The pale skin on his face was scarred like Jay and Hand's but, Lars noticed, mottled with bluish blotches in no particular pattern. As he neared them, the pilot rolled up his sleeves to show the scars on his arms.

"Real fucking aliens," he said. He looked at them then down at his arms. "Shit, man, sorry—habit. Bet only granny over there can read the name. Everybody calls me Patches."

"Lars," said the wolfman. At least the collar translators still worked in this dimension. "The houseplant's Frank."

Auntie Hand kept her arms covered under her bangled robes. Still, Patches seemed to be reading her face, the brand under her throat.

"Sheeeit, lady." Patches whistled and shook his head. "Sheeeit. You, like, a ghost or something? Hasn't been anybody with that name in, like, two hundred years."

"Something," the witch said, "like a ghost."

"Man, it was dumb luck I was out there," Patches said, "just going for a ride to clear my head, you know? Watch the tide come up, contemplate the ephemeral nature of existence and all that shit. Then the ICA beams me out a distress call—the weeds are looking at a weird tree stuck in some rocks and a hairy dude and an old lady shimmying up to the wall. Says they all just tumbled out of a portal in space-time. I'm thinking, *Devil's Tits*, right? I go out to meditate with the tide and come face-to-face with disruptions in the fabric of the *universe*? Heavy, you know? Pick up the big guy just as he's choking a serpent to death then come get you guys just in time—you gotta watch those sea worms. You saw those teeth, right? Wicked."

Another scarab soared close overhead, followed by a flock of spider-like birds the color of corpses. Lars said, "Look, thanks for the save—we were ten seconds to fucked out there. But did you see anybody else? A chick like you, purple tendrils, big sword on her back?"

"Nah, dude, nobody like that. ICA only reported you three." From some pocket in his coveralls, Patches pulled a long, curved pipe and lit it with a small torch. "Real fucking aliens . . . Probably need to register with the Council Authority as transdimensional refugees. They'll want your passport, grandma, that whole drill." He inhaled, held it, then exhaled rings of green smoke. "Course, you all might be arrested, being illegal aliens. Whole Federation's antsy. What are you, anyway, some kind of death-badger? This fucking tree, too, get a load of that guy. Looks like he fought a lumberjack and lost."

Frank sagged. One of his branches looked like it was going to swing.

"Frank," Lars said, "the guy saved our asses."

Patches was chugging on his pipe again. Auntie Hand seemed lost in the sight of the city. Her eyes were wide, almost horrified, behind her red lenses.

"I wouldn't worry, my dudes," Patches went on. "We had this alien come through a few years back, looked like something straight out of the ocean cities, squeaky little guy. Now that fucking dude is famous—he's like the richest guy on the planet. Lives right here in Imperium, too."

"Cosmic Christ . . ." Lars muttered. "What's this guy's name?" A few *years* back? It had only been a couple of days since the jump out the airlock, even with the subspace detours they'd taken.

"Arcturus," said Patches as green smoke curled from his pale lips. "The *Fish* Man."

"Can you take us there? To the Fish Man?" Lars said. "I got a hunch he can help us find our friend. Probably whip us up a princess-seeking dildo that flies on ghost farts."

"Yo, you know about the Emporium? Guy's got *all* the toys." Patches was re-lighting the pipe. He shrugged. "I don't know if I can do that, dude. ICA's gotta be waiting on a report. Probably best if I take you to them, let the Authority process you and all that. Coast Guard'll find your missing sword chick. If the serpents leave anything."

Lars snarled. Here, under these moons, the wolf bristled just under the surface of his skin. It wanted to claw its way out—and through Patches' smarmy-ass face. He fumbled in his shredded pocket for the singing angel gun that had turned Quillian to mercury, but the fancy little pistol had gotten lost in transit. Hard to keep track of shit across dimensions. He still had knives, though. Lots of knives. He flipped one up from its sheath and leveled its blade at the pilot's blotchy, scarred nose. Frank loomed behind him. The pilot's eyes went wide.

"Yo, it's cool—don't get all alien aggro. I'll take you to Fish's place." Patches cashed his pipe and tucked it back into its pocket. "If they'll let us in. Guy's got, like, his own army."

"He'll let us in."

Patches shrugged again, then turned and opened the scarab's passenger compartment. "All aboard."

Tight fit, Lars thought—Frank'll have to crawl in like an alleycat. The tremuloid climbed in as best he could, crunching against the door frame and trailing a mess of twigs and loose leaves. Lars waved branches out of his face and stepped in. The scarab rumbled as its engine powered up. Auntie Hand stood on the platform, robes whipping in the wind, as clouds of electric flashed by and took her shape.

"Auntie," Lars called, "Let's go."

"It's all changed," said the witch.

"No shit," he said. "It's been two hundred million years or whatever. Don't get hung up on it. Let's just find Jay. Whole mission's a bust without the princess."

"Don't lecture me, beast." She looked again at the sprawl of the city. "I've broken the laws of time and space to return a monarch to her throne. The throne of what, a city of pathetic peasants grown fat on pigs' blood? It sickens me."

The old woman glanced once more at the skyline, sneered, and hobbled into the compartment, the door closing behind her. Inside, Lars heard the unmistakable snap of a poptab can. Frank had his prehensile branch coiled around a tallboy, his roots jammed up against a six-pack cooler. The wolfman held out his hand—the universal sign for *Beer Me*—and soon he had a cold one snapping open, frothing at its mouth. It was a bitter, metallic brew, but godsdamn and Cosmic Christ he sat back and savored every sip as Patches lifted off, and the city was beneath them again, this time safely beyond the walls and windows of the scarab—everything awash in twilight and moonbeam, the haze of dusk, every chance patch of white glowing like his sheets under a black light from the Negastar's ultraviolet.

215

CHAPTER XLVI

The scarab kept low over the city, swerving around other insectoid aircraft and flocks of corpse birds and shadow creatures on black, smoking wings. Auntie Hand huddled in her clanking robes, whispering things even the translator chips wouldn't render intelligible, her mechanized hand moving as if on its own. Frank's sucking limb was polishing off his third brew, and Lars was nursing his, thinking of *Sheila* and Budge and Jay and the transdimensional clusterfuck he'd gotten himself into. *Swallow the sun and moon . . .*

Patches jerked the scarab around a cluster of dark towers, and Lars almost choked on his borrowed beer: Ahead, glowing in strange light, was a castle. Even in the context of that city, it was menacing—polished red stone smashed together in beautiful chaos, as jagged as flowers made of ribs and teeth, or a bloody growth of ice.

"Fuck is that?" Lars said, tapping the window glass.

Frank's trunk creaked as he managed a wooden shrug.

"Home," said the witch.

"Cosmic Christ. Looks like Dracula's ski lodge."

"*Sangre City*," Auntie Hand said. "Imperial seat of the royal family for over a thousand years. See that tower, the one like a mouth? That was mine." The old witch grinned, showing her sharpened fangs.

"Maybe Jay headed there. Stroll through the old homestead."

"Not without us," said the Hand, coins and bones jangling on her robes as she gestured toward Lars. "Not without her living weapon."

"Ah," Lars said, "there in the spooky castle lies the locus of righteous vengeance. Of fucking course."

Neon spilled through the windows, flashing across the witch's eyes. "She's lost out there among slaves and gutter trash, searching. I kept her away too long, she doesn't know her ass from a paper bag in this city. Your friend had better know where to find her."

Lars gulped his metallic brew. "Fish ain't much of a friend. Tried to take my ship, the little gremlin. But if anybody knows something, it'd be Fishman. He's a wily son of a bitch."

The scarab began to descend, the neon-gilded facades of spiked towers rising quickly beyond the windows. The craft slowed, twisted, darted, and came to a stop midair as outside a trid billboard, floating on its own tachyonic motor, blinked an ad for a space dildo.

Lars crushed his can and tossed it with the others. "I think we're here."

Patches' muffled voice filtered through from the cockpit, followed by the fuzz and static of a radio. Then the scarab was moving again, into a tunnel of neon and trid, holographic sex toys reaching for them like hungry serpents.

○

Everyone waved them through. From the landing pad, full of fancy hoverships and scarabcraft, to the mansion's cathedral doors and into the loud and buzzing party, vampires in security armor told them to keep going, Mr. Fishman was expecting them.

"This is so weird, bro," Patches muttered as party lights played across his round goggle lenses.

Lars burped in the direction of one of the security guards. "Sorry about the beer."

"One love," the pilot said nervously. "You dudes needed it more than I did. Just, you know, no need to wave any more hardware around, yeah?"

Fish's mansion seemed to exist both in and outside the city, occupying a sharp rock formation not far from the red castle. It was built into, and from, the rock, a gothic cathedral of dark stone at once dwarfed on all sides by towers and looking down imperially on the city's labyrinthine streets far below. It was exactly the type of garbage house Lars would've expected a Bizarro Fish to have, the anti-Emporium for the Fucktoy King. But the sounds of partying—music, voices, glass clinking—gave him some hope that if he couldn't finish his mission or get back to his universe, maybe he could at least get shithouse-drunk and cuddle up with some vampy hanger-on in Fish's richboy entourage. The amphibious fucker'd tried to ship-nap *Sheila* and had spaced him almost to death, but for a good lay and never-ending booze, he might be willing to let bygones and all that.

Partygoers stared and parted as Lars made his way through the crowd, followed by Patches, Frank, and the hobbling Hand. Lars almost expected a record scratch, everyone to stop frozen like he'd blasted them with a Medusa beam. Holographic portraits of alien genitalia shimmered on the stone walls, and the DJ kept to an unholy mashup of trance and chamber music, the industrial beats sending waves through the light of the holograms. Most of the partygoers were Jay and Hand's species, in varying shades of paleness, wraith-thin to grossly fat, and with head tendrils tied and clipped in their own fashionable ways. A few, though, were marked with dark gray tattoos instead of scars, and in place of tendrils their heads were mohawked with fishlike fins. Among them mingled other species, stranger, composed of red mud or white light or green, iridescent plantflesh. Lars guessed they were other dimensional immigrants, though who knew what happened in pocket universes. That shit was beyond the physics they'd taught in his little stilt-school on Terra. Hell, he hadn't made it past basic algebra.

"Where's the bar?" Lars asked one of the finned vampires.

Before she could answer, an armored guard gestured toward a stained-glass door. "He's waiting. Mr. Fishman doesn't like to wait."

"Tell him to hold onto his space dildo," Lars spat. "It's been a long day."

The guard, eyes hidden by reflective glass, said nothing.

Lars looked back at his companions. They were a sad-looking bunch: the mottled pilot, the battle-ravaged tremuloid, the ancient witch. He'd been happy on his own, hadn't he? Jetting galaxy to galaxy, wolfing out and getting paid. *Universe's ultimate lone wolf.* It said so on his business cards. But since taking on Jay's righteous mission, he'd been a lot less lone. Whether he wanted to or not, he'd accepted them as his pack, covering their asses when a true lone wolf would've tucked tail and bailed. Now he found himself the drunk uncle in a family of space monsters and nowhere near drunk enough to play the part. He grabbed a glass out of a partygoer's hand, ignored her gasp, and sucked down the thick green booze.

"You guys wait here, grab yourselves a drink," he said, wiping the liquid from his beard. "I'll ask the fish where Jay is."

As he pushed through the crowd, the stained-glass door began to open, nothing but shadows visible inside.

220

CHAPTER XLVII

For all the theatrics, Fish's office wasn't the fucktoy emperor bondage chamber Lars had been expecting. It was just a room, with bland antique furniture and giant pop-art portraits of the dildo king, broken only by the wall of TV screens opposite the door. Fish stood facing the screens, his back to Lars and crew. Gas lamps and blue screen-glow lit the room.

"She figured out the puzzle box," Fish said, turning. Even in the low light, Lars could see he was impeccably dressed in a shiny paisley three-piece laced through with silver thread. He was visibly older, his gills and scales shriveled and pale at the edges. One of his hands glinted—a chrome-plated prosthetic. Behind him, the screens played scenes of the coastline, of receding water and white beaches and the malevolent coils of serpents in the distance.

"Looks like you figured that one wrong, huh?" Lars said. "Universe didn't unravel. Frog Mother didn't swallow shit." The wolfman plopped onto a snakeskin sofa and put his hands behind his head, admiring Fish's wall of TVs. "Those are your eyes on that beach. Hope we put on a good show."

Fish's scaled lips parted in a grin. "Uppercutting a sea serpent," he said, his voice turned gravel. "Impressive. And you don't even seem drunk."

"Give me a minute. I haven't found the bar yet."

Lars leaned forward. The sea monsters on the screens were making him uneasy. Tide was still rising.

"I just have one question, then I'll be out of your scales," he said. "With your web of eyes out there, you see what happened to Jay? Did she come through?"

Fish looked at his metal hand for a moment, some kind of fish-man emotion flashing across his face. "It was my idea, the lookingweed. Keep an eye on the breach, I said. The Council listened, and that was the first step." It was clear the amphibian was about to launch into a speech, and Lars wished he had another drink. Make it a whole bottle. That vampire slime wasn't half bad. "We have to watch for breachers, I told them, for aliens, the dangerous kind, the kind who destroy lives and worlds. The serpents had already taken an arm and both legs when they found me." Fish knocked on his thighs, and each rang metal. "The box, too. Down the throat of some monster. But you know me, Lars—even just a glance at the Emporium in Canal City, you know I'm resourceful. I trained as an engineer once, specializing in erotic electroanatomy and weaponized biomachinery. Designed new limbs myself. The Council was so impressed, they gave me free reign, whatever I wanted. I rebuilt the Emporium, jellying local fruits for my line of artisanal lubes and examining the local anatomy to customize coital pleasure enhancements. In return for their aid, the Council asked for my help with prosthetic design, scientific enhancement, weapons engineering. From one Emporium, I built an empire."

"An Emporium empire," Lars said, yawning. "What'd I tell you, huh? Dream come true. You're hot shit in vamp city. So just consult your creepy Big Brother eyeballs, tell me to find the princess, and we'll fuck off to the red castle and leave you to your sex party and dildo empire."

"The princess who wrecked my shop, kidnapped me, and chased me into open space?" Fish said. "Haven't seen her. But I've learned a few things since I've been here, Breaxface. Your princess is from a family of killers. I mean nasty—the draconian iron-fist enslave-the-populace sort. The royal family glutted on the blood of slaves while the rest of the kingdom ferried to the Nega-sun and back, mining the star for negativium to fuel their war machines. She's got fistfuls of the stuff, Breaxface. Those little vials she promised you and me, they're nothing—she stole bricks of it when she and her witch escaped the revolutionary forces, the rebels who overthrew her family and established the councils. Since the Liberation, every citizen of the Council region has been taken care of—energy and profits from sun mining redistributed to everyone, universal basic income, universal healthcare, slavery and hierarchy abolished, peace established across the planet. For two centuries, negativium has powered art and science instead of war. Sure, a guy like me with some knowhow and lube-jellying expertise can amass extra wealth, but no one goes sick or hungry, and even with the rotating duties of public maintenance, everyone is free to pursue their dreams. What do you think your princess wants to do? Leave all of this as it is? Preserve the peace?"

Jay's mission of righteous vengeance: Kill the killers who killed her family. It sounded noble enough. She'd been just a kid, would have been murdered herself if the witch hadn't smuggled her out, if Hand's story was to be believed. Witness to mother, father, brothers, sisters cut down by a horde of angry rebels. Wasn't that still wrong? Didn't she deserve her revenge?

Enter Fish's history lesson. Vampire kings of Sangre City growing rich on the backs of slaves, literally bathing in their blood. Two hundred years of peace and prosperity with Jay's family stone-dead and out of the way.

"Prove it," Lars said.

"I don't need to," said Fish. "Ask anyone. Ask the old woman you've got following you. Go to the castle and see for yourself. It's a museum now, with Imperial artifacts collecting dust, a whole tour with dioramas and holograms displaying the history of the rebellion. Original lookingweed footage from the storming of the castle showing the revolutionaries cutting through walls of blood to release slaves from their chains."

Lars thought of the old witch, hissing through her teeth at the slaves and gutter trash. Didn't matter to Hand whether the planet was all puppies and rainbows with Jay's family in the grave. The witch wanted vengeance, with Jay on the throne. Everything in its proper place.

"Ain't my problem, Fish. The vamps can sort it out when I'm back shaking my dick in my own universe. I just want my paycheck and my ride home." Under the multicolored gaze of Fish's pop-art likenesses, he felt the moon juice from the planet's lunar trio buzzing in his veins. Electricity crackled between the fingers of the amphibian's chrome hand.

"It doesn't matter where the princess is," Fish said finally. "None of you are leaving this party."

Fish held up his prosthesis, and metal broke apart, transformed, re-building itself as a large, shining, humming dildo.

"You gonna fingerbang me to death?" Lars snarled. Fur bloomed across tattooed skin, knuckles cracked and lengthened into claws. Jaws lengthened into salivating snout. "*Better get some of that sweet jellied lube.*"

From Arcturus Fishman's dildo-appendage, a rope of light lashed out, looping to become the chain of a laser chainsaw. Orange light reflected in the fish-man's wide eyes, across the silver threads of his suit. Bursts of electricity coursed through the threads themselves, and the paisley suit sucked up into itself, forming a paisley-patterned armor chestplate, exposing Fish's smooth cloacal groin and steel robotic legs. Out of each of his metallic thighs, crossbows emerged, loaded with barbed cock rings, and from the back of the paisley armor sword blades fanned out like wings. "I always wanted to be called Razor," he said.

Lars hunched on all fours and howled, full wolf. "*Okay, pal. Let's lycanthroparty.*"

CHAPTER XLVIII

Sex toys attacked from everywhere. Laser-blasting butt plugs, flying vibrator drones, fucktoys fashioned for foreign anatomy retrofitted with helicopter blades and automatic weapons. They came from the shadows, from hidden pockets and doorways in the walls of the office. At the center of them, slashing with his giant dildo laser chainsaw, was Arcturus Fishman, half amphibian, half Terminator. Lars could smell fluids on the sexual predator drones, a dozen different sources at least. *What the hell, Fish,* the werewolf thought, *you couldn't wash these things first?*

He batted away a pair of strange waggly things wielding circular saws, took a laser beam to the tail, and smelled the burning of singed hair.

"You took everything from me!" Fish was shouting. "You destroyed my whole life! I lost my work, my home, my arm, my legs! And now you want to destroy this world." He fired the cock rings from his thighs. "Not on my watch, *Breaxface*."

Black blood splashed, shielding Lars from the razor-edged cock rings. Behind him, the stained-glass doors hung open on shattered hinges, and Auntie Hand stood in their rainbow light, the gears in her hand clicking. The witch's diviner, the fish-man's laser chainsaw: It was about to be a prosthesis-versus-prosthesis battle royale up in fucktoy emperor's office. Back in the doorway, looming, Frank finished slamming two of Fish's armored guards together and dropped them haphazardly to the floor. No sign of Patches, but Lars couldn't blame him—this wasn't his fight.

Fish hovered on his sword wings, shouting. "This is *my* house, bitches! You evil bastards! You world-ruiners! This is *MY HOUSE.*"

Dildo drones blitzed the witch, wolf, and tree. Blood shields rose and fell as the drones zigged and zagged, crashing into the solidified gore; blood ropes lassoed attacking dildo craft and yanked them out of the air. Long wooden limbs slapped at the swarm of sex toys as Frank joined the fight, foliage falling with the damaged drones. Cyborg Fish's blade-wings rippled as he launched himself at the werewolf, laser-blade swinging. The robophibian soared, silhouetted by his bank of TV screens. Beneath him, Lars rolled forward, snatching Fish by both hydraulic ankles and hurling him into the wall of TVs. Even before Fish hit the screens, the wolfman was on him, claws tearing at the seams where fish-flesh met the metal of his legs. Wolf and frog crashed in a showering of sparks, and the screens went dark, the room now only lit by gaslight and laser beam. Fish's gills fluttered as he screamed, and the dildo saw slashed at the wolfman's back, burning fur and flesh. Fish screamed harder when his legs wrenched free of his pelvis, wires and bio-rigging dangling from the stumps.

"My legs! My fucking legs!"

Lars tossed the prosthetics aside as Fish still slashed. The giant dildo laser chainsaw found its way under the wolfman's arm, cutting deep into the side of his ribs. Even with his lunar healing factor, the pain made him howl. A claw wrapped around the fish-man's throat, just above the collar of the paisley armor. Gills, struggling to breath, tickled the werewolf's palm. Fear spread across Fish's face. The chainsaw fell limp, its laser blade sheathing.

"You're making a huge mistake, Lars," Fish said. "They're using you. And when they're done with you, you'll be nothing but an animal. A pet."

"*I'm nobody's pet,*" Lars growled.

The amphibian's breathing was growing shallow. The last of the sex toy attack drones were falling, exploding in small bursts of sparks and fire. Fish still in hand, Lars stalked to one of the couches, sat the legless cyborg upright, and let him go. Fishman sighed, sucking breath.

"Lars," he said. "Lars ... if you go ... if you find a way back ... take me home."

"*Sure,*" the wolfman grumbled, already beginning to snap back to human self. "*Now—where's the bar?*"

CHAPTER XLIX

Vampire utopia. A planet federated and cooperative, where the basic needs of every space vamp were met. Even if tensions were rising between councils, that was still a hell of an accomplishment for the last two hundred years. They'd killed the monarchs and thrown off their chains. Jay's family had been tyrants, and she was the last scion to the bloodline of the vamp-king dynasty. As they made their way back through the party, Patches confirmed everything Fish had said, right down to the red castle being a crusty old museum.

"Liberation Day, they end the Freedom parades at the big front gates and everybody yells anti-imperialist stuff at the windows," the pilot said. "Scary place, dude. Lots of weird shit in there."

The witch said nothing. Her wounds were healing slowly after the run-in with the sexual drones, but even without the cuts, she'd have looked like death. Frank had a slime drink in each branch, already tottering. At the stained-glass door, a few straggler guards had raised their swords, but a word from Fish made them stand down. They'd gone muttering into the wrecked room to assist their broken employer, glaring through reflective lenses as Lars and crew found the bar and loaded up. The partygoers kept their distance, and that was fine with the werewolf. He'd had enough of vampires. Enough of this whole damn planet-slash-universe.

"What kind of weird shit?" Lars said. "Any puzzle boxes that look like they could open the gates to hell?"

Patches shrugged and drank something cold and bloody. "No idea. I don't do museums. Too many ghosts—I'm a big avoider of ghosts and haunted things."

"Zoinks, Shaggy. Me too."

The pilot gave him a quizzical look, but Lars was in no mood to discuss cartoons.

"Auntie," he said, "what happened to the key Jay used? You think she still has it? Fishman lost his in dimensional transit."

The witch scowled, a mustache of blood shining on her lip. "If I didn't need you, I would drain your veins right now till your heart shriveled like a raisin. You disgust me." She waved the drink in her diviner hand, spilling a little of the black liquid as she did. "All this lot, these vermin, these *slaves* disgust me. They should be on their knees in my presence."

"Slow it down, grandma." Lars sipped at his own drink—more of the thick green stuff. Glass to his face, it smelled strong and earthy, and the finish reminded him of fermented meat. "You're gonna get us all thrown in some Commie Council dungeon. If they're not already on their way. As much as I want to blackout on this slime and dance the Transylvanian Twist with one of these fish-finned lovelies, I think it's best if we roll out of here. We find Jay, we grab the key if she's got it, I say toodles to all of you and fuck off back to the big ol' universe I'm used to. Auntie: you, Frank, and Jay can do whatever the hell you want—retake the thrown, eat everybody in the city, I don't give a shit anymore. I'm tired. I'm hungry. And I still haven't gotten my rocks off since the princess cock-blocked me on my shore leave. I'm done. Now let's find Jay and the key, then I'm going home."

He finished his drink in one swig and tossed his glass to the barkeep. He was halfway toward the front door when he realized no one was following him. Growling, Lars stalked back to the bar—where Patches was talking to a pretty little vamp with bleached head-tendrils and purple freckles on her shoulders. Frank and the Hand were nowhere in sight.

"Patches, the fuck? I thought we were all rolling."

The pilot shrugged. "Oh, nah, bro. I'm good here. Best party I've been to in months."

Lars grabbed the sleeve of the lanky vampire's flight suit. "How am I supposed to get around this city," he growled, "hitchhike?"

Patches' eyes were still hidden behind the goggles, but Lars could see fear on his splotchy face. "Yo, dude, I don't know." He fumbled in his pockets, and keys jangled. "Here, here, take the scarab—just, like, don't crash it. I only have liability insurance."

Lars took the keys. They felt strange without a rabbit's foot dangling from them. He missed *Sheila*. "Where'd the tree and the old lady go?"

"Slunk off, man. You know, into the shadows. Like ninjas."

"A gigantic walking tree and a hobbling old woman slunk off like ninjas?"

"She's got that black magic, right? 'Imperial hexsmith.' That lady's the boogeyman. *Wander too far into the dark and Auntie Hand'll get you . . .* That's what they'd tell us when we were kids. Who knows what ninja-type stuff she can do."

Lars scratched his nuts and sniffed the crowd, searching for the familiar stenches of tree sap and patchouli. The stink was there, but it was everywhere, dissipated and lost in the smell of the mob, no distinct trail left to follow. *Cosmic Christ*, he thought. Now he'd lost the whole damn crew. He was trapped in this little nightmare universe with no way home. He didn't even have a change of socks. The girl with the bleached tendrils had disappeared, and Lars almost felt sorry for interrupting Patches' schmooze. He shoved the keys into the pocket of his fatigues.

"Party on, Patch," he said. "Thanks for the wings."

○

The office was still a disaster zone of broken sex toys and TV screens, but somehow Fish had reattached his legs and was walking among the rubble. A guard tried to block Lars from entering; the werewolf snarled.

"It's okay," Fish said. His metamorphic paisley suit had resumed its three-piece double-breasted shape, complete with titanium bowtie. But Fishman looked haggard, defeated, like someone had just kicked his ass. Lars reminded himself that he was the one who'd done the kicking.

"Hey, Fish," the wolfman said. "You still want to save this shithole planet and go home?"

The amphibian jerked his prosthetic hand, and the laser chainsaw blade snapped out, blazing orange. "What's the plan?"

CHAPTER L

Up close, Sangre City was twice as menacing as it had been from the air. The castle's walls and turrets jutted from the grounds like the bones of some eviscerated demon, crystalline crags of red translucent heartstone pulsing inside with shadows of swirling darkness. Even with the museum's pixelated trid billboard projecting over the gates and the plastic pocket of brochures bolted to the wall, the castle still looked like a place where you went to die, screaming, in a dungeon lousy with rusty chains. A thermal-scan padlock hung heavily on the front gates, where, Lars imagined, Patches and the rest of the city had their Two Minutes Hate at their former monarchs every Liberation Day.

The werewolf turned to Fish. "You want to pop those knife wings and leap this? Or should we just bust through like the wrecking balls we are?"

Fish had been a different creature since they'd made for the scarab. Less the hellbent-for-vengeance killer cyborg, more the eager dildo-fisted sidekick. The possibility of a way back home had thawed him, at least on Lars. He still wanted to laser chainsaw Jay into space-vampire sushi, but the plan Lars had outlined was simple: If Jay had made it through with her key intact, grab the puzzle box and skedaddle through the time warp back to Universe Prime. If she lost it or had gotten herself perished, find the Hand and figure some other avenue through the spooky breach. As they set Patches' scarab down in the museum's tourist lot, parking in a handicapped zone to be closer in the event a quick escape was necessary, Lars had made the amphibian promise to keep a sheath on his chainsaw if Jay appeared, at least until they had their ticket home. Fish had reluctantly agreed.

Fish grabbed the thermal lock with his cybernetic hand, and the device beeped with some technological whizbang. A second later, it slipped free from the black gates, thudding on the concrete. The fish-man grinned. "Perks of being half android."

"Yeah, yeah," Lars muttered, "you're fucking useful for something."

The castle's doors, arched slabs of more blood-red heartstone, hung open just wide enough for someone smaller than a werewolf to slip through. Lars grabbed a door in each hand and wrenched them wider, the giant hinges creaking with the movement. Inside, the castle was too polished and well-curated to be a fortress of nightmares. Holographic gaslight lanterns glowed white-hot in the carved bone sconces, the skull-and-steel chandeliers. The kitsch of vampire history occupied every available space along the red crystal walls, shimmering under security force fields and labeled each with its own informational plaque that Lars couldn't be bothered to read. Viewing screens framed in faux-tarnished bone played lookingweed footage, just like Patches had said: Vamps in rags swarming the hallways of the castle, falling on shadowed guards and gilded royals like locusts. In the walkway between the exhibits, chevrons of red light blinked the direction of the path.

"It's all here," Fish said soberly. "The whole bloody history, if you feel like reading the plaques. Jay's family terrorized this world for a thousand years. She would restore that. With you as a weapon, her dog on a leash, she'd take back the throne."

Lars barked a laugh. "Cosmic Christ, Fishman," he said, "I know I'm a big scary monster. One and only wolfman in this universe or the next. But how exactly would Miss Princess plant her flag on this *whole world* with just me as her attack dog? Even Frank's knocked me on my ass. I know these councils have gone all hippie-dippie co-op and shit, but any army would kill me." He nodded his beard toward the nearest screen. "Those slaves took down an army. They'd have my head on a spit in ten seconds flat."

"Then why did you take the princess's contract? Why agree to her mission?"

"Something to do, Fish," Lars said with an overdramatic shrug, "something to do. She was flashing a lot of cheese. Might've been only pennies to her, but that much neg would've been a lot to me. Retirement, the good life on some paradise rock. Figured I'd think of something along the way. Or that she'd get sweet on me." He scratched his groin absently. "Anyway, I don't fucking know. And I don't know Jay's plan. It was just 'vengeance this' and 'Ragnarok that.' She didn't get real specific."

"I don't know, either," Fish admitted. "But I do know that the witch you had with you is very dangerous. And powerful." The amphibian looked around the polished heartstone room with his dinnerplate eyes. "And that this is a bad place."

Lars felt a tingle in his fur, and the virus in his blood swirled like the darkness in the walls. A chill scraped down his back from hindbrain to tailbone. "Fuckin' A, Fish. Grayskull, Hell House, and the Temple of Doom all wrapped up in one sealed and holo-labeled package. Rebels should've burnt this place to the ground and pissed on its ashes."

A sound like metal scraping stone echoed through the hallway from some further chamber. Lars fumbled in his torn fatigues for the hardware Fish had given him back at the mansion—a couple of sawed-off silver-slug repeater shotguns, dozen shots each barrel. Knives and concussion pistols were strapped to each leg, in case of emergency. The wolfman jerked the guns, both cocking with a heavy click.

"Either the janitor's dusting the crown jewels," he said, "or the party's about to get started."

Fish nodded, smiled a lizard smile, and unsheathed his laser chainsaw. The chevrons blinked a path toward the sound—and the duo followed.

234

CHAPTER LI

The scraping continued to echo as Lars and Fish followed the blinking chevrons, the horror of the deposed royals and the glory of the revolution shouting at them from every exhibit and artifact, until finally they came to a wide atrium ceilinged in glass. Beyond its dusty panes, the planet's three moons shone in their dissimilar phases alongside the purple-black sun. In the room, two rows of shadow armor, still smoking with hexed shade after more than two centuries, lined the walls under half-burned banners that Lars assumed were the royals' coat of arms: Three white circles in the mouth of a black serpent against a field of crimson.

Scrape . . . scrape . . .

"Ah, shit," Lars muttered, shoving the shotguns back into the holsters on his belt.

Against the furthest wall, carved into the heartstone with images of serpents and dragons and wolf-like beasts was a throne of crystal fangs—and Jay slumped across it with her stolen broadsword. She drew the blade idly across the vampiric canine between her knees. Black blood caked on her mouth and chin, and at the foot of the throne, tossed across the wide steps, was the corpse of a fellow vamp dressed in a red-paisley knockoff version of Fish's three-piece suit. From the nametag under the pocket square, they figured him for the curator or a tour guide. What a mindfuck—eaten by a princess your whole museum says died two hundred years ago.

Fish tensed. His gills fell flat on his scale-encrusted neck, and the orange laser-chain lashed.

"Easy, Fishman," Lars said. "Don't make surf-and-turf the second course."

Fish lowered the saw, but the amphibian was still rattled. Hell, so was Lars. Jay looked every bit the evil villain, bloodspattered, black-clad, sitting in the stone maw of a wall-to-wall hellscape. She stopped scraping her sword and seemed to notice Lars for the first time.

"Jay," said the werewolf. "You okay? We've been out looking for you. Where'd the nether spit you out?"

The princess shook her head, tendrils falling loose around her scarred face. "It's all a lie."

Holding up three fingers, he said, "Scout's honor. We even crashed this asshole's party to get a bead on you."

"Not you," said Jay, "my whole fucking life."

She stood up, and Lars could see that she'd strapped into one of the suits of shadow armor. It fit like a black, smoking glove. The movement of the shadows blurred her edges, and her body seemed to half fade into the dark inner swirls of the heartstone behind her. "I didn't remember much. My mother singing in the gardens as my sisters and I poked at the lookingweed. My father riding a sky serpent back from a faraway battle, looking every bit a hero and a king. It was like some fairytale." She spat, missing the corpse on the stairs by an inch. "It was a fairytale. She only let me remember those moments, and the blood as they were cut down. The ones who weren't eaten were burned alive in the gardens. She told me my family had ruled with justice, compassion, that the rebels had been vicious barbarians jealous of our power. She said that without my family to rule, the world would be chaos, and the rebels would fashion themselves dictators, or fall on themselves in backbiting, and the people would suffer. She said my people needed me. That they thirsted for revenge just like I did—that I needed to avenge my family's deaths not just for myself, but for the world."

Lars let his eyes fall onto the ornate carpet between himself and Jay. He couldn't quite make out the pattern, something gothic and terrifying in its design. His own family had been dirt-poor refugees, tilling muck in the floodyards of the Sierra Coast. Most of them were probably dead by now from radiation wafting across the ocean, or from starvation, the yards never yielding quite enough. He hadn't seen them since the Terran Security Council had banished his wolf ass for unknown contagion and the massacre of his crew. But it was what it was—he'd come from nothing, never been anyone, never felt the weight of having to answer to anyone but himself. Jay, the survivor princess, carried the weight of a planet—and it must've felt a lot heavier with Auntie Hand's bullshit piled on top.

"Look, Jay—" he started.

"Have you seen all this?" she said, waving a hand. "They were killers. My father, my mother, my sisters . . . Behind that door is a big stone pool with an altar in the middle—they would hang the most beautiful slaves by their feet and cut them throat to groin, then swim in the guts and feast. Their own people."

Fish's laser chainsaw pointed in the direction of the corpse, but Lars shot him a look. No use starting any arguments on moral relativity. They had a mission. Puzzle box, interdimensional chute-the-chute, then home free. They needed Jay's key.

"I saw it," Lars said. "You're right—they were shitty. Know who else's family was shitty? Everybody's. And yeah, the witch fed you a line, probably one she thought you needed to hear. But the planet seems to be doing okay. Fish here says it's just shy of vamptopia—everybody's getting what they need."

"I saw them. The people." She was looking at the rows of armor like they were about to come to life and zombie shuffle. "The vortex dropped me in the city, near the edge. Even with the new towers and the wall holding back the sea, I still knew my way home from the shore. The streets still follow the same paths. Maybe you're right, Lars—maybe everyone is getting all the blood they need, each with a coffin in a high-rise and free medicine and a job to do in town.

But there's still suffering here. Still sickness, still those who are forgotten and left behind."

"That's life, Jay. In this universe or any other. Even the best of us can't save everyone." He stepped forward, hair on his neck bristling as his boot touched the haunting carpet. The gaslight holograms in the bone chandeliers were beginning to flicker, and darkness rose from the empty armor like the shadows of ghosts. For all its amusement-park artifice and museum sheen, Sangre City was a tomb, a place of death—and Lars was feeling more than a little creeped out. "Why not put the sword down, forget the whole vengeance thing, and let's all go get a beer? Pour one out for the old king and queen."

Shadows flared from her breastplate, and Jay's galaxy eyes turned hard.

"Are you kidding?" she said. "I can still *save* this planet. I can rule the way I always imagined my father did. I can be better than he ever was."

"That ain't just vengeance, that's regime change. You're gonna need an army for that."

"Not an army," Jay said. "I told you before: just you."

Lars shook his head and scratched his beard. That's all they ever said, Jay and the Hand—they needed *only* him. For what? He wasn't a fucking one-man battalion. He was a werewolf. There was a big-ass difference.

"I'm just one guy with fur and some teeth," he said. "And I'm fucking done. I coulda used the neg, and it's been great getting into all kinds of life-threatening shenanigans with you on this little mission—but it's high time for me to get back to my ship, pop a cold one, and fuck off into the black. Adios, sayonara, so on and so forth. Now, if you could just bust out that puzzle box, give it a turn, and let Fish and me warp back to the big fat starry-skied universe we know and love, we'll owe you a round. Top shelf, no well stuff."

Jay's broadsword crackled with blue electric.

"I can't do that, Lars."

"*Can't* because you lost the box—or *won't* because you're gonna make us do this the hard way."

Bringing the sword up to grip it with both hands, the vampire princess allowed herself a smirk—Lars could almost see her razor teeth.

"Won't."

CHAPTER LII

Jay struck first. From the corpse on the floor, ropes of blood snaked wickedly for Fish and Lars as the princess sprinted through the rows of empty soldiers. As she moved, her armor cloaked her body in darkness and left shadow clones in her wake, each Jay-shade darting in its own random path before dissipating into smoke. The bloodropes lashed at Lars' arms and ankles and wound themselves around Fish's paisley torso. Gears whined, and the amphibian's sword wings unfolded, cutting through the blood. Another rope came for him, but Fish sliced with his laser chainsaw, the bright orange blade sizzling as the blood lost its hex and splattered. Ropes coiled Lars' left boot and pulled—until the wolfman pulled the trigger on one of the shotguns, and a solid silver-alloy slug cut through blood and blew a glittering hole in the strange carpet. Jay was on him then, a bloodwall ahead of her like riot shield. Lars managed one warning shot, the slug sticking wetly before the wall dropped and the broadsword slashed electric from her darkness. Metal clanked metal as the wolfman caught the blade in the sawed-off's trigger guard.

Through gritted teeth, the princess said, "I don't want to hurt you."

"Color me convinced," Lars said.

He pushed hard on the sword. The smell of all the vamp blood was making the wolf in him hungry. Jay's pale face, all rage, flickered into focus between roiling shadows, and Lars knew that if he didn't duck away soon, one of them was gonna end up snuffed. He skidded sideways and dropped his gun, listening to it clatter as Jay stumbled. She fell forward, off balance from the sudden lack of pushback, and Lars punched into the dark, landing a softened blow somewhere in her guts. She slowed for a moment—but it was enough. With the three moons shining in from the skylight, the virus in his veins was soaked in lunar juice. He changed rapidly, fur sprouting and bones refitting, flesh mutating from man to beast. Straps broke; weapons clattered to the floor. Lars Breaxface, Werewolf in Space, dropped to all fours, snarled, and howled at the moons.

Mid-howl, a bloodrope surged from the shadows of Jay's armor, noosed his throat, tightening to a strangle. Served his ass right for the horrorshow theatrics. He ripped at the rope with both claws, but the gore was thick, and kept pulsing. Overhead, the hologram lanterns began to glitch, casting the room in gaslight stroboscopics, or maybe he was just losing consciousness. Then a flash of orange, and he was heaving breath, his neck free, Fish gliding over him on those ridiculous wings, pyrotechnic chainsaw hand raging.

"*Okay,*" the werewolf coughed. "*Truce.*"

Shadows moved among shadows among shadows. Between Jay and the rows of guard armor, clouds of hexed darkness were swirling the room.

"I can't let you leave, Lars," came Jay's voice. "I can't kill you either."

Then another voice, the familiar rasp of an old woman who'd been smoking since she bought her first training bra:

"But he doesn't need all of his limbs."

And through the blood he could smell her: patchouli oil, morning breath, the dust of the desert in her dry skin.

The darkness began to clear, shadows slipping back into plate and mail. Jay stood at the foot of the throne with her sword still raised. Lars followed her gaze—to find Auntie Hand and Frank filling an arched doorway. The Hand hobbled in, leaning on one of Frank's outstretched branches.

"Go ahead," she said, "cut off a leg or two."

"Auntie . . ." Jay started.

The old witch held up her wooden hand. "I'm sorry, little bug. That I told you so many fictions. But," the witch's eyes flashed, "I needed you to get here. To be strong. This is the first step to restoring the throne, with you as rightful heir."

"They were horrible," Jay said, sword beginning to waver. "They killed so many people."

"Don't be such a bleeding heart," muttered the witch. "They did what they had to. What they *could do*. They *ruled* this world. You don't conquer a planet with benevolence—you conquer it with fear."

Auntie Hand, squinting through her red lenses, dragged Frank into the chamber. The tremuloid looked at Lars, and his eyes, what eyes were left, seemed filled with apology. As best he could with wolf claws, Lars offered a conciliatory thumbs-up. *Fuck it*, he wanted to say, *we all have our roles to play*. The werewolf growled as the witch leaned in to inspect Jay, the two vamps dwarfed by the throne wall's immense hellscape relief.

"Your mother's armor," Hand said approvingly. "Fits you well."

"I should kill you," Jay said. She held the broadsword in strike pose, but her face had drained of anger. She looked the frightened orphan she'd been when Hand smuggled her out of that castle all those years before.

"*Don't*," Lars said. "*Turn the key—we can go. Leave the witch here.*"

Jay's grip tightened, and she drew the sword up—and slid it into its sheath.

"Good girl," said Auntie Hand. She turned to look at Lars and the knife-winged Fishman. "Now, let's get on with it. I'm sure one of us has tripped an alarm, and it's only a matter of time before the peasant police make their way into this sanctum. Frank, can you please?"

The tree covered the ground between himself and Lars with surprising speed. Perhaps he hadn't been so wounded by the sea serpents after all—or more likely, the Hand had done her healing hoodoo again, same as she had on Cairn, a trade to do her bidding. As Frank tangled the werewolf in every grasping limb he had, Lars didn't give a fuck *how* the tremuloid had regained his strength—the wolf just wanted free from it. Wood creaked as he wrestled against the restraints. He heard Fish utter a weak battle cry and felt the heat of the laser chainsaw, then: the gust of a snaking tree branch and the hard thunk of a cyborg amphibian hitting stone.

"*Fuck is this, Frank?*" Lars growled. "*I gave you my beer, man.*"

"There are sometimes more important things than beer," said the witch. She was busy feeling along the wall of the hellscape with her diviner hand, patting the asses of beasts and demons until she came to the right section and pressed the tongue of a lupine monster. White light glowed from her clockwork palm, and above the throne a chunk of the wall burned away, revealing an orb of black rock.

Ah shit, Lars thought as his blood began to writhe in his veins. His shoulders strained against Frank's hold, and he could hear the wood begin to splinter. *That ain't just some rock.*

He could feel it flooding him, blood burning: The mother lode of moon juice.

"The Dark Moon," Auntie Hand said. "The heart of our fourth satellite, harvested and imbued with the negative energy of our sun, according to the rites of prophecy."

The rock—the Dark Moon—spun on an invisible axis, glowing in a miasma of pulsing violet light. Frank's grasp was beginning to give. Lars felt the wolf taking over, red blur closing in his peripheral vision. All that remained in focus were the Dark Moon and Auntie Hand. The werewolf howled. A branch burst with a boom, then another, raining sap and splinters across the sanctum. Frank dropped the wolf, limbs recoiling in distress, Lars launching bloodthirsty and moondrunk toward the old witch.

CHAPTER LII

Budge's ink worked its magic. Against the otherworldly force of the Dark Moon, the minotaur monk's tattoo-bound spells seared through the arcane designs on Lars' arms and abdomen, fighting to keep the mercenary's wolf-self in check. The Dark Moon still pulled, but the monk's hex-ink held, funneling energy from fists to chest, from claws to lungs, centering, and the red blur dissipated from the edges of his vision. Lars felt himself take control, tension leaving his jaws and fingers. At the foot of the throne, he skidded to a stop in a hail of splinters and tree sap and snarled at Auntie Hand.

"*Fuck your prophecy,*" he said. Behind him, Frank was twitching in pain, a couple of ragged stumps bleeding amber sap where his limbs had exploded, and Lars felt like a real asshole for doing the exploding. But Frank had plenty more branches on his old, scarred-up trunk, and Jay had her gloved hand outstretched, already pushing sap back into the wounds. Lars shook his head in half-apology. He couldn't slow down now. He had a universe to get back to.

Wooden claw crackling, the witch stood under the whirling Dark Moon and busied herself with some detail of the hellish bas-relief. Some old stone tongue or fingernail. She didn't seem at all

246

concerned about the werewolf stalking up the stairs behind her. Lars glanced back, hoping to see Fish at his heels with the laser saw charged. Instead, the amphibian was crumpled in a paisley heap against the far wall. Gills flapped lazily on his neck, and his bulbous eyes were sealed shut. Lars was on his own. The Dark Moon made his blood boil in his veins, and he had to clench his teeth to swallow the bloodlust. *Heart of a moon hexed with nega-sun,* he thought. *Swallow the sun and moon...* Fuck that. He wasn't swallowing anything. He was getting that key from Jay and wormholing off this rock. The planet's proletarian revolutionaries had taken care of bloodthirsty monarchs once, let them do it again. He wasn't anybody's hero.

"Jay..." he said. "*The key. The box. Use it.*"

The warrior princess kept her soldierly poise behind the throne of fangs.

"I can't," she said.

Lars loomed over her, shoulders hunched and bristling. Saliva dripped from his teeth and pooled on the seat of the throne. "*Let me go,*" he growled. "*Fuck your mission. Kill 'em all, I don't care. But you do it on your own.*"

"When the world is in its twilight," came Hand's voice, as if reciting scripture, "the great beast will rend the sky, and violet fire will burn out its eyes. The beast will swallow sun and moon, and serpents will consume the rest in darkness."

The old witch hobbled toward him slowly, her robes emitting their trademark jingle. Even plotting the deaths of millions, she still seemed so much the grandmother. *The Big Bad Wolf wearing Grandmother's face.* Lars shook his head and snarled. He'd had enough of the witch and her hocus-pocus. It'd been too long since he'd had a meal, and just then the Hand looked like four feet of witch jerky. He could feel the Dark Moon's power flowing through him, zigzagging the network of tattoos like a circuit. He was as strong a werewolf as he'd ever been, no Dys-7 bullshit, no berserker mode, no lunar-battery weak sauce. He was Wolf—and he was going to eat that witch's throat out.

Lars leapt. Then dropped right out of the air.

He hit the stone hard, pain blazing as one of the crystal teeth of the throne pierced his left leg. He shook his head, dazed, and standing over him was the Hand, Jay subserviently behind her.

"The . . . fuck?" he heaved. He tried to swipe for the witch's legs, but he couldn't move.

"Pay attention, beast," Hand said. Rustling her robes, she knelt beside his head, leaned her face close to his, and sniffed. "You forget too easily. Do you remember how I held your blood back on that grub bitch's planet?" She grinned at him like she was debating whether to eat now or take a doggy bag. "In my hands, your veins are puppet strings."

Once again, he wished he was back in *Sheila*'s pilot seat beating off into a tube sock and staring out at a sea of stars. He'd followed Jay on her righteous mission because it promised a paycheck and he didn't have shit else to do. But shit else was looking pretty good right now—anything anywhere, even a stilt-shack in his shithole town on his shithole home planet, with a brood of kids and a wife with no teeth. At least he'd be alive. His heart was beating like the double bass in a speed metal tune. *You were right, Budge. This shit's gonna kill me.* He felt the fingertips of the diviner hand press against his chest, and the wood was cold, even through his fur. As the fingers pulsed with electric sorcery, the hair across his body stood on end.

"Ink-based hex," the Hand scoffed. "Amateur work. Looks like a wild animal did this."

He felt it first in his wrists, the tight binds of Budge's tattoo voodoo loosening. The witch lifted the diviner, and he saw the ink flowing out of him, a growing ball of black liquid swirling in the magic grip of the clockwork hand. There would be nothing to keep the Dark Moon's energy from overpowering him now—nothing to keep the wolf at bay.

"Fish," Lars shouted, struggling. He couldn't move an inch. Flash frozen, neck to tail, from the inside, he might as well have been blasted with a Medusa beam. *"Fish—could use some laser action here."*

"Your guppy is out cold," said the Hand as she shuffled toward the Dark Moon. The ink that had been his binding tattoos spattered across the stone floor, oozing into cracks. "And you," she spat at Lars, "there are rodents in the sewers beneath this castle who've got more brains. But you're what my princess dredged up from the cesspool of that cancerous universe, and you're the only weapon I've got to teach these rebel scum who the really owns this planet. Now, with that pathetic hexcraft out of the way . . ."

Auntie Hand's crimson eyes gleamed behind their lenses. Her clockwork claw whirred as she reached toward the Dark Moon, into it, breaching its rock and pulling out a black shard pulsing with sparks of purple. For a moment, she looked at it, frowning, and Lars wondered if maybe she'd messed up her sacred prophecy, busted up her holy Dark Moon.

"I was a young girl when this spell was cast," the Hand said. "Can you imagine it? I was younger than you, little bug." She nodded absently toward Jay, then stood over the frozen Lars. "I was a knockout back then. My tits were fabulous."

"*Bet they still clean up nice,*" Lars croaked. He felt himself beginning to lose control, swelling with the Dark Moon's super-juice. It wouldn't be long before he was full-on beast—a rabid animal seeing red. Again, Hand hunched over him. The shard sparked. She waved her flesh hand over his snout, and the veins inside obeyed. His mouth splayed wide. Drool soaked the fur on the sides of his face.

"They do," the witch said, and pressed the shard of Dark Moon into the werewolf's gaping mouth.

CHAPTER LIV

The taste of the rock was live wires and cigarette ash. As the witch dangled the shard of Dark Moon between his jaws, his tongue burned, his teeth thrummed, and frothy spit pooled in his throat, choking. At the edges of his vision, the red berserker blur crept inward.

"Wait." Jay's voice came from some corner of the room. "Auntie, stop."

Auntie Hand snatched the rock from his mouth and whipped to face the princess. "Stop? Little bug, I'm doing this for you. This animal..." She sneered at Lars. "This loaf of hair is the weapon of prophecy. You said it yourself, my princess—you looked all over that sick universe to find it. We have the weapon. When Imperium falls, the rest of the cities will cower."

"I don't trust him." Jay was standing over him, glaring. "Like you said, he's a wild animal. He just tried to kill me. What do you think he'll do if we make him a monster and let him loose?"

"The prophecy—"

Jay shook her head. "The prophecy is wrong. We don't need the beast," she said, staring down at the frozen werewolf. "We only need his blood."

The Hand looked at him over her red lenses, a shark-toothed grin spreading across her scarred and sallow face. Lars choked back more spit. Jay was right—not that he'd tried to kill her, but that he goddamn would the second they set him free. *Shared my beer, my bed, my tunes, my starcruiser . . . Just to get stabbed in the back by this whole fucking crew.* Jay, Frank, Hand . . . Even Fish had slashed him with that laser-saw back at the mansion. His friends, or the nearest approximation he'd had in a long time, since Budge or maybe earlier: since the crew of the salvager, who'd saved his life and in turn had been a werewolf's lunch. He reminded himself: This was why he rolled solo. *Lone wolf.* You couldn't trust anybody, in this universe or the next.

The witch snatched the shard away and let him close his mouth. He coughed and growled, teeth still vibrating from the Dark Moon's electric. He wanted nothing more than to eat the vampires' hearts out, their livers, maybe floss with their intestines and wash it all down with a keg of dark beer. As he imagined clamping his jaws on the witch's wrinkled neck, she spread her razor mouth wide—and clamped her jaws on his. Rows of jagged teeth found their way through fur and skin to arteries throbbing with adrenaline and wolf blood. He again tried to move, to lash out or pull away, but all he could do was lie like a frozen slab of beef as the vampire witch drained him. His heart slowed. His fingertips grew cold, then his arms. His tail was numb. As his lycanthropic blood pulsed into the witch's mouth, he felt the pull of the Dark Moon subside, the red blur receding, hands snapping back into human fists. Little Red Riding Hood in reverse: This time it was Granny ate the Wolf.

"That's enough," Jay said. "Don't suck him dry. We may still need him."

Auntie Hand dropped the wolfman and stood, shard of Dark Moon still in her claw. Gore caked her face from nose to chin. "Princess . . . little bug . . ." The witch's breathing strained. She struggled with the words. In the silence of the throne hall, Lars could hear the cracking of her bones. "I am your servant . . . always . . . *This was all . . . for you. To be—who you were meant to be. My queen.*"

Hand's freeze spell began to loosen, but drained of so much blood, Lars could still hardly move. He watched as the witch, bones twitching beneath her loose and weathered skin, opened her mouth and dropped the fragment of Dark Moon down her own throat. She swallowed with ceremony—and the blood of the wolf, now flowing through her veins, took over.

Swallow the sun and moon . . . Lars thought. *Well, this is gonna be shit show.*

Jay was backing away, a look of horror on her face. From far off, Fish was shouting—screaming. Under the whirling Dark Moon, long thatches of ghost-white fur began to sprout across the witch's skin. Fur stretched across her scarred face as bones broke apart inside, reforming into a vicious snout jagged with yellow razor-teeth. The witch hunched and grew, tail lashing, robes jangling until they tore. As the white fur spread down the scars of her arms, her good hand shifted and lengthened into a bestial claw—and the hand beneath the clockwork diviner re-grew. The stump regenerated into a second wolf claw, and the diviner's straps strained and broke, the old wooden prosthetic falling hollowly to the stone floor. In the triple moonlight, the wolfed-out witch stamped her foot and howled, the stone beasts behind her pathetic facsimiles of the yeti-furred vamp-wolf hulking beside the throne. As she howled, her cosmic eyes glowed electric, wild and bulging, before bursting in a spray of sparks and light, and in their place burned the purple energy of the Dark Moon.

Even as she stood, the Hand Wolf grew, swelling with nega-lunar power. She towered taller than Lars ever had, growing still, eyes burning and fur bristling. The witch had chosen the form of the Destructor, and it wouldn't be Mr. Stay Puft—it would be her own damn self, as a giant alien were-beast. The plan had gone off just as Budge had said, except it wasn't Lars gone super-wolf—on Jay's suggestion, the witch had switcheroo'ed that little piece of prophecy. The Big Bad Wolf would bring the wolfpocalypse . . . it just wasn't gonna be Lars Breaxface. Now the old vampire witch, juiced up on his blood and Dark Moon magic, was what she'd wanted all along: A living weapon to terrorize her planet.

"*Freeze!*" someone was shouting. Someone else: "*Oh gods . . . what is that?*"

Out of the tunnelways, the Johnny-come-lately Imperium community police had made their way to the throne room. Four volunteer peace officers in threadbare uniforms, not a gun among them. One clung desperately to an electrified lasso—the others had nothing but their empty hands. Jay was already drawing her broadsword but seemed unsure of whom it was meant to skewer: cops or monsters.

Lars called hoarsely, "Get the *fuck* out of here!" But the cops, either by blood magic or pure terror, were frozen in place. The Hand Wolf roared and leapt, clearing the length of the room in an instant, knocking over suits of shadow armor that smoked as they fell. A bite through the throat of one officer. Another decapitated by the swipe of a claw. The other two, fleeing, and Frank valiantly attempting to wrangle the wolf-witch, only to lose two more limbs to her gnashing teeth. Sap and splinters rained, and the Hand Wolf barreled into the tunnels of the castle, white fur turning black with vampire blood. As she disappeared, screams echoed—and the howls of the wolf-witch faded into the distant noise of the city.

CHAPTER LV

Lars crawled to his feet. He felt like a freeze-dried zombie, death-flavored astronaut ice cream, but even half drained of blood, the werewolf virus was at work healing its host. The bite on his neck was sealing over with new skin, and blood cells were replicating, filling up his desiccated veins. He shook his head, scratched at the rags on his chest, and yelped at the pain. He looked down and his mind suddenly cleared: his left still human, but his right arm—his right arm was werewolf. The bones cracked and recracked under his tattooed skin, shifting back and forth between wolf and man. *Ah, fuck* . . . Somehow his wolf-self was on the fritz. Fine time for his blood to glitch—when there was a giant alien werewolf vampire witch monster on the loose. He knew the witch had caused it. The draining of his viral blood had left his power all out of whack in a way he'd never felt before. The wolf virus was clamoring to fix itself.

Jay stood dumbly with her sword out. Fish had stopped screaming. Frank was stuffing leaves against his wounds to stop the sap from hemorrhaging. Lars grabbed one of his silver-loaded sawed-offs from the floor and, in one fluid motion, had its barrel a sword-length from Jay's throat.

"Gimme one reason not to blow your fucking head off."

Jay let her sword blade drop. Her eyes were still on the tunnel where the Hand Wolf had escaped. "I just saved your life, for one."

Lars' grip tightened on the shotgun. His hand metamorphosed around the stock, but he kept his trigger finger steady. "Fuck you did. You played me. Recruited me on your little mission just to have the Wicked Witch of the Beast turn me into some monster. You didn't want a massacre—you wanted B-movie Armageddon."

"You're half right," Jay said, "You were just a means to an end. A way to punish my family's killers and take back my throne." The warrior princess shifted her gaze to the uniformed corpses on the floor. "Auntie wants to destroy everything. I thought she wanted justice for my family, but she doesn't—she wants the end of the world, and for me to rule over its ashes."

"No shit. That's your wolfpocalypse prophecy at work," said Lars. "Wolf eats up the sun and moon and everything, serpents take care of whatever's left. Ragnarok-'n'-roll."

"I want to *save* my people, Lars. I need you to help me do it."

Lars sniffed. She was sweating, and he liked the smell. The scent of fresh blood from the corpses was making him a little hungry, too. He blinked and tried to focus on the gun. "Shit, why didn't you just cut her head off while she was still just a little old lady in a bedazzled muumuu? Cosmic Christ, now she's a fucking werewolfasaurus."

"I don't know." The ornate scar on her chest rose and fell quickly as she breathed. She said, "I couldn't kill her looking like that. Like the woman who raised me. But that," she gestured toward the tunnel, "that monster, I can kill. I just can't do it alone."

"You're not going to kill anybody," Fish shouted from across the throne room. He was up on his sword wings, hanging in the air like a frog-headed angel. "You're gonna be thirteen slices of princess sashimi." He charged through the air, chainsaw ablaze. With a grunt, Lars swung the shotgun away from Jay—and aimed it at the flying amphibian.

"Not yet, Fishman," Lars said, brandishing the barrel. He then shouldered the shotgun and turned back to Jay. "We help you with your monster problem, you give us that key. And throw in as much neg as we can carry. Maybe one of these fuckin' shadow suits too. It'd look good in *Sheila*'s hold. I could put a bottle opener on it or something."

"Anything you want," said the princess.

Fish squawked, "Just kill her, you ape! *Take* the key! You want to get mauled by her grandmother or whatever? That crazy wolf-thing that just stormed out of here? It's coming back, I promise you. It'll kill all of us. We'll be monster food—a Breaxface breakfast with a side of Fish sticks."

"You won't find it," Jay said. "I hid the key. This armor doesn't have pockets anyway. Help me save the city—the world—and I'll give you the box. You can go back home."

Lars shrugged and shoved the shotgun into the ragged waistband of his ripped fatigues. Gray fur kept growing and shrinking across his tattoos, and his shoulders lurched with wolf-mutation. "You got a deal."

"Breaxface," Fish started, "but she—"

"Save it," the wolfman said. "No other way home, Fish."

As Frank slunk toward them, still nursing his trunk wounds, a thundering beast-howl cracked across the city and shook the ground beneath their feet.

A shadow fell over the castle. The light of the three moons vanished, and above them, through the skylight, the Hand Wolf lumbered into view—HUGE. *Super-kaiju Rita-Repulsa-Make-my-monster-grow ultra-gigantic huge.* The apocalypse beast loomed skyscraper high and titanic, fangs as big as houses foaming with waterfalls of bloody spit. White fur crisscrossed with black bleeding wounds as the monster's skin swelled and split. In what seemed like slow motion, the Handzilla swung a barge-sized claw, and a building burst and crumbled. Neon flashed and shorted, smoke and dust billowed in wild clouds. The Hand Monster's eyes still burned, each socket a blazing sun of hot white-violet. She turned her massive head down as if seeing through the castle's skylight, and a long black tongue split her teeth—licking her lips.

Lars thought of Budge's teaching and the mountains of that moon. The power channeling through his tattoos and surging through his chest. *Get your head outta the lilacs, Breaxface.* He was a few tattoos short now, all that magic ink just a stain on the floor. Now all he had were Budge's mutterings, the chants as ancient as the light from dead stars. He muttered a prayer to the Hot Cosmic Jeezus and any other gods in earshot, or hell, really only to himself, a whisper and a mantra to get his shit under control. He couldn't do this. He needed the tattoos and a beer. That was the only way. Monk spells and malt beverage—he was powerless without them, just what the witch had said, an animal. His body kept shifting. Wolf, man, wolf. In the shadow of the Hand monster, he breathed and remembered the old minotaur's meditations. The quiet mountains, the smoke of roasting beets. Blackness and nothingness and the geometric music of the infinite universe. Lars remembered. He took another breath, and his bones began to quiet, fitting themselves easily into werewolf form.

He soaked in the three moons and the negasonic magic of the Dark Moon and belted out a full-throated werewolf howl. Among the ruins of the throne room and his beaten and ragged crew of transdimensional companions, Lars grinned a wolfish grin and growled, *"Let's slay us a giant-ass monster."*

CHAPTER LVI

"So, what's the plan?"

It was Fish piping up, flashing that neon-orange laser chainsaw hand of his a little too eagerly. They couldn't see Handzilla anymore; the werewolfosaurus had disappeared behind a half-demolished tower, and anyway the glass of the skylight had been mostly covered with ash and debris from the crumbling buildings. But the ground still shook with her footsteps, making the holo-lantern chandeliers swing and the shadow suits of armor rattle on the castle floor.

Lars shrugged. *"Fuck if I know. Punch her, blow her up, shove a rocket-sized stake through her heart. Throw some water on her and watch her melt? Oh, what a world, what a world . . ."* The werewolf whirled to face Jay. *"Any ideas?"*

"I . . ." the princess started. "I don't know. The prophecies aren't a roadmap. They only say the beast will tear apart the ground and the sky and then the serpents and darkness, and then fire. The elders never mentioned a killswitch for the apocalypse—they *wanted* this to happen."

The castle shook. Inside, it was almost quiet, the Hand Monster's howls and the city's destruction distant noise beyond the thick heartstone walls. Lars could only imagine the panic in the streets, the piles of dead and dying. Nothing grander than what a few regular city-busting bombs could accomplish, but infinitely more terrifying. Bombs don't have teeth, or eyes of violet fire. Bombs don't laugh and howl when they kill you.

"*Well, Fish,*" Lars said, "*say your prayers to the Frog Mother. 'Cause this is suicide.*"

Lars started for the exit, when Fish squawked, "That's it!"

Jay and Lars exchange a look. The amphibian was cackling, gill flaps wagging with each staccato intake of breath.

"What's 'it'?" Jay said. "Is your Frog God going to hop out of her swamp-heaven to help us?"

"No . . ." Fish said. "No, but the Frog Mother . . . 'Holy Frog Mother, from whose pond we all have sprung, in whose mouth we shall all be swallowed.' The prayer, Lars—you remember. The Frog Mother will swallow the world, and then the world will be born again."

Lars growled, "*Fuck is your point?*"

Fish's laser chainsaw flickered away, and the mechanism at the end of his arm whirred and transformed back into a webbed metal hand, pointing at the Dark Moon. "I'm talking about death and rebirth, Lars. Alpha and Omega, right? The cycle of all things. And the cycle of this thing is we have to make the monster swallow that whole magical piece of moon."

Before Lars or Jay could respond, Fish added, "You saw her skin, right? All those oozy, nasty bits? Gross, really, probably get infected and gangrenous, and then you got a big problem. But what I'm saying is this: The witch's body can't handle all that power. Even with your werewolf blood. She's too big already, just from that little shard she ate. So, what if she eats the whole thing? All that magic . . . *pop!*"

"*Like a frog in a microwave,*" Lars said.

Fish choked. "Like . . . *what?*"

Jay sheathed her broadsword and stepped toward the Dark Moon. Its purple light played across her face, lighting the intricate scars that laced the skin. Lars almost felt guilty for wanting to eat her heart and liver only a few moments before. To be fair, she *had* let the old witch blood-trap his ass and guzzle on his veins. But seeing the warrior princess beside her throne, in the disco light of that magic moon-heart, he remembered the first time he'd met her, the cat-infested bar on Victor's Halo, and the brawl with those Siskelian ass-clowns, the run from StatSec, the jaunts across the black in *Sheila* and the rest of the trouble they'd gotten into. They weren't family, and they might not've even been friends. But they were a team, sort of. A motley crew of mostly losers who were the only hope this planet had of slaying this city-killing monster.

"*That's stupid,*" Lars said. "*We do it old school—with fists and teeth.*"

"No. He's right, Lars," Jay said. "I saw it, too. She's barely holding together." The princess turned to Fish and nodded toward the Moon. "If this is how we destroy her, how do we get it up there? Cover it in blood and hope she's hungry for a snack?"

"*Let me at it,*" Lars said. The werewolf strode up to the whirling Moon. Its energy pulled him, made all the fur on his body stand on end. He snarled, tensed his claws. His fist flickered human, then back to wolf. *Think of Budge, you mutt,* he thought to himself. *Don't even think that berserker shit.* He gritted his teeth and reached for the Dark Moon—only to be blown off his feet, zapped straight through and thrown ten meters into a pile of shadow armor. He landed in a splash of smoky shadow, a hard metal gauntlet poking his grundle.

Fish flipped out his sword wings and soared up to the orb. "Maybe it's wolf-proof," he said, smirking. The amphibian reached with his metal hand, only to suffer the same fate as Lars. A surge of energy from the circling stone, *zap*, and the cyborg fish-man roared overhead, crashing in a heap just beyond Lars' own landing spot.

"It's not going to work," said Jay. "None of us can hold it. Not without help."

She was looking at something on the stone floor—a severed hand, shriveled and brown. No, not a hand—not really. Lars recognized it then: Auntie Hand's clockwork prosthetic. The wooden diviner she'd used to pluck the shard of Dark Moon that had made her go full-on super beast. Jay lifted it, inspected it, looked at her own gloved left hand. She shook the glove loose, letting it drop with a small, echoing click. Even her hand was marked with her name: thick curlicues of scar tissue looping over white-white skin, across tendon and bone. "Lars," she said, "you have to it."

"*Do what?*" the werewolf growled.

"Take my hand."

"*Like—hold it?*"

"No, motherfucker, I mean *cut it off*. Bite it. Eat it if you want."

Fish's eyes went wide. "Holy Mother, are you nuts? You're gonna cut your *hand* off? No way, we you need to do your crazy evil vampire ninja stuff on this monster, okay? Let me tell you what it's like to lose your hand—it sucks. Yikes," he muttered, shaking his own prosthetic, "cutting your own hand off. That's crazy."

The castle was shaking harder now. Everything rattled, and from the tunnels they heard crashing as museum exhibits fell to the quakes of the Hand Monster's steps. Cracks webbed across the dirty skylight.

"We don't have time," Jay said. She pulled the broadsword from her back and, in a flourish, held it hilt-first toward the wolfman. "Here. If it's easier."

Lars swiped the sword away and bit deep into the princess's wrist. Teeth buried into bone till it crunched, the black hot blood of the vampire spilling across his lips and tongue. It was delicious. Jay grit her fangs in pain but didn't cry out. She closed her eyes, brow furrowed, and the blood began to slide out of his wolf-mouth, into the wound, coiling like smoke in reverse back into open veins. The hand was just a snack, and Lars chewed it up and swallowed. At the foot of the throne's steps, Frank, who'd lost more than a few appendages himself in the last hour, had a look of sympathy in his myriad yellow eyes. Fish looked horrified.

Jay breathed deeply. With her right hand, she fit the witch's wooden claw to her own raw stump. Black blood began to flow from the wound, only a thin ribbon at first, then more, spooling through the gears and hexworks of the diviner, the arcane prosthesis becoming an extension, a part of her. She flexed the fingers, and gears whirred, making a fist.

"All the fucking blue gods of the sea," Fish muttered. "Lars, did you really have to eat it? I mean, she offered the sword and everything . . ."

Lars' hulking wolf-shoulders shrugged. *"Missed breakfast."*

They both shut up when they realized Jay was making for the Dark Moon. Walls shuddered. Glass fell from the ceiling, a couple of the skylight panes finally shattering from the tremors, and both Lars and Fish ducked for cover. Oblivious to the hail of glass, Frank shuffled up to the throne in reverence, offering a branch to the princess. She took it, and the battle-torn tremuloid lifted her to the magic, swirling rock. She reached with the witch diviner—into the violet miasma, fingers piercing the rock's black curst—and grasped it. The Dark Moon pulled effortlessly from its hidden chamber in the wall, as if weightless. Frank set Jay down, the Dark Moon dwarfing her, at least as tall as the vampire and three times as wide. It stopped spinning on its axis, but purple sparks still flashed around its nega-black surface.

"Okay, boys," she said, "Now what?"

Lars was ready for that question. He'd already been wondering that same thing—how the shit were they supposed to get the Dark Moon up to Handzilla's snout to toss it in? He doubted Fish could buzz the princess up that high on his fancy sword wings. Then he'd remembered:

"We got wings," he said. *"Parked in the handicapped. Right outside."*

As glass and debris fell across the room, the four would-be monster slayers dashed for the parking lot, Jay dragging the Dark Moon in their wake.

CHAPTER LVII

Lars Breaxface had seen all manner of destruction. Wars and genocide, space-barge crashes and asteroid explosions. The wreckage of cities on his home planet, still glowing faintly with radiation, and of course, Dys-7, the massacre he'd caused all by himself before he figured out how to control the wolf. But, except in ancient movies, he'd never seen giant kaiju monster destruction. Giant kaiju monster destruction was its own thing altogether.

The smell slapped him like a dick in the face. Smoke and dust and newly dead bodies. Blood and burning metal. Torn bowels and crushed concrete. And the faint, omnipresent stink of old lady and patchouli. The streets outside the castle were obscured by clouds of dust, the occasional fire or sparking neon sign flashing through the smog. Rising from the dark clouds were the city's cyber-gothic skyscrapers, several of them burning or smashed in or truncating at jagged wounds of half-standing walls where Handzilla had knocked the whole top of the tower right off. Small black dots were falling from the windows of the smoking towers, and it took Lars a moment to realize they were people—vamp people, the people of this night-planet, jumping to their deaths. People were screaming, somewhere,

265

everywhere, and the sky was chaos: beneath the nega-sun and the trio of moons, a ragtag armada of armored zeppelins and darting scarabcraft had assembled in a ring around the white-furred wolf-witch, blasting her with laser weapons, rockets, harpoons, whatever they had on hand. The city had no military—it'd been labeled a tool of the monarchy and disbanded after the revolution—and police forces, even the uniformed corpses the Hand had left in the throne room, were all volunteer. They weren't prepared for war with a mega-beast.

Hand was menacing. Half hidden behind a gleaming pyramid, the giant were-creature swiped at the attacking aircraft with huge, deformed claws. She caught one of the zeppelins and crushed its graffiti-scrawled envelope in one hand, tossing it like trash as it erupted in fire. The ring of aircraft started to retreat, joining the swarms of others who were already fleeing or zooming up and down from the surface to rescue those trapped in the skyscrapers' upper floors. White flocks of corpse birds screamed above the smoke and flames, the mocking clouds of lightning among them trying to take avian shapes, everything in the sky hauling ass now away from the apocalyptic Auntie Hand. Through her pale fur, the witch's name-scars cut like ridges of flesh, pulsing purple as the nega-power coursed through them. Around the glowing scars, her skin swelled and split, bubbled and burst, only to close up again—the werewolf virus working furiously to heal its host—leaving the beast's white yeti fur slick with hot black blood.

"Holy Frog Mother, save us," Fish prayed.

"*Hot Cosmic fucking Christ*," Lars muttered.

"Come on," Jay said, dragging the Dark Moon through the castle's front gates. "Before there's no one left to save."

○

Patches' scarab was where they'd left it, though there was a small red-and-black security cruiser parked beside it and, taped to the scarab's windshield, a paper ticket. Seemed that the team of volunteer rent-a-cops lying gutted in the castle had paused on their way inside to write them up for improper parking. *Fuck it*, Lars thought, *if anything's left standing, ol' Patches can deal with it.*

"Who's flying this heap?" Jay asked. The Dark Moon was pulsing with light in her newly-attached clockwork hand. It hung from her fingers like a black stone balloon, hovering beside the princess as if outfitted with anti-grav. Its proximity pulled at Lars, threatened to incite either berserker mode or seizure, his skin and bones still twitching now and then with the glitch, though he'd gotten it more or less under control. His blood, healing, had nearly replaced itself, and he'd gotten used to the magnetic force of the Moon. But the planet's orbiting moons were pulling too. Above, gleaming in the clear black sky, they were the lunar-power mother lode, and Lars knew from experience that a moon-juice source like that could keep a werewolf raging indefinitely. Maybe the Hand's Dark Moon power-up was overloading her a little, but if she figured out how to stop the skin splitting, how to stop growing, she'd be unstoppable. In the always-night of the vampire planet, with those three moons shining down, a werewolf could wolf-out forever.

They had to blow the bitch up fast.

Fish grabbed the cockpit hatch with his metal fist. "I'll do it."

"*You? pilot?*" Lars grunted.

"It's been a long five years on this rock," Fish said. "I've learned a lot of things, and not just how to make sex lube for space vampires. Besides, you think I want to be anywhere near that monster's mouth? You think I want to fall out of the back of this thing and be dinner? No thanks. I want the front row seat to Exitsville. Ejection seat, rocket-powered, with parachute."

"*Lotta confidence, Fishman.*"

"I'm a realist."

Jay cleared her throat. "We don't have time for this. Let's go." She was already opening the hatch to the scarab's passenger compartment. "Frank?"

The tremuloid went first, snagging a few branches as he squeezed through the doorway. Then the princess nodded for Lars. The wolfman took one last look at the monster in the distance, swatting at the attacking police scarabs like a grizzly besieged by bees. This was it—they'd knuckleball that magic rock down her gullet, and if Fish and Jay were right, she'd pop like a possum butt-plugged with an M-80. End of Handzilla, apocalypse canceled, and a one-way ticket back to Universe Prime.

Lars kicked aside the empty beer bottles from his first trip in the scarab. Their presence made him thirsty, and he could see in Frank's eyes the battered tree was thinking the same. After monster slaying, they needed to grab a brew. Let bygones be bygones and all that.

Jay pushed the Dark Moon into the compartment. It only barely fit, its top scraping the ceiling. She didn't even bother to close the hatch. They'd need it open to execute the plan.

As Fish lifted the aircraft into the sky, wind whipped in through the doorway, carrying with it the city's infernal smog. Over the PA, Fish's garbled voice announced, "Heading straight for her. Most of the others are pulling back. Some gunfire still spraying, though—these guys couldn't hit the broad side of a whorehouse."

"Tell them to stop shooting and join the search-and-rescue," Jay said. "We've got this. We're the cavalry."

Standing in the doorframe with the city beyond her, the vampire looked every bit the badass she was, even with one hand stuck in a rock. Shadows smoldered like black flames across her armor, and the broadsword's hilt stuck up silver and gleaming behind her head. She'd tied her head-tendrils back in a slack bun, but even then the tendrils' ends lashed in the wind. Her face was drawn, lips tensed, and galaxy eyes sparked beneath a furrowed, scar-laced brow. Lars hoped for all their sakes it was as easy as a drive-by drop, and they'd be home free. They needed a win.

The scarab banked, and suddenly there she was: Auntie Hand, monsterized. Her snout was twice long as the scarab, each razor fang longer than Lars, and red-black froth dripped from her shredded lips. Fish hadn't flown them within swiping distance yet, but the wolf-witch had noticed them, had picked them out of the swarm of aircraft. No doubt she'd sensed the Dark Moon on board.

Jay braced against a wall. "Here she comes."

Lars breathed and let the wolf blood course through his veins. He clenched his claws and howled. Just a drive-by drop . . . but if shit went wrong, he was ready.

The scarab lurched, climbed, and banked hard again. Through the open hatch, they could see below: the wolf-witch's monster mouth, wide open.

"*Throw it!*" Lars growled.

Jay pushed—but she didn't let go.

"*The fuck?*"

Before Lars could say more, he saw fear flash across the face of the vampire princess. She was struggling, pushing, but the witch's hexed prosthetic wouldn't let go of the Dark Moon.

"It's stuck!" Jay shouted.

Over the PA, Fish was yelling, "Drop it, drop it, she's—"

Then the universe rolled like a hamster ball. Upside-down, end-on-end, spinning. Lars crashed headfirst into the compartment ceiling. Frank's branches scraped against him as the tremuloid struggled to find a hold. The Dark Moon had wedged between a seat and a cargo locker, and from it Jay hung in the air, attached only by her wooden hand, where it remained stuck in the crust of the rock. Metal wrenched, and the tail section of the scarab tore free. Where the back of the cabin had been, two giant violet-flaming eyes stared up at them, blank and demonic.

A grating, heavy voice erupted from the Hand: "*You . . . lit-tle bug . . . you would . . . stop me . . .*"

It was almost a question. With her free hand, Jay unsheathed her broadsword, energy whining down its blade. She shouted, "If not me, Auntie, who?"

The vampire werewolf witch-monster threw its heavy head back and howled. The sound shattered the scarab's windows, and then Lars heard nothing, total silence, dulled. Then the slight whine of a high-pitched ringing, his ears throbbing, hurting like hell but the wolf blood's healing factor was already at work patching up his eardrums. Even the monster's howl was apocalyptic. The wolfman scrambled to an upside-down seat and dug in his claws. Plan A had gone to shit—it was time for Plan B. Berserker mode. Eat his way into her chest like a starving rat and start tearing up organs till the old witch keeled over. He felt the Dark Moon's energy surge and readied himself for the leap—

—until the universe flipped again, the scarab dropping like a stone out of the air.

CHAPTER LVIII

The scarab fell away as Lars, still juiced on Dark Moon, launched himself through the torn-open tail section. Leaping across the city, he felt like a lycanthropic Spider-man, without the webs, which were kind of important actually, he realized, as he found himself loose in the air without a parachute, nipple-high to the big beast. The Hand Monster's roiling skin was only meters out of reach, and he was falling like a goddamned idiot, somersaulting in the air towards near-certain death.

Something wet and black swallowed him whole.

His first thought was he'd been eaten by the Hand-beast. But he hadn't passed her jagged teeth, and the hole he was in didn't stink of monster breath. It smelled like blood.

Vampire blood.

He clawed through the wall of blood surrounding him and looked around—he was in a bubble of monster gore, suspended in the air by thick umbilicus of bloodrope. Not far away, Jay was standing midair on a round, dripping platform of blood, her boots sinking a little into its hexed surface. She still held the Dark Moon, weightless as ever, and her other hand was outstretched, manipulating the dark blood that erupted from the monster's skin. Lars found himself in a kind of half-cocoon of blood, hanging from the witch's thigh by a long bloodrope like some blood-clot dingleberry. Not far away, Frank hung from a web of bloodropes looped through his upper foliage. The sound of an explosion reached him, then the heat of it, and Lars looked down to see the wreckage of Patches' scarab burning in the middle of an already wrecked street. *Fish . . .* No sign of the amphibian or his parachute, at least not in one of Jay's blood-magic lifejackets. *Sorry, pal. Woulda gotten your frog ass home if I could've.*

Lars and Frank shook as Handzilla walked, slow and lumbering, fighting gravity with her enlarged mass. As Jay glided over to the wolfman on her blooddisc, he saw the glint of metal in the corner of his eye. Then a flash of neon orange. Soaring on sword wings was Arcturus Fishman, amphibian archangel, with laser chainsaw ready to slice up some monster ass.

"Fish," Lars said. "*You're not a corpse.*"

"Not yet," said the amphibian. "But it was close, *too* close. You remember what I said about not wanting to be anybody's dinner? Still true, don't get me wrong. But also I think it's time to this nasty old lady learned the name *Arcturus Fishman . . .*" From the stump at the end of his arm, the chainsaw blazed.

The wolfman grinned. "*Groovy.*"

"Lars," Jay called. "There's nothing we can do. Even if I can fly us all up there, she'll see us coming. We lost the element of surprise. We need something to really hit her, something bigger than the firepower those cops are spraying. Something that will knock her off balance. If I can surprise her, I can get the Dark Moon in."

Fish frowned. "All I brought is the saw. Left the rest of my toys back at the mansion." Then the amphibian's eyes brightened, and he began tapping furiously at a holo-interface on his mechanical arm. "Calling reinforcements. I don't know what's left, after you sons of bitches wrecked the place. But maybe there's a drone or two. Radio my security team, too, if they're still standing."

Doesn't matter, Lars thought. The Hand Monster wasn't going to be fazed by some goggle-wearing rent-a-cop or self-lubricating dildo bomb. There was only one thing that would shake this beast-witch: wolf-on-wolf ultraviolence. Straight to the chin.

"*The Dark Moon,*" Lars barked. "*Break me off a piece.*"

"Are you fucking crazy?" Jay said, nodding up at the Hand. "You see what you're attached to? The Moon *created* this. It's what turned her into this creature."

"*One sliver. A speck. Not a whole chunk—I'll hit her, you drop the Moon.*" He looked up at the gigantic wolf-monster and wondered if maybe he really was fucking crazy. What did he know about the Dark Moon's powers? Maybe it didn't matter how much you bit off—maybe all it took was an atom to make you monsterfied for life. What choice did he have? Auntie Hand had to go down. And he was the son of a bitch to make sure it happened. He growled, "*Now.*"

"Fuck you," the princess spat. "I don't need two giant wolves trashing my planet."

"Agree with the lady," said Fish. "You don't know what this thing will do. You have to science it first—test it, determine its properties, measure against control groups. So far, it seems to, uh, just turn whoever eats it into a mega-monster. You shouldn't risk it. We might have to kill you too."

From the way Frank was looking at him, Lars could tell the old tree was with them—three against one on the Operation: Make Lars Humungous. Lars started swinging in his blood bucket, toward Jay. Because sometimes democracy fails. Yes, his plan might end up with him plowing across the planet in a gigantic werewolf berserker rampage until the others devised a way to King Kong his ass off a tall building, but Lars didn't think so. He was controlling his wolf self better than he ever had. Even with the Dark Moon close, he calmed his mind, kept it zen.

Around them, the Hand was walking glacially and buildings crumbled and, high above, the motley armada had all but scattered, their paltry barrage of harpoons and laserfire waning. It was now or never. Jay's gauntlet clenched into an armored fist, and her other hand—the diviner—moved toward him, pulling monster blood with it. "Lars, don't—"

But he was already there. On his blood-bucket's next swing, he flopped over, into the air, toward the Dark Moon. Jay pulled it away, but not fast enough. He fell on top of it claws first, slashing, and then, just as before, the Dark Moon repelled him, shooting him upward toward the mega vamp-wolf's mega wolfgina. But he'd gotten what he needed, could feel it sizzling under his fingernail. The tip of his claw was sparkling like he'd just finger-banged a unicorn. He'd breached the moon-heart's magical miasma, if only for a second, and scratched off a speck. He hoped it was enough. As the wolfman soared upward, he licked the dust from his claw. To himself, he muttered, "*It's morphin' time*," just before shit went crazy.

CHAPTER LIX

Lars was Alice, and the Dark Moon dust was an Eat Me cake. He was Ultraman engaging his Beta Capsule. He was Mario tripping on the mother of all mushrooms. It wasn't anything like the body-horror snapping and stretching of werewolf transformation. He felt like he was wearing an inflating werewolf suit, a heavy thing but coursing with power—full-on Incredible Hulk mode. He was growing huge.

Riding the momentum from the Dark Moon's force blast, Lars landed full-sprint on all four claws in the dirty white forest of the witch-monster's pubes. He thanked the gods of physics he hadn't landed headfirst in old-lady monster cooch. There wasn't enough booze in the universe to drown away an experience like that. He didn't have time to get caught up in the beast's nethers. He was running, clawing, straight up Auntie Hand's abdomen, leaping chasms of torn skin, waterfalls of dark blood, glowing walls of scar flesh. As he ran, he grew. He could feel it, his werewolf body hulking out, swelling. His clothes—everything from underpants to combat boots—fell away in shreds, and soon he was nothing but wolf, feeling the wind on his ball sack as he bounded up the body of the beast. The Hand Monster's fur was no longer a forest, suddenly it barely reached

275

his knees. Her cuts only cracks now, the scars minor tripping hazards. She had noticed him, finally. From the corners of his eyes, he saw the barge-sized claws coming toward him, but he still hadn't slowed—he was raging. Rushing on moon-power and nega-magic. He was running between her saddlebag werewolf breasts, up on his hind legs, both hands clenched in heavy fists. Above him, the Hand's jaw didn't seem so gargantuan now—it was just a jaw, wolfish and ragged, and soon Lars was beneath it, fists ready, the wolf-monster's hands stopping in surprise.

Then Lars Breaxface what he was born to do.

What he'd done to that Siskelian smuggler in the Pickled Quasar.

To Quillian Nine's trash-golems on Canal City and Cairn.

To the hell-mouthed sea monster in the drainpipe of the tidal wall.

What he'd done a thousand times to a thousand other assholes in barfights and on battlefields and anywhere he'd had to call down the fury. He was what he was; he did what he was always meant to:

He punched the monster in the chin.

Werewolf fist made contact with monster jaw. Shockwave boomed from impact. Giant bones split, and giant razor teeth flew. He was bigger than the wolf-witch's head now, and still growing. He vaulted over the monster's shoulder as she stumbled, and as he scraped to a landing on a nearby pyramid, he saw Jay and Fish buzzing above the Hand's open mouth.

Boom time. Drop it, Jay . . .

But she didn't. The Dark Moon, it must've still been stuck to that prosthetic mitt. The Hand Monster staggered, but her hellfire eyes had locked onto his two flying companions. From below, boulders of debris crashed against the monster's hide, courtesy of Frank. Distracted and concussed, Handzilla turned, and her mouth began to close—almost. Lars had shattered her jaw like an earthquake: skin and fur split in two from chin to throat. As she tried

to move it, the two halves of jawbone splayed. Black blood coiled up from the cracks in her skin, winding around each piece of jaw, pulling them apart as Jay wielded the power of the witch's diviner, blood magic turned up to eleven, and between the jagged jaws, trailing a comet's tail of shadows, Jay dived—the Dark Moon ahead of her, pulling her down like a weight.

Princess and moon-heart disappeared into the Hand Monster's throat. The monster froze. Lars was scrambling on the pyramid, trying to steady his new gigantor bulk to launch a second attack. He felt the stings of laserfire on his back, a few of the ballsier cops edging forward from the swarm to attack the newly giant Lars. He didn't even bother batting them away. His skin healed almost as quickly as it burned. Auntie Hand was Target Number One. He had to focus. Jay's bloodropes fell away, and the wolf-witch's jaw was already sealing up, her werewolf healing factor also in overdrive, pulling flesh and bone together like a zipper. Lars crouched at the apex of the pyramid, tensing his mega-arms for another leap. He looked down and noticed his own skin starting to split and bleed, a faint purple glow tracing through his old tattoos. He closed his eyes and felt something behind them, burning. Well, shit—maybe he was gonna go full-on Ragnarok Wolf after all, flaming eyes included. But before he did, he was going to save the princess from the belly of the beast—he could do that much, at least.

He perched on the pyramid's apex and dug his claws into the steel structure, preparing to launch his new giant self at the monster's chin for another hyper turbo sucker-punch.

"Yo, she-bitch," he snarled. "*Let's go.*"

Then his claws started to slide—the pyramid was growing underneath him, the broken buildings around him soaring skyward, and Handzilla herself towering over him.

Oh cosmic fuck . . . The pyramid wasn't growing; he was shrinking. He was all out of sparkle-magic Dark Moon power-up, and his gigantor-ness was wearing off. Apparently a scratch-and-lick from the magic moon-heart bought you time enough for one big punch. Or maybe it was a symptom of the fritz, his wolf blood not quite back to one hundred. Cosmic Christ, he thought, even Ultraman got three minutes as a giant kaiju-fighter. Lars was pretty sure he hadn't even hit two. The cracks in his skin began to heal. The glowing tattoos beneath his fur faded, and in seconds, he was back to his regular werewolf self, regular werewolf-sized, stranded sixty stories up on the top of a cyberpunk pyramid as the giant vampire were-monster— who had just eaten his sort-of friend and did not seem to be exploding from Dark Moon overload as planned—lumbered toward him, eyes blazing. As the final crack in her chin sealed over, her wolf snout stretched into a smile, and even missing the few teeth he'd punched out, that megalodon grin was scary as hell.

CHAPTER LX

Maybe it wouldn't have been so bad being the witch's giant attack-wolf. Sure, he would have been a near-mindless city-killing freak beast with flaming eyes, but being gigantic, even for a brief moment, had been pretty rad. And at least he'd be more or less alive. At least he wouldn't be about to die buck-ass naked in an alien universe. And his cock would've been huge.

There was no space princess with magic blood cocoons to save his ass this time. At that moment, she was either fighting her way out of the Hand Monster's guts or halfway through digesting, along with the big black rock that was supposed to be super-beast kryptonite. He was stuck, and the super-beast was coming toward him mouth first. So she planned to eat him too. Whatever. It seemed fitting, he and Jay dying together in the intestines of Handzilla. If it weren't for his wolf blood and her mission of righteous vengeance, there wouldn't be a giant beast ravaging downtown Vampville.

Plan C, Operation: Make Lars Humungous, had somewhat flopped, but if she was intent on gobbling him up, maybe he could still backtrack to Plan B, Operation: Rip Monster Apart from Inside. He hunched atop the pyramid and let out a wicked werewolf howl that echoed through the broken city. He wouldn't get swallowed easily like some chocolate-flavored cum wad; he'd be a hairball with claws.

Something buzzed past his tail, and he snatched it out of the air. A thick, smooth tube of polished chrome scuttling on an anti-grav motor.

"Specially engineered for maximum zero-grav and subspace satisfaction," came Fish's voice from behind him. "Propulsion's a new feature, though—like a vibrator on overdrive. A great gift for your more adventuresome user of zero-gravity erotic appurtenance. Pop this baby into an orifice and ride it 'round the cabin while you climax like a supernova. One year warrantee included."

Fuckin' space dildos... Lars coughed out a laugh as best he could, given his werewolf anatomy. He released the buzzing dildo, and it put-putted around to join a few others flying around the sword-winged cyborg fucktoy salesman. From his little swarm of sex toys, two sets of fuzzy, zebra-striped handcuffs zoomed toward him, dangling from heavy-duty anti-grav engines.

"For airborne S&M play," Fish explained. "Can't always wait till you're in outer space to get that weightless feeling."

Lars snapped one cuff from each pair to his wrists. They lifted him off the pyramid, holding him above its point, eye level with Fish, his thick werewolf arms spread like he was on the first letter of the "YMCA." All things considered, the cuffs were comfortable, but he felt like wolf bait on a fuzzy hook. The monster was close, moving slowly but purposefully toward them. Buildings crumbled with each step.

"Jay," Lars said. "*She's in there.*"

Fish's head drooped. "I know. The wooden hand wouldn't let go. She didn't have a choice. It was that, or abandon the plan."

"*Not fucking working. Where's Frank? He was down throwing rocks at Goliath a second ago.*"

"Don't know," Fish said "Saw him stop a piece of building from falling on some people. Then the princess went in. I lost track."

A lone corpse bird passed by, squawking and dripping some kind of slime from its sallow skin. It made Lars hungry just looking at it—until the Hand stepped close enough to smell her breath. Like a meth addict who'd been drinking battery acid. The stench burned his sensitive wolf nostrils, and his stomach turned.

"Look, Lars," Fish said, nodding toward his swarm of toys, "all I've got here are a couple of souped-up prototypes outfitted for anti-grav. Flying fucktoys. Nothing with any firepower. You guys destroyed all of that when you broke into my house. I'm just one little amphibian with a pair of wings and a laser chainsaw for a hand. I can't take on a world-ending colossus. I couldn't even beat *you*. We need to fly out of here. Out of the city, straight on to the next syndicate. Maybe they have something there that could blow a hole in this monster. But apocalypse-wise, Armageddonly-speaking, I'd say Imperium's lost, and so is the princess. We failed."

Lars couldn't believe it. Jay'd been so damn sure that Fish's Dark Moon plan would work. Swallow, overload, ka-boom. But it hadn't—and in less than a minute, they'd be the next course in Auntie Hand's all-you-can-chomp buffet.

"*Fuck it*," he growled. "*Let's go.*"

Then, from the Hand Monster's open mouth, a skull-shattering shriek erupted. It swelled, climbing in pitch and volume. The monster threw her head back, eyes closing as she shrieked, Lars and Fish both shaking from the vibrations of the sound. *Jay*, Lars thought. The warrior princess must've been hacking her way out of the wolf-witch's guts after all. The monster's eyes opened—and from them, columns of violet-black fire shot straight up into the sky. Out of her mouth a wider column beamed, swirling nega-fire searing through her teeth. The shrieking continued, a high singing tone more felt than heard. The network of name-scars across her skin burned deep purple and then the black flames ruptured through the flesh, a web of holy magic Dark Moon nega-fire engulfing the alien witch-monster. In a fireworks finale of jet-black fire and violet sparks, the giant werewolf Auntie Hand exploded, her body bursting along the seams of her scars, and her massive wolf head popping off, sailing over the tidal wall toward the sea of hungry serpents, as white fur and hot, hot blood rained across the ruined city.

The shrieking ceased, and the silence was deafening.

As the smoke cleared, Lars saw a black balloon flying over ground zero, right where Handzilla's chest had been. No, not a balloon—a bubble. A bubble of monster blood. And it was gliding down to the burning, gore-spattered crater below.

"*Fish,*" he said, "*get us down there.*"

CHAPTER LXI

At the center of the crater, the sphere of blood bloomed, and Jay stepped onto the scorched pavement, covered in organ bits and entrails but alive, intact, and holding her tech-laced broadsword. The bubble melted into a puddle behind her, black and glistening like an oil slick.

Lars unlatched the fuzzy cuffs and dropped to the ground, Fish and his dildo army buzzing behind him.

"*You did it,*" he said. "*Slayed the monster. Saved the world.*"

Jay smirked, sheathing her sword behind her back. Entrails clung to the jagged ridges of her shadow armor. "Had some help. That was a hell of a punch."

Lars shrugged. "*It's what I do.*"

"Top-notch heroics," Fish cut in, drifting toward Jay. "Have you ever thought about modeling? I have a new line of high-tech bondagewear you'd look fantastic in. What's your bust size, 36-C? How do you feel about nipple armor? It'd be a great business opportunity. Everybody loves a hero."

"I'm not going to wear your metal bras, frog man."

As Jay waved off the eager amphibian, the battle-weary wolfman dropped to all fours and stretched his haunches. He'd been in wolf mode too damn long now. He was tired. He needed a beer. His hands began to twitch, and in moments he was back to his human self. It felt good, if a little breezy.

"You're not wearing clothes."

"Price you pay for going gargantuan, princess. I'll pick up some new threads when we're back in my 'verse."

"About that . . ." Jay began. "Wait. Where's Frank?"

Her starry amethyst eyes darted around the wreckage of the crater, and a look of worry crossed her face.

"I bet he's fine," Lars offered. "That old log is a tough son of a bitch."

Fish said, "Yeah, but the monster—she could've stepped on him, right? Or he could've been caught in the explosion? She really blew up, with nega-fire and everything."

Lars shot him a look. The fish-eyed cyborg was oblivious.

Concrete scraped concrete on the far side of the crater, and from a caved-in liquor store, right on cue, a pile of rubble and monster guts fell away to reveal the dusty and battered foliage of a ragged tremuloid that had seen better days. Frank lurched out from under the debris, dragging a case of some glowing vampire booze.

"Frank," Jay called, "you okay?"

As if to answer, the beat-up tree sat himself on the charred pavement, ripped the case open, popped the cork off a bottle, and began sucking the liquor in through the prehensile branch.

Jay smiled a shark-toothed smile. "He's okay."

Surrounded by his whirring sex toys, Fish headed for the damaged tremuloid, offering medical assistance in exchange for a healthy swig of whatever spirits he'd looted.

"About our ticket home, though," Lars said. "Pop out that puzzle box and let's all vamoose. I've still got some brews in *Sheila's* hold. Those kegs from the fart alien. We can all kick back and toast to victory."

Jay's smile faded. She turned to look at the ruined city, the smoke and fire, the survivors just now making their way from wherever they'd hidden away. "I can't, Lars."

"Taking the throne back, huh? Mission of righteous vengeance succeeds. Guess the old witch wasn't totally wrong."

"I'm not staying to be a queen."

She stopped to wipe a spot of blood from her scarred cheek. Hell of a woman, this magic ninja alien vampire princess. Kills the monster, rejects the spoils. On some level, Lars had to admire that. Selflessness wasn't exactly in his nature, but he could grok it on occasion.

"I'm going to do whatever I can to help," Jay said. "I caused this. It's the least I can do."

"All right . . ." Lars said. What else was there to say? Good luck? Toodles? "Good luck with that," he added. "Toodles." He scratched the hair on his chest and belched. Goodbyes were weird. One more check in the pro column for flying solo. Nobody to say adios to. "So, about our payment? I seem to remember a contract for a haul of negativium for services rendered. And one of those suits of armor. I'll take an IOU on that, if it's cool. I can't even tell if the castle's still standing from here."

"Still playing the mercenary," Jay said.

"A werewolf's gotta eat."

Smirking, the princess reached up and unlatched the spiked spaulder on her shoulder. "It's a good thing I kept all this close by."

Beneath the piece of armor were the two vials of negativium and beside them, shining in the moonlight, the small, golden puzzle box—the key to the door between universes. She took the vials of neg out first and started to offer one to Lars, then paused. "You want Fishman to hang onto this for now?"

"Hell no. That's a shit ton of money. My big score," Lars said. "Besides, Fish is playing nice now, but I think he's still pissed about us busting up his shop back in Canal City. Might figure it's restitution."

The crater was littered with blackened ropes of the wolf-monster's yeti fur. Lars grabbed up a smaller strand, one about the thickness of a licorice rope, then took the vial of negativium from the princess, knotted it in the monster hair, and hung the whole thing around his neck. The vial nestled among his chest fur and faded ink, for now dangling like a ridiculous piece of jewelry.

"Not bad," said Jay. Then, calling to the amphibian, "Mr. Fishman? Payment. As promised." She tossed the vial, and Fish caught it with his flesh hand. He flashed a wide frog-lipped smile and raised his mechanical arm, a small compartment irising open near its elbow. He tucked the vial inside, gave a webbed thumbs-up, and went back to boozing with Frank.

Jay then unfastened the key from its hiding place on her shoulder and offered it to Lars. The wolfman took it, dwarfing the delicate box with his thick tattooed hands. This was it. The monster was gone. There was no more mission. He had his ticket home. Back to *Sheila* and the big empty and whatever trouble he could find there, among the stars.

"You sure?" he said. "Back there, you've got infinite worlds. Here, it's just the one. Kinda boring, if you ask me."

"One world is sometimes enough," she said.

He snorted, and his stomach growled. The dust was getting to him, and he was still wicked hungry. The princess's hand hadn't been much of a snack. He called for Fish, who was sucking on a genie bottle of glowing liquid. "Time to rock and roll. Wormhole train's leaving the transdimensional station."

Reluctantly, Fish handed the bottle back to Frank and started making his way across the desolation. The big tree took a swig with his drinking appendage. Then, with significant creaking, he lifted himself off the rubble. Still carrying the jug, he lumbered toward them, dragging a few feet behind the cyborg amphibian.

"Hey, Frank," Lars said. "Sure you want to stick around this rock? Still got a hell of a stash of beer back on *Sheila*. A keg's got your name on it for saving my ass from those sea monsters."

The battered tremuloid took his post behind the armored princess and straightened his posture, eyes as clear as they could be with Frank up to his sapwood in gin and juice. He looked just as he did back in the neon bar on Victor's Halo, only a little more roughed up: ever the loyal bodyguard.

"Yeah," Lars said, giving the tree-man a nod. "Figured as much."

He stepped back, holding the puzzle box out like the sacred magical artifact it was. Nearby, Fish stood with his fingers steepled, goggled eyes magnified and fidgety. Lars held his breath—and tapped the surface of the box.

Nothing happened. He tapped it again, caressed it, gave it a little two-finger action. Still nada. Shaking his head, he handed it back to Jay. "You mind? I don't know the combination to this lock."

The princess slid her new wooden fingers across the box and blue sparks surged through the designs of its engravings. An unnatural wind picked up, blowing from everywhere at once, a thunderclap boomed, and just above the center of the crater, the breach opened: a deep black void ringed in blue lightning.

Lars took one last look over his shoulder at the world's three white moons. He could live there, if he wanted. For a while anyway. Settle in some remote mountain town and meditate like Budge under these moons. Let them recharge his blood, get him back into balance. Howl at them now and again, when he was in the mood. With his wolf blood, the difference in cosmic vibrations didn't seem to matter, not like it had with Jay and the Hand. In the moonlight, among the rubble, he felt good. Better than he ever had.

But what about *Sheila*? What about the great wide universe out there? All the crazy shit it had to offer? What about his stash of beer? *One world is sometimes enough*, Jay had said. For some people. Not for Lars Breaxface, Werewolf in Space.

"All right," he said. "We're out. But if a storm starts kicking up, just remember what ol' Lars Breaxface does when the earth quakes and the pillars of heaven shake and some evil witch-beast tries to call down the wolfpocalypse."

Jay smiled again. "And what's that?"

"I'll tell you next time," Lars said, and stepped through the portal.

CHAPTER LXII

The world between worlds was calm. The scent of burnt yams was still in the air. Crickets fiddled their nighttime rags. Stars danced their disco in the sky. The trail to Budge's campfire was well worn, just as he remembered it, big crescent divots of hoofprints beaten into the dirt. He had to tell Budge he'd done it—he'd stopped Ragnarok, with a little help here and there. The old bull-headed bastard wouldn't believe it. Budge tended to get a bug up his ass about prophecies, thought they always found their way of coming true. Fate finds a way, the old monk would say. Lars didn't believe that shit for a second.

When Lars reached the minotaur's fire ring, though, there was no Budge. The ashes were white and long cold.

"Fuck it," he said out loud. Whether it was a trick of netherspace or some cryptic lesson from the real, magical, dimensionally ambiguous Budge, he didn't know. He kept on walking, steering wide around the spot where the monk had pelvic-thrusted him over the cliffside. As the wolfman strolled butt-naked and whistling down the mountain trail of the forest moon, everything around him faded slowly to black—everything but the stars.

CHAPTER LXIII

Beyond the breach, they tumbled into chaos and explosions. Lars tripped out of the portal first, a clumsy Fish collapsing onto him. The wolfman howled as the amphibian's metal angles dug into his exposed fleshy parts. Fish muttered his apologies.

Around them, the Library was still booming. They were right back where Lars and crew had crossed over to the vampire dimension, more or less. The breach hadn't reopened in the temple's cat-infested reading room where Jay had first unlocked the box and sent them all down the rabbit hole. Instead it'd dropped them outside the collapsing temple, about halfway back through the stacks toward the landing port, where *Sheila* was gassed up and ready to rocket.

"What the hell is *happening* here?" Fish screeched.

Only moments had passed, Lars realized. Somewhere in that temple, Boris was exploding, the witch's last victim. He'd been in the vampire universe for almost a day, but here it'd been a matter of seconds. The witch had said time worked differently in the pocketverse. Even now, Jay must've been days and weeks into her new life, whatever life looked like in the aftermath of Handzilla's rampage.

"We pissed off some Librarians."

"Librarians?"

They were jostled by the crowds—aliens of a thousand shapes fleeing the imploding temple. The cyber-mummy custodians of the City of Books darted overhead on paper wings, all of them heading the other way. They didn't give the naked, human Lars a second glance. If they were looking for him at all, they were looking for the wolf.

"C'mon," he said. "My cruiser's in the parking lot. Let's lift off this dive."

Fish didn't hesitate. He soared behind Lars on his sword wings as the naked wolfman pushed through the panicked crowds, dodging toppled food carts and the occasional burning book. The vial of negativium bounced against his chest on its monster thread.

As the crowds trampled book after book, Fish shook his head and muttered, "A travesty."

"They'll print new ones," Lars barked, elbowing a squid-faced woman out of his way. "Now haul ass."

○

Sheila was right where he'd left her. He caressed the flames painted across her nose, looped his fingers along the six graffiti letters of her name, and laid a deep, heartfelt kiss on the bare spray-painted titties of the eponymous brunette on the fuselage. Then he fiddled in nethers of the cruiser's undercarriage and until he felt a pelt of soft fur. He tugged on it, and when his hand reappeared, it held a dirty pink rabbit's foot keychain, from which hung his spare set of keys.

The lock clicked, and the hatch to the cargo hold opened. He was home.

He sucked in the smells of it—stale beer, old socks, unidentifiable fast food remains. Everything just as he'd left it. His crates of canned meat, the big strapped-down bags of Fish's Rubber Room weapons cache, and of course, the rack of beer kegs. Lars knelt under the tapped keg, yanked the lever, and out poured the hopped nectar of the gods directly into his mouth. Foam frothed over his beard and down his chest, but he didn't give a fuck. He guzzled ale till he choked, spit it out, and guzzled some more. For one sweet gulping moment, he was in frothy paradise. All the dude ever wanted was his beer back.

"Lars?" Fish was looking at him like he'd caught him fucking a floating eyeball. Dull explosions boomed outside, and the space cruiser rocked.

The wolfman stood up, body hair glistening with spilled beer. "Grab a seat," he said. "And hold onto something. No telling what these Librarians will do with their sacred temple tumbling down."

"Wait," said Fish. "Where are we going?"

"Fuck if I know, man. Universe is my oyster. Where do you want me to drop you?"

Fish slumped against a shipping crate. With his wings sheathed and his mechanical arm in hand mode, he didn't look so much like an amphibian avenging angel. He looked like a guy who'd lost both legs and an arm in a shitty accident. "Well," he said, "you've destroyed my life twice now. I have nothing and no one, not even those last few prototypes. They got lost in the portal somehow. I have nowhere in the whole universe to call home."

"Shit, Fishman," Lars said, pausing at the corridor to the cockpit. Fish had a point: Jay's mission had obliterated the amphibian's world once, then did it all over again in another universe, and Lars had been right there tearing it up with her. He thought of all those long hauls in the black alone, *the ultimate lone wolf.* Fuck good was a lone wolf if he, say, got his ass stuck atop a pyramid or eaten to death by a giant monster? "You got a home, Fish—you're looking at it. Room enough for two if you don't mind sleeping in the hold."

Fish grinned. "Not at all."

○

On the way past his bunk, Lars nabbed a pair of patched-up fatigues from a pile of stale laundry on the floor. He took a whiff, and they passed the sniff test, or close enough. He yanked them up, going commando and not even bothering to buckle the fly.

294

In the cruiser's old, familiar cockpit, he nestled his ass into the carefully cultivated divot of the pilot seat and shoved the keys into the ignition, the sound system's speakers roaring with the booming sound of a revving '67 Impala. Holographic displays raised in overlay across the control board, and his fingertips tapped with instinct, acting on muscle memory even before he could think. In seconds, the engines were fired up, and victorious fucking death metal was raging from the stereo.

Sheila lifted off the landing pad. Engines flared, and the old cruiser blasted into orbit and beyond, into a field of real, shimmering stars stretching halfway to infinity and back again, leaving the cube-shaped Library planet in her quantum wake.

On the navigational bits of his holo-display, Lars tapped the coordinates for Freewheel. Seemed like as good a place as any to start. A thousand and one places to get fed, fucked, and drunk, and once he fenced a bit of the neg around his neck, he'd be the casino world's high roller numero uno. Werewolf VIP. He engaged the futtle drive, and stars streaked by the windows in long white lines as *Sheila* zoomed into subspace. Nodding his head to the thrashing double-bass, he leaned back, punched the big red button for auto-pilot, and settled in to watch the psychedelic rainbow of subspace rushing by. Color melted into color, and the craziness of the whole batshit adventure, from Pickled Quasar to monster battle, stripped away with every passing lightyear. He felt all right. Better than all right. He'd helped save the world, and held himself back from full-blown werewolf berserker mode. No Dys-7 repeat, not on the vampire planet or ever again. He'd tamed the beast. And now he was home sweet home, with a fortune in negativium, a weapons cache to outfit a small army, a new friend with a knack for guns and fucktoys, and a cozy pair of pants, the universe—*his* universe—speeding past him, kaleidoscopic and infinite.

All he needed now was another beer.

LARS AND FISH WILL RETURN IN

LARS BREAXFACE
AND THE STARKILLER UNICORN

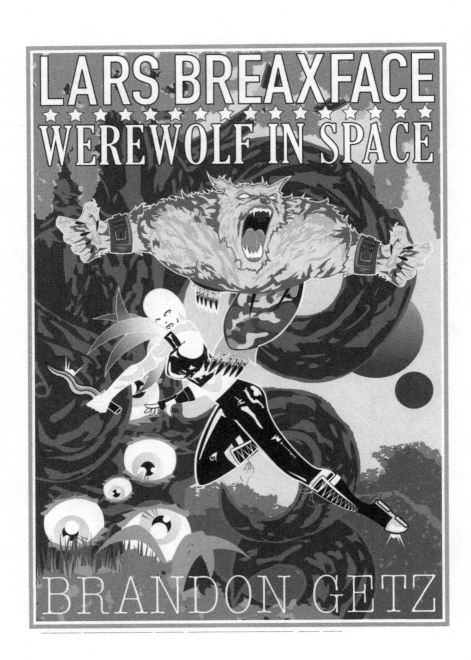

LARS BREAXFACE
WEREWOLF IN SPACE

BY BRANDON GETZ

Acknowledgements

Too many people to thank, and I'm gonna feel like an ass if I forget anybody. But I'll try. First, I have to thank Greg Leunig for getting on my case to write something for the now-defunct JukePop Serials (RIP) for like two years. Thanks also to the motley crew of Breaxface fans who read and voted on JukePop and kept me chugging along chapter by chapter. A humungo-gigantor thank you to all the artists who contributed work to this project, especially to Jonas, who started it all off with his amazing cover art of the titular hero in his porn-bedazzled cockpit. To my main beta readers, Jason Peck and Nic Eaton, thanks for the feedback and for catching shit that I didn't. To Nate and Shaunn at Spaceboy Books, a wolfzilla-sized thanks—Nate's excellent edits and rad design work helped to make the book you hold in your hands. And lastly, thank you to my partner, Hillary, who supported this nonsense the whole way and who told me to submit this story to Spaceboy and unleash the space werewolf on the world. Cheers.

About the Author

Brandon Getz earned an MFA in fiction writing from Eastern Washington University. His work has appeared in *F(r)iction*, *Versal*, *Flapperhouse*, and elsewhere. *Lars Breaxface: Werewolf in Space* is his first novel. He lives in Pittsburgh, PA.

About the Artists

Jonas Goonface is a friendly ghost that haunts coffee shops and draws comics about cannibals and space samurai and Satan and stuff. He recently collaborated on *Godshaper* with Simon Spurrier for BOOM! Studios.

His work can be found at http://jonasgoonface.tumblr.com

Brian Price is an artist and graphic designer in the orbit of Pittsburgh who stays up half the night drawing like a madman. He is currently working on two graphic novel projects: a paranormal detective comedy and a historical superhero tale starring an escaped slave dressed as the devil protecting the Underground Railroad. Follow him on Instagram @brian_price_

Melissa Ciccocioppo is an artist residing in Pittsburgh, PA. She graduated from the Art Institute of Pittsburgh with an Associate's degree in graphic design. Soon after graduating, she picked up her first bar of polymer clay and was immediately hooked. She decided to keep her full-time job at the wacky local coffee shop to pursue her new love for sculpting and created Bambi's Clay Design. Her specialty is fun, colorful jewelry and small sculptures of animals and other made up creatures. She loves taking commissions, so don't hesitate to contact her with a custom order!

Shop: www.bambisclaydesign.etsy.com

Facebook: *Bambi's Clay Design*

Instagram: @industrialbambi

Megan Shalonis is a Pittsburgh artist known for her stylized paintings of houses, campers, and flying saucers. She also curates monthly art showings at the Bloomfield Crazy Mocha coffee shop. Find her on Instagram at @megalons and purchase work at https://meganshalonis.bigcartel.com

Kate J. Reed is often a writer and sometimes a drawer. She is always a reader, a mom, and a partner. She has published short stories in *Copper Nickel* and *Literati* and co-edited the *Railtown Almanac: A Spokane Prose Anthology* for Sage Hill Press. She's pretty excited to be in this badass book!

Ryan Yee has created work for properties like *Pathfinder, Star Wars,* and *Lord of the Rings.* He has also been working with Wizards of the Coast on *Magic: The Gathering* since 2009. He has now been featured in the galleries and illustration annuals he loved staring at as a kid. He currently lives in Pittsburgh, Pennsylvania, and works as a lead concept artist for Schell Games, where he continues to draw and create worlds fifteen-year-old Ryan once dreamed about.
More at www.ryanyee.com

Kim Piper (Twitter: @penandpiper) is an animator, artist, and writer who turns, werewolf like, into a chemist during the day. She brings characters and creatures to life using nothing but pixels, pens, and coffee. Loves: Sci-Fi, Neil Gaiman, *Buffy the Vampire Slayer,* martial arts, and powerful stories told through any medium. *Ara of the Wanderers,* a pixelated RPG developed by Kim and her partner Nick Barr, is forthcoming at www.araofthewanderers.com

Ken Town is an artist pretending to have a day job. He gets his lip piercings stuck to people. His art is about navigating darkness. That's why he usually draws cartoons. See more of Ken's art on
Instagram: @rocketTango.

Higu Rose is a black artist and resident terror of Chicago, IL. Based in fiction and autobiography, their work focuses on experiences of being queer, isolated, and mentally ill. Their narratives are a constant endeavor to understand the self and society, with a snarling desire to love and live. Higu is the worst kind of cool guy. Bad teeth. Don't know math, neither.
Find their stuff at www.swamp-monster.net or follow them on Twitter @higoons

Bill Homan is a New England native now living in the Pittsburgh area. A special effects artist, potter, photographer, and visual artist, he is also the longsuffering spouse of author Gwendolyn Kiste. Some of his illustrations can be found in *A Shadow of Autumn: An Anthology of Fall & Halloween Tales.*

Felicia Cooper is a puppeteer, dancer, actor, educator, and maker. Her work is primarily centered around illustration of movement as a language for expression and the dissection of a human compulsion to find order in chaos through narrative. She has completed artistic residencies with Bread & Puppet Theater, The Children's Museum of Pittsburgh, Pearl Arts Studios, and has been the recipient of a grant from the Pennsylvania Council on the Arts. She has also worked in collaboration with the Irma Freeman Center for Imagination, Harvard University's Project Zero, Dixon Place's Puppet BloK!, DRAP Arts Festival, Pittsburgh Festival of Firsts, The National Puppetry Conference at the Eugene O'Neill Theater Center, and others.

Maggie Lynn Negrete is a feminist artist who adapts her medium in response to the dialogue she wishes to create with the audience. Her artwork consists of installations, illustrations, and prints with themes focused on women's history, fantasy, and the occult. Uniting these mediums, Maggie's design sense manifests through black and white linework with nods to Gilded Era illustration, the current renaissance of sign painting and is influenced by her heritage of typographers and illustrators.
Find her at www.mgglntcreates.com

Nate Taylor is a graphic designer by day, illustrator by night. Any free time that isn't consumed by drawing monsters is spent daydreaming about Myst island.
More at www.illustratornate.com

Ross Kennedy owns and operates Armature Tattoo Co. in Pittsburgh's Bloomfield neighborhood. His first graphic novel, *Revenants*, written by Wendi Lee, takes place in a post-apocalyptic Pittsburgh full of bloodthirsty creatures. He is currently working on a sci-fi noir photographic novel called *Kasper Hardy* and is collaborating *with Lars Breaxface* writer Brandon Getz on the gritty superhero comic *Arcane*.
Follow his Instagram @rosskennedytattoo

Nic Eaton is a part-time writer and full-time human from Queens. He dabbles in art and has done only two notable things in his life thus far, one of which is illegal in 16 states.
Find his artwork on Instagram: @nice.doodles

Scott Elliott Javier Patrick is a designer and illustrator living in Pittsburgh, Pennsylvania. Drawing inspiration from the natural world, Scotty takes great pleasure in bringing life and identity to his projects. Scotty is currently single and available.
Follow his adventures on Instagram @scottycurious

Spaz is an artist, cheerleaderologist, and former frontman of all drag-queen punk band Paul Lynde 451. Originally from Greensburg, PA, at age 14 he invented a cartoon character for the school newspaper and named it Spaz, which later became his graffiti tag and alter-ego. Spaz's activities include go-go dancing for bands and for a club, performance art, conceptual art, and emceeing punk shows. He was once in a *Pittsburgh Post-Gazette* article about people in Pittsburgh who go by only one name. He's best known to people under the age of 30 as the subject of the Anti-Flag song "Spaz's House Destruction Party."

Michael Jackson is an award-winning filmmaker and visual artist. His films have screened at Cinequest, Santa Barbara, and Sonoma where he won the 2017 Best Drama Short Film Award and the 2017 American Diversity Award at the "Latino Short Film" Film Festival. In 2014, Michael moved to New York City where he created a series of intertwined film shorts called *Harlemites*.
Michael's visual art can be found at www.mitaja.com

J.A. Waters has lived all over the U.S. and so home is just wherever he happens to be. Making the internet beep by day, by night he likes to draw the characters that tumble about in his head. Sometimes, J.A. likes to write a bunch of words that describe the weird stuff those characters are going through. With their powers combined, you'd normally get a comic book. In J.A.'s case, you just have a bunch of sketches and a whole lot of fun.
Find him at www.jawaters.com

Matt Phillips is a cartoonist, philosopher, swordsman, and Tormund Giantsbane cosplayer living in Pittsburgh. He's the creator of the webcomic Jesus Christ Supercar, about his car being possessed by the Lord and Savior. He just bought an axe from Cold Steel.
Find his comics at jesuschristsupercar.thecomicseries.com

Brian Gonnella is a conceptual artist & illustrator from Pittsburgh, PA. He earned a BA in English writing and film studies at the University of Pittsburgh but has been working professionally as an artist for almost a decade, and has exhibited work nationally at gallery and museum level. Inspired by cartoons, punk and graffiti, he has developed an animation/painting technique using spray paint and acrylic paint pens as a primary medium, coupled with a tedious

stenciling & layering process that could be described technically as something between stencil graffiti, comic illustration and Japanese ukiyo-e paintings.
More at www.briangonnella.com

Peter Boyer is a freelance artist from Burbank, CA, (now residing in Pittsburgh!) with artist roots stemming from his pops, Ken Boyer. Drawing day in and day out, he also enjoys old comic books/cartoons and David Lynch movies. And perhaps a tad obsessive with Ancient Egyptian lore.
You can look him up on Facebook or directly talk to him through e-mail: murgatroidpuss@gmail.com

Joe Mruk is a freelance illustrator, designer, and educator living in the East End of Pittsburgh. Since graduating from Cal U in 2010, he has become involved with the music community in Pittsburgh, working on designs and illustrations for bands and media kits for festivals. He has conducted drawing classes at Wash Arts, and coordinated and served as an instructor at a summer art camp for Lakota youth for three years on the Pine Ridge Indian Reservation. Find him at www.redbuffalo.org

Index of Artworks

About the Publishing Team

Nate Ragolia was labeled as "weird" early in elementary school, and it stuck. He's a lifelong lover of science fiction, and a nerd/geek. In 2015 his first book, *There You Feel Free,* was published by 1888's Black Hill Press. He's also the author of *The Retroactivist*, published by Spaceboy Books. He founded and edits BONED, an online literary magazine, has created webcomics, and writes whenever he's not playing video games or petting dogs.

Shaunn Grulkowski has been compared to Warren Ellis and Phillip K. Dick and was once described as what a baby conceived by Kurt Vonnegut and Margaret Atwood would turn out to be. He's at least the fifth best Slavic-Latino-American sci-fi writer in the Baltimore metro area. He's the author of *Retcontinuum,* and the editor of *A Stalled Ox* and *The Goldfish*, all for 1888/Black Hill Press.